What Heals the Heart

The Pullman Station Series Book One

Jen Telger

ISBN: 979-8-9855291-0-4 (paperback)

ISBN: 979-8-9855291-1-1 (ebook)

Also by Jen Telger

Sticks and Stones: Book Two in the Pullman Station Series

For the Lass and the Lad

Contents

PART ONE

Maple Street

May 1985

The gunshot blast punched my eardrums as a sharp, acrid odor stabbed at my nostrils.

"Annabelle Walker, you get outta here before I shoot you clean through!"

My brain and body engaged. Time to go!

I veered around patio furniture, dodging potted plants as adrenaline pumped through my eleven-year-old body and launched me up the side yard, breathless.

Jump the fence. JUMP THE FENCE!!

Can't. Too much cargo. Around the fence. GO!

Feet and hair flying, I rounded the fence and skidded across our driveway, collapsing on the steps of our veranda as the heady perfume of lilacs in full bloom replaced the bitter smells of fear and gunpowder. Wiffle balls dribbled everywhere. I patted my body, searching for new holes, but found no blood. Come to think of it, the blast had sounded more like a starter pistol.

Such was life living next to old Nattie Dennings, our next-door neighbor in the long, yellow house on the left. A run-in with her left most folks in town confused or terrified—maybe both. Many of them would gladly sell their soul to the devil to avoid such a thing. I didn't have that luxury, though.

Breathe. You're fine. Only Nattie. She shot at you! But you're fine ...

It was always this way when I had a run-in with Nattie, which was pretty much every time I got within a stone's throw of her front window. Fancying herself a bit of a lookout, she squinted from behind the sheers on the regular. God save whoever lacked the good fortune of an alternate route. Some folks called her a nasty old busybody. Knowing her as we did, we kids called her "Batty Nattie."

***

July 2005

Lake Geneva, Wisconsin

As always, heading toward home turns the soil in my mind, harvesting old memories and readying for new ones. Ever since the phone rang earlier this week, scenes from my Pullman Station days, including the starter pistol incident, have been swirling about in my head. Nearly six months have slipped by, with one thing after another, and a visit is long past due.

This one will come with tears, of course, as occasions such as this often do. Still, talking with old friends will be soothing; to reminisce about our childhood that, to us, had been magical. So many fun times to recall, although a few scars will give us pause in our stories, as well. Still, it's nice to be heading home.

My husband, Mark, and I took our places in the front seat of our Nissan. Our kids, Grace and William, rode in back and, from the moment we closed the doors, they started in.

"Mom, tell us about the olden days, again," said Grace.

"Yeah, tell us about the old times!"

Mark quickly looked away from me, stifling a snort of amusement. Nothing like the youthful enthusiasm of eight- and ten-year-olds to tempt an existential crisis in their thirty-something mother as she heads to a memorial.

"Geez, guys. You make it sound like I got to school by horse and buggy."

"You know what we mean," Will persisted. "Tell us about your crazy neighborhood again."

"It was not crazy, Will! Well ... Yeah, okay, so there was a little crazy. But lots of wonderful, too. The best childhood a kid could ask for."

I thought for a moment. "Things don't look the same anymore, of course. Everything seems ... smaller, I guess. But when I was your age, it was heaven."

"C'mon! Tell us about Cilla! Pleeease..."

"Yeah, and Nattie!"

I glanced in the visor mirror and found two grinning faces looking back at me, as was the one across the console, reveling in anticipation of a good tale.

"Go on, Annabelle. We do have five hours to kill, after all," said Mark.

Of course, it's a story they've heard pieces of countless times before, the details of which have been filled in by various friends, neighbors, and even Cilla and Nattie themselves over the years that followed.

Many of the harsher parts remain a mystery to Grace and William; time enough to hear about those when they're older. But while I have no intention of enlightening them just yet, the lessons are worth learning.

***

Growing up, my family lived in the small town of Pullman Station, Minnesota. Though I'm married now, people back home will always know me as Annabelle Walker, the tall, skinny girl with long, dark braids and most unfortunate house placement. Not that our house itself was terrible. Located on Maple Street and protected by big, beautiful trees, it nestled in a sun-dappled stretch under a leafy tunnel that extended all down the block.

The house was fine, all things considered; white with black shutters and a single-car garage at the back of the driveway. We also had the only suitable backyard in which my friends and I could play ball.

The veranda out front proved a special treat. Surrounded by lilac bushes and low hedging, it had a swing hanging just around the corner that was the perfect place to sit with an ice-cold lemonade on a hot summer day or with company over for a visit on a Sunday afternoon.

The day Nattie shot at me, however, I used it as a resuscitation device of sorts; the cool white paint smooth against my flushed cheek, encouraging my heart back into my chest so it could return to the business of pumping again.

The only thing that held a candle to snags with Nattie was an episode with Cilla Prescott. As it happened, she lived in the white house with green shutters on the other side of us. Calculating, vengeful, and pig-headed, Daddy used to say that the devil would be tickled to have such a diligent scorekeeper in his ranks when she finally passed. That always got a look from Mama, but Daddy and I would dissolve into giggles. I reckoned he was right.

Cilla was in no way better than Nattie, mind. Both women were mean as pissed off copperheads and sneaky into the bargain. But while Cilla would just as soon cuss several layers off your hide as look at you, Nattie was bat shit crazy.

Mama didn't like when I called Nattie or Cilla names. She said our Christian duty required us to be kind and care for all God's creatures, regardless of their disposition.

"Besides, Annabelle, if you do it behind their backs, you're like to slip up and do it face-to-face one day."

Daddy didn't mind the names. Judging by the number of times he'd heard Jesus Christ called upon as unsuspecting solicitors cannoned off one of their porches, he figured old JC himself wouldn't get within bible-chucking distance of either one of them. Being shot at by Nattie—starter pistol or no—only reinforced that theory. Therefore, our Christian duty lay firmly nestled within the caveat of self-preservation.

Once I'd finally reached our house that day, and the smooth paint had started to take effect, I lay on the palliative veranda waiting for the blood to reoxygenate my brain, now that my heart had remembered the mechanics of pumping again. Nattie had nearly gotten me. Her piercing shriek rang in my ears, slicing my eardrums to ribbons. But the time had come for me to do the collection, and so I had. Lord knows, no other kids would dare set foot within a mile of Nattie's front door, let alone go sneaking through her side yard to retrieve wayward Wiffles.

Seeing how we played at my house and how Mama always had Daddy and me doing our Christian duty, everyone figured I should be the one to Zamboni Nattie's back lawn. As far as I was concerned, it took a lot more balls to walk into her yard than I could ever carry back out.

Most of the time, I managed to grab and control six or seven Wiffles while running for my life. Once in a while, one would come back over the hedge before collection time, always at night and always in unusable condition. Each one would be sliced clean through, save for a twist of ragged white plastic left to emphasize its grisly demise.

That day, though, Nattie had pulled a new trick out of her bag. The starter pistol—who knows where she picked that up—had fired right above my head. Thinking about it as I leaned on the steps made my queasy insides go all watery again, bullets or no. I was pretty sure she'd shoot me for real, given a chance.

The blood gradually returned to my head, and I sat up, gathering wits and balls around me.

"Crap."

I'd dropped one when the pistol went off, which meant the next collection loomed one hooked at-bat closer already. No way I was going back. If the fallen Wiffle ended up as a mangled hedge grenade, so be it.

Welcome to Pullman Station

Pullman Station is a rather sleepy town. In fact, the name came from railway workers back in the day who used to joke that no one ever got off there, so the passengers in the Pullman cars could remain asleep, and the name stuck. It's a small, quiet, peaceful place. Maybe if Mama and Daddy had known how things would play out between Nattie and Cilla, they might've found a different house equally as charming.

***

Our backyard was longer than it was wide. That meant anything hit by us right-handed kids during a ball game inevitably landed in Nattie's yard with a fair amount of regularity, and Nattie had a keen sense for when the collection was due. Besides spying on Cilla Prescott, the only thing that kept her from watching out the front window was watching our games. Peeking through the high hedges between our backyards, she'd wait for Jimmy Drummond or Sasha Perkins to drill one over. It seemed that those idiots ought to do their share of the collection, Christian duty or no.

"Okay, Jimmy, that's the third one today. You're on collection."

"Nuh-uh! It's not my fault Sasha can't throw a decent pitch. Make him do it!"

"No way, man! I'm not going over there. Probably come back cursed with leeches on my eyeballs or something. Besides, you're the one swinging at everything in front of your face. Not my fault you have bad eyes."

"Fine. Fine! I'll do it," I'd relent. And so, it would go.

During the summer, games took place whenever three or more of us gathered, and weather permitted. If we had a full house, we'd have the twins, Sasha and Natalie Perkins, and Jimmy Drummond, Sasha's best friend, playing. They all lived on the back side of our block. Jimmy's little sister, Maisy, who was almost six, liked to tag along, too. If we were really lucky, we'd also have Jimmy and Maisy's older sister, Pansy, and her boyfriend, Garrett.

We'd rotate through who pitched, fielded, and batted, depending on how many of us we numbered on a given day. Sometimes, we only had one pitcher, one fielder, and one batter, which meant you better hit hard enough to reach at least third so your ghost runner could get home on your next one. If you didn't, you might get stuck with both of you on base, and then you had to sacrifice your ups. Our pitcher also switched sides every half-inning so the defense could throw for an out. We loved the game and were a tight crew, so we made it work.

Mama kept a garden at the back of the yard where she grew all sorts of flowers. Crown tulips, black-eyed Susans, snapdragons, daisies, irises, and lilies all called that space home. Behind the garden stood a red board fence. Anything hit beyond the fence was a home run, while anything hit beyond the hedges on either side was foul in every sense of the word.

A big patch of pampas grass in the back corner acted as first base. That made the first baseline twice as long as any of the others. Anyone who made it that far had a good chance of getting to second, which was a pole that held one end of the clothesline on the other side of the yard. The corner of the garage was third, and the distance between there and home plate was as abbreviated as the first baseline was long.

The stretch between second and third always proved tricky. While the shortest of the runs, most hits flew in that direction, so someone nearly always stood there to catch or at least tag a runner. If we hit too hard, there was a chance of losing the ball to Nattie's graveyard, and everyone knew the price to pay for that.

Hanging wash was our only saving grace. Problem was, it was still a bit of a crapshoot. Land a ball between two lines, and you might reach third while the fielder wrestled with a face full of softener-scented bath towels. Rebound one off the front line of whatever was up, and you'd probably punched your ticket back to the patio. Knock one into a pair of undies, though, and you were pretty much guaranteed a home run.

Our pitcher's mound lay about ten feet in front of home plate, this in a depression caused by a long-since rotted old tree stump. It never occurred to us that the "mound" was anything but. At least if a batter drilled one straight out, the pitcher had a head start toward hitting the dirt before getting a stinger to the eye.

Inevitably, most of Mama's crown tulips got dethroned early season. The destructive display exploding with vibrant reds and yellows received raucous appreciation before we remembered to be decently contrite. The patch of baby pampas grass had a base worn into the front after the first few games. By fall, many of the grand white plumes lay trampled from overeager runners and search-and-rescue efforts for disappearing pop-flys.

Occasionally, a kerfuffle broke out over whether a ball had been lost in the pampas grass or had instead died just across the hedge in Cilla's yard. When that happened, our best bet was to take a Popsicle break. By the time our tongues turned neon orange or Sasha managed to produce an impressive string of green Yo-Yo drool, our wits would return.

Rather than trying to retrieve anything from that yard, agreeing to disagree always proved the safest bet. Right-field fouls were rare, so we started the inning over, accepted the loss of a ball, and enjoyed the love of the game.

***

Everett Coleman lived around the corner, his backyard abutting ours at the red board fence. A kind, rather soft-spoken man whose own son and daughter had long since grown and flown, Mr. Coleman loved having the neighborhood kids around. His wife passed not long after the birth of their second child, and he'd remained a bachelor ever since. The current head librarian at the local library, Mrs. Chisholm, watched the Coleman kids for several years while Mr. Coleman worked as a mechanic at the auto shop. These days, though, he could often be found puttering in his gardens as we clambered over the fence to retrieve a home run. He always met us with a smile and friendly banter.

"How you kids doin' today?"

"Hi, Mr. Coleman," we'd wave. "We're good. No flower explosions yet!"

He'd chuckle at us. "Well, if you need to, you know you have your pick over here."

Everyone, adults and kids alike, adored Mr. Coleman. Quick with a smile and a clever story and always game to sit and chew the gristle of a problem with you, he had a way of putting a body at ease. He was never cross, never judged, and never gossiped. But in his eyes, you could tell he knew things. In fact, he was the one person in town everyone thought might know the truth about what had come between Nattie and Cilla. Everybody knew Mr. Coleman worked for their husbands at the shop all those years ago, and the families had been friends. But if he was privy to anything, he wasn't saying a word.

All of the neighborhood kids had two extra reasons for appreciating Mr. Coleman. First, he let us cut through his strategically placed yard on our way to each other's houses or the pool. In doing so, we avoided having to run past Nattie's or Cilla's out front. That, in itself, was worth our undying devotion. Whenever we were tearing through, we heard his soft chuckle, followed by the higher-pitched "Hooo…" that invariably punctuated his delight. He was aware of what a precious gift he was giving us, and I think he may have enjoyed it even more than we did.

Second, he always let us cut posies from his garden when we'd obliterated one of Mama's beautiful spring blossoms and needed a mea culpa offering. His glorious peonies were always a big hit in the event one of her tulips bit the dust. A kinder man you would never meet, and he sort of balanced out the two old bats flapping around our side of the block.

***

Save for the odd character or two, our neighborhood was a pretty sweet place to grow up. It was our kingdom, our blissful hidey-hole carved deep within a chaotic world of grown-up problems that had yet to reach their icy fingers down our collars. Kid law reigned, and hearts governed. We were free, untethered, and unconcerned with forces that would all too soon compel us to reconcile the world we lived in with the callous inequities of life.

***

"Mom, I hafta go," came William's voice from the backseat.

Grace and Mark, already rapt with attention, let out groans.

"Will, you were supposed to go before we left." Gracie chided.

"I did! But I hafta go again."

"Ten-four, good buddy," Mark said as he switched on his turn signal and took the next exit. After a quick stop for the bathroom and snacks, we set off again, ready to settle back into the summer that changed my life.

Of course, life being the secret-keeper it is, we didn't always have all of the details required for a full picture. Events of decades past simmered quietly in their respective pots on either side of our house, but all we could see was the steam.

Little Girls Lost

Back Bay, Boston 1921

Nine-year-old Priscilla Dixon curled up in the farthest corner of her closet, willing herself to dissolve into the wall. The sounds of stumbling feet and crashing glass below were tattooed on her eardrums, persisting, no matter how hard she pushed her fingers into her ears. The paranoia and nonsense would come next, frightening and confusing her as she prayed for it to pass. For now, it was only the horrible insults.

"Damn it, Sarah, you're drunk! You're always drunk. You're a useless, disgusting pig and an embarrassment to this family. How can you do this to me?"

"Oooh! It's always about you, isn't it, Eggar? Always poor Eggar not getting what he wants! Except that you do get what you want, don't you?" Sarah screamed back at her husband, slurring her words as usual. "You just take what you w-want and to hell with everybody else!"

"That's enough!" Edgar boomed. "How dare you speak to me like that? Everything around you is because of me, you stupid cow. The house you live in, the beautiful things I can afford, Priscilla's schooling. All of it! Why don't you just crawl back into your piss-rank hole and pass out? That's where you're happiest anyway."

It hadn't always been like this. Priscilla's mother, Sarah Dixon, had been the belle of the ball during much of her youth. Beautiful in a way that transcended the mere prettiness of other girls, Sarah began to attract much older men at an early age. Confident, clever, and funny, she commanded an audience with ease, steering them in whichever direction her heart desired.

At twenty, she'd set her sights on the gregarious and wealthy Edgar—several years her senior and on the radar of many young ladies in Boston—during a summer spent with her aunt. She'd promptly brought him under her spell, and he proposed a mere three months later, delighted by the attention and jealousy that his stunning fiancée aroused in other men.

"I'd be dizzy with a dish like that, too," they'd say, nudging each other as they waggled their eyebrows up and down. "Lots o' skirts running after guys like us, but that one's something else!"

At twenty-two, Sarah had given birth to Priscilla. The picture of familial bliss and perfection was cemented two years later, when little Penelope—Penny, as they affectionately called her—followed. But Sarah's life wasn't at all what she had hoped it would be.

Living in an elegant four-story brownstone and being married to Edgar, a successful financier, Sarah wanted for little, save for her husband's attention. When the girls came along, he continued to live life in the fast lane. And while he still appreciated Sarah's beauty and the stir it caused when she arrived somewhere with him, he was much less interested in a mother of two children than in the childless arm candy he'd married.

Sarah had always enjoyed the parties and galas, playing the role of the unavailable-yet-tempting young wife to an old-money up-and-coming tycoon. She held engaging conversations with wives and held her liquor with their husbands, which enchanted the men, and her own husband, all the more.

It was the transition from brilliant social star to mother of littles that was the first straw; despite having a part-time nanny and housekeeper to help, there was no one to sweep Sarah off her feet or fawn over her every lash flutter anymore. Instead, Edgar insisted she take an active role in raising the children, and so, her days became filled with wet nappies, biscuit crumbs, scraped knees, and messes. Sarah eventually scrapped the nanny and threw herself into their lives with vigor, pretending not to care that Edgar now directed his affections elsewhere.

Sarah and the girls went on regular outings in Boston Public Garden. They often took a picnic for lunch during the warmer months and spent a lazy afternoon exploring and playing hide-and-seek amongst the flower beds and statues. Other times, they enjoyed the lovely Swan Boat rides on the pond, during which Penny insisted on throwing any leftover crumbs to the ducks on the water. Each time her toss cleared the rail, and they raced toward her haphazardly thrown fistful of morsels, she clapped and squealed, her light auburn curls bouncing around her face as she giggled.

"Look, Prissy, look! I'm feeding the ducks!" she'd say, proud of herself for doing things her big sister could do.

"Well done, Penny!" Priscilla would praise.

Sarah pulled the girls to the Garden on their Flexible Flyer to play in the snow and watch the ice skaters during the winter months. They came home rosy-cheeked and exhausted but happy and full of chatter for their father. After filling their bellies with a delicious dinner, it wasn't long before they were cleaned up and crawling into snuggly, warm beds in the nursery.

Regardless of the weather, those they met along the way always fawned over Sarah's little angels, smiling at them and complimenting her on what a wonderful mother she must be to have two such adorable and well-behaved girls. Both were beautiful, taking after their mother. Starving for the attention, Sarah soaked up the praise, and they quickly became her avenue to enjoying the spotlight once again.

***

Priscilla and Penny spent nearly all of their time together. When they weren't at the Garden, they pushed their dollies in prams on the front walk, cooing and scolding as they saw fit. They created nests in their closet in the colder months and pretended to sleep rough, trying to keep warm. Though two years apart, they were best friends and constant companions and needed very little in terms of outside friendships.

When school started for Priscilla, nothing much changed. Edgar insisted on private tutors, of course, which didn't do her social expansion any favors.

"I will not have my children mixing with rabble from God-knows-where," he said. "You will find the best tutors money can buy and see to it that my daughter does well. That is your job, after all."

Edgar was always affectionate toward the girls, who adored him and were the one thing that kept their parents united, but the two adults might have been neighbors for all the affection they showed each other. Treating Sarah more as a minion than a wife and keeping her further bound to house and children resulted in their marriage all but dissolving.

Though unable to understand all of the words or insinuations, Priscilla was aware of the attitudes and tones she witnessed between her parents. Still, she had Penny.

***

In September 1918, a second wave of the Spanish Flu pandemic flooded into the United States via military facilities in and around Boston. While a mild first wave known as the "Three-Day Fever" had taken place farther west earlier that year, this was much deadlier. The virus found a warm nest within the confines of troop barracks and trenches in Europe, and the close quarters of war caused a wildfire spread of the contagion. As wounded soldiers arrived home, hospitals and medical personnel—already depleted in number due to wartime service and the failure to utilize trained African American nurses—suffered the massive burden of spreading infection into the bargain. They became taxed beyond capacity.

In November, citizens gathered in celebration of Armistice Day, despite a rapidly rising death toll, fanning the flames of the biological bonfire and creating a societal inferno. Thousands upon thousands dropped dead, some within mere hours of showing symptoms, while others hung on for days before succumbing to the slow-motion horror of suffocation. Spouses, children, siblings, friends—were all lost in the blink of an eye. The shocking and widespread devastation of this new pandemic on the heels of war drove many mad with grief.

For Sarah, as for most parents, the idea of losing her girls was more terrifying than anything else she could have imagined. The simple gauze masks recommended by the government seemed a rather paltry defense against this unseen and viciously destructive intruder. Sarah reluctantly kept her active five- and seven-year-olds home, safe within the confines of their brownstone, allowing only their housekeeper access, and put an end to the parading of their beauty and manners amid the fear of their potential loss.

Edgar continued to come and go as necessary and fell ill in the early Spring of 1919. It was sudden and ruthless, yet, miraculously, he recovered. Sarah dispassionately and thanklessly cared for him until he was once again independent, leaving the girls in the care of their housekeeper in a separate area of the house, with the windows open whenever possible. It was the best they could do under the circumstances, which were better than those of most others, and Sarah was grateful.

Once better, Edgar returned to work and his relatively regular routine. Though exposed repeatedly during his care, Sarah, inexplicably, never fell ill. Little Penelope was not so lucky. Somehow, despite all the precautions in the world, the little girl succumbed a scant nine hours after her symptoms began, and the remainder of Sarah's carefully constructed world came crashing down.

Like her mother, Priscilla didn't contract Influenza; for whatever fateful reason, it spared them. But to her, it felt as if her mother would have preferred for her to die rather than Penny.

Sarah became distant in her grief. Rather than engaging Priscilla and guiding her through her confusion and loss, she would often seem entranced in a far-off world, not hearing, not remembering plans or promises, forgetting Priscilla's birthday, and snapping when Priscilla innocently pointed these things out.

Becoming more and more reclusive, Sarah rarely left her bedroom, save to retrieve another bottle of whatever would numb the pain from the vast wine cellar below. Having selflessly nursed her indifferent husband back to health, it felt unjustifiably cruel that she should lose one of her girls.

Lonely and isolated, having been robbed of her only playmate, Priscilla began sneaking out on her own, exploring a smaller, nearby park and eventually finding refuge beneath the lilac bushes. As her mother continued to decimate the wine cellar, Priscilla spent more and more time in her hidey-hole, creating an imaginary kingdom where she was no longer Priscilla Dixon but merely "Cilla."

As winter approached, it became impossible to trudge through the cold and snow to her haven. So instead, she spent hours indoors, reading, playing with her dolls, and dreaming of remote places where bad things never happened, and there was never a reason to cry. She missed Penny terribly.

It didn't escape Cilla that her father and mother lived in separate universes even when in the same room, which they avoided whenever possible. She heard the arguments and felt her mother's drunken wrath seeping through the floorboards and walls, her father's repulsed criticisms hot on its heels. It was hard to know which was worse: her mother's drinking, her father's scorn, or her own penetrating loneliness.

Unable to concentrate or remember things, Sarah told fantastic tales, slurring her words and believing entirely that what she was proclaiming was the truth. Edgar shunned and ridiculed her. Tutors and nannies avoided interacting with her, and Cilla was left resenting how her mother's demons had poisoned their home.

As the months and years passed, the downward spiral was unrelenting. Sarah became equally difficult when sober as when drunk. The worst was when she saw things no one else could. The fear in her eyes frightened even Cilla, who became hardened and stoic toward her mother. While she hated Sarah for retreating when she'd needed her most, she pitied her for her decline in the face of losing Penny.

Sarah frequently turned violent during the hallucinations. When this happened, Cilla would run up to her bedroom and hide in the closet, wishing that Penny was there to keep her company as she waited out the storm raging below.

***

In April 1926, Sarah Dixon left this world. Having been relentlessly beaten by addiction and sorrow and looking more like a wretched 70-year-old than a 36-year-old former beauty, her body finally gave out. Her mind, however, had departed that spring day seven years past when half of all that she loved most had been lost.

Upon her mother's death, Cilla's father took little notice of the fact that she remained. Not troubled by the loss of his wife and consumed by the current economic contraction, he spent many nights in his library poring over financial reports, making phone calls, and scribbling notes on his desktop until the wee hours. A few short weeks later, having gained significant self-reliance and independence during her mother's drawn-out battle with her demons, Cilla was done waiting for someone to care.

Just shy of fifteen years old and wise beyond her years, young Cilla left the miserable life she'd known for so long. Stealing a large amount of cash from her oblivious father and packing only the bare essentials, she stubbornly set out to make what she could of the world on her own.

Moving Forward

Back Bay, Boston, April 1926

B oston was a large, vivid city full of people from all walks of life and all manner of lifestyles. On the other hand, Cilla was a young teenager from Back Bay with a lot of money and little experience with how the world worked outside her father's home. Her desire to shed her old self and learn the world's ways was far outstripped by the dangers therein. She would need every scruple she possessed to avoid the risks of this cosmopolitan city or, worse, the local constabulary. But she had become resourceful during her mother's decline.

Cilla's clothing was outdated and her hair unkempt compared to other girls—something she would need to rectify posthaste to pull this off. Her one saving grace was that while she'd hidden from her monster mother whenever possible, she'd also spent a lot of time observing her various tutors over the years. In addition, she'd logged countless hours spying on her father from the gap between the pocket doors of his library late at night. That had allowed her ample time to practice her carriage and tone, if not see to her physical appearance.

Adequately educated, Cilla was proficient in math and reading and, therefore, could keep track of expenses and create lists as if sent on errands by her mother. With an excellent vocabulary of measure with her station in life and academic skills well in hand, she set out for fine new clothes and a chic haircut. While procuring these in her current attire might cause a few heads to turn, her adequate funds would likely allow for any questions to be quelled. Being possessed of at least some of her mother's former beauty and charm, she found she could get away with quite a lot, which would have otherwise been suspect, had she been an ordinary urchin with such an unusual pocketbook.

As she explored the downtown and observed its people, developing her real-time strategy for success, Cilla became aware of hunger gnawing at her belly. Stopping in at a lunch counter for a takeaway roll, she spotted a 5&10 across the street. Technically, it would have everything a girl might need except a bed.

She ate sitting on a bench outside the 5&10, observing the patrons and front window dressing. The ladies who came and went appeared a bit more common than in Back Bay but still quite presentable. Cilla studied them with intensity, trying to learn what she could. Finally, courage in hand and heart in her throat, she stepped inside.

Cilla wandered the store, trying to be inconspicuous, but looking at all the items on offer. Everything from dishes to baking equipment to clothing and make-up was available. A conversation between two women looking at dresses caught her attention. While they didn't appear to be poor, neither were they especially well-to-do.

"I don't know, this doesn't seem quite right," one said to the other as she held a dress up in front of herself.

"Well, then, what about this one?" her friend replied, holding out another.

"Hm ... I don't know. It's fine, I suppose. It just seems a bit ... plain. They all do. It's not that I need to be the bee's knees or anything; I just don't want to be plain old Doreen, you know? I want a little pizzazz, for once."

"In that case, I think Filene's Basement is in order. My friend, Virginia, finds the most wonderfully swanky clothes there on the cheap. She's always raving about the place."

Hearing this, Cilla knew her saving grace had arrived. She just needed to find Downtown Crossing and Washington Street.

***

Upon locating Filene's Department Store, Cilla strolled the basement looking at the fine clothes. Once again, observing those around her, she did her best to select items that would make her appear older than her fourteen years. Having purchased a few pieces of finery, including a new dress, fancy bag, hosiery, and shoes—which proved a bit trickier to master than she had expected—she changed, stuffed her old clothes in the new bag, and headed upstairs.

At the Beauty Balcony on the Mezzanine, Cilla discovered that spoiled little rich girls weren't all that uncommon. The staff welcomed her face, her money, and her unexpectedly polite manners with relief and open arms.

"What a dish we have here!" said one attendant, calling others over to see.

"Such perfect pale skin—and those cheekbones!" raved another.

Everyone fawned over her like a belle getting ready for the ball. They pampered her, carrying on with chatter as if they never got to work on a specimen like her. She wasn't used to such flattery, but it felt nice.

"Now, we simply must use a light hand. This doll's face needs to shine through. Why, you'll have the fellas falling all over themselves, thinking you're the cat's meow!"

Cilla watched the mirror intently, memorizing techniques and products to repeat the process later on her own. The result was an easy-yet-sophisticated style that added years of maturity to her face without making her appear overdone or like a little girl playing dress-up. Finally, a trip to the Michel Kazan Beauty Salon for a haircut sealed the transformation.

***

Now that she looked the part, Cilla needed to find a place to stay for the night. The problem of where had perplexed her for some time. While she didn't know anyone in town, she couldn't have risked staying with them anyway. She had thought about sleeping rough in a park somewhere but quickly dismissed the option after observing the city by day.

As the sun sank low in the sky, she felt tired from all she'd had to organize, do, and pretend since leaving the house that morning. Her feet ached in the new shoes. Surely, she could sleep for days.

A hotel seemed the safest bet on short notice. The most considerable risk wasn't so much her age—after all, she now looked much older and could play up her genetic gifts—but rather, as far as she knew, her father might appear anywhere in the Boston area at any time; something she needed to avoid. Then again, maybe he hadn't even noticed her absence yet, and wouldn't recognize her anyway if he had. Still, it was one less thing to worry about if she didn't stick too close to home.

Only a few hotels came to mind, and, to her frustration, they were located mainly in Back Bay. The Fairmont Copley House, The Lenox, and Loews: all names familiar to her from eavesdropping on her father's evening conversations, but all within his immediate locale and, therefore, not viable options.

The Omni Parker House, however, was downtown and nearby. Though only about a mile farther from Back Bay than the others, and still between there and the financial district, Cilla grabbed her courage by the throat and readied herself for her most challenging performance of the day.

***

Nestled among massive feather pillows and thoroughly impressed that her bravado had worked, Cilla congratulated herself on managing to land in the lap of luxury for the night. Again, her father's money managed to silence any protests or suspicions that may have entered the minds of the staff at the Omni Parker House. They'd simply accepted her payment, provided her with information regarding available services, and shown her to her room. She could get used to that.

Cash-on-hand, however, would need to be given a bit of a breather if she planned to survive long-term. Still, an extra day spent planning and being posh might not be entirely out of line considering what she'd been through over the last seven years.

There would be time a-plenty in the morning to ponder such necessities. For now, Cilla let her eyelids fall, reveling in the feeling of true safety and comfort for the first time since Penny died.

Fritz

"I feel bad for Cilla," Grace announced. "Is that what made her so mean?"

"Well, she wasn't mean then. She was pretty resilient, like most kids. But a lot can happen to a person over the course of almost sixty years. And a lot happened to Cilla."

"Bad stuff?" William asked.

"Some. But a lot of good stuff, too."

"I don't get it." He flopped back on his seat.

"Just keep going, mom," said Grace. "I wanna hear more about Nattie and Cilla."

June 1985

Other than possibly Mr. Coleman, no one seemed to know why things went south between Nattie and Cilla. Nor did anyone know why the two of them had become so antagonistic toward the world. Nattie, Cilla, and their husbands Jack and Marlon had been best friends for years. After Marlon passed and Jack followed a year later, everyone figured the two women would be closer than ever. Instead, Nattie went a bit 'round the bend, and Cilla stopped being nice to everybody. Whatever had happened, those two hated each other's guts.

Living between them was a bit like hunkering between gasoline and gunpowder. One tiny spark, one rumor on the wind, and the whole works would blow sky-high, shrapnel flying and everyone ducking for cover. You were likely to be caught up in a mess of trouble looking left or right. Still, Mama made us fulfill our Christian duty on the regular, asking if they needed this or that from the Piggly Wiggly or the post office.

For her part, Cilla was perfectly capable of doing for herself. Still, she wanted to also take advantage of anything offered to Nattie. Nattie, however, didn't like to drive and preferred to caustically accept the offer of errands run on her behalf. Problem was, if one of them discovered you were doing for the other at the same time, you'd get an earful.

***

Nattie had her spying ways, of course, finding out what was up in the neighborhood from her posts behind the window sheers and hedges. And Cilla was no different. But she had an accomplice. Fritz, her moderately unhinged tunneler of a Dachshund, frequently burrowed into other yards on the block. When she let him out, Cilla left him to his mole-ish inclinations, and he'd manage to dig his way over to our yard any number of times each year.

Thankfully, he didn't do much damage beyond the underpass itself. That is unless he continued over to Nattie's and doubled down on his chaos, which was somehow always our fault. Fritz would gleefully Shawshank his way under her side, and then Cilla'd come storming over, cussing a blue streak and demanding that Daddy retrieve her four-legged fortune hunter from Nattie's yard. Nattie, vexed to the point of apoplexy that a Prescott occupied her premises, would likewise take her fury out on Daddy when he came to fetch the little trailblazer.

For his part, Fritz remained unwaveringly single-minded in his endeavors, never bothering to come when called. On the contrary, he would take off whenever he sensed anyone about to put an end to his speculating. He put up a rather nasty fight if caught, giving the impression that his name was more mental classification than loving identifier. As such, Daddy couldn't win for losing and hated the stubby-legged reprobate with a passion.

Occasionally, Fritz would get lucky enough to be taken on a proper walk, always a reasonably good indicator that something Nattie said or did had Cilla especially nettled. A stroll presented the perfect pretext to survey the neighborhood and instigate further discord. In this, Fritz was happy to help. For all his turbulent lack of trainability, that dog would crap on Nattie's front lawn with the obedience of a Catholic monk, which pleased Cilla to no end. They'd continue for a block or two, then turn for home, stopping only long enough for the little demon to verify ownership of the fresh dung heap on display.

Once in a while, Nattie would see the deed happen. She'd come charging out of her house, madder than a hornet, hollering at Cilla to shove off.

"Cilla Prescott, you get out of my yard!" she'd scream. "Take that filthy mongrel to your own yard to drop his duty!"

Cilla would keep her nose in the air and continue along, saying, "He's an animal, you nitwit! I can't control where he does his business."

It usually took a few good dumps before Nattie got fired up enough to go stomping over to Cilla's. A paper bag full of dried turds clutched in her hands, she would spread the collection on the front porch for all to see. Cilla would leave the mess until dark and then slip out to dispose of it. No way she'd give Nattie the satisfaction of seeing her handle the poo. Not that it mattered in the slightest; Nattie was the one scooping and collecting the stuff. Simply sweeping dry turds into a dustpan and tossing them out didn't seem like much of an insult if you asked me. In my opinion, Cilla masterfully wielded the upper hand on that one.

The biggest problem with Fritz, however, wasn't his tunnels. Nor was it his desire to remain unbound or his curious toileting habits. Simply put, he was mean. He didn't like belly rubs, ear scratches, or snuggles. He didn't play fetch or jump for Frisbees or do tricks. Instead, he was as nasty toward most people as Cilla. Daddy was known to whip out his slingshot and snap Fritz in the behind with a pellet or two, this to deter him from thinking of our yard as an exotic travel locale, thereby saving Daddy the trouble of returning him. No matter: either too pig-headed like his owner or too dumb to care, having his hindquarters stung by BB's never bothered him much.

On more than one occasion, Fritz had scared the bejesus out of five-year-old Maisy Drummond. Therefore, she was deathly afraid of any dog, regardless of size. Whenever she heard anything sounding vaguely like a collar with jingly tags, she took off for home, her little legs blurring as she sped along, screaming like a tornado siren.

One day, she jumped off the school bus, shrieked as if stung by a bee, and shot off for home. With each stride, she became more hysterical. Turned out, the zipper on her Windbreaker jingled when she ran, but in her mind, trouble was on her tail.

For some reason, scaring Maisy was the only thing that ever prompted Cilla to reprimand Fritz. He could do as he pleased to anyone else, but she drew the line at the littlest Drummond. In fact, she appeared to draw it for herself, as well. She'd holler at any one of us other kids, but when it came to Ms. Maisy, you'd witness the only smiles you'd ever see out of Cilla Prescott. Lucky little squirt.

Speaking of scary dogs, one time, a foul ball managed to scoot its way down our driveway and into the street when a Doberman from one of the rental houses down the block happened to be out for a walk. Maisy ran and grabbed the ball from the gutter, not seeing her waking nightmare. As she stood up, her eyes locked with the beast's.

The Doberman, twice her size and glad for an opportunity to play keep-away, broke free from his owner. Maisy took off like a shot, blasting her afterburners and rocketing up the driveway into the backyard. Poor girl almost expired right there on our patio.

As the dog went after her little hand, slobbering all over her, we screamed for Maisy to *"Throw the ball!"* as she screamed in terror. Jimmy finally wrenched the thing from his terrified little sister's grasp and threw it as far back down the driveway as he could, the crazed hound in hot pursuit, careening into his frantic owner along the way. In the dog's defense, he wasn't exactly mean, just big, severe-looking, and slobbery. But none of that mattered in the slightest to Maisy.

Later that afternoon, the lunatic's owners invited Maisy and her parents over for a visit. Shaking the dog's paw was meant to show her he was friendly. While it may have made the owners feel better, it nearly finished Maisy off.

Any dog could be a threat for a child as small as she was, even the Yorkshire terriers down the other end of the street. Therefore, she took no chances. Whenever she headed to our house, it was via Mr. Coleman's yard and the red board fence. Bypassing the sidewalk, the Doberman, and Fritz entirely—provided Fritz wasn't tunneling—became her main goal. Truth be told, there were few things cuter than her head of light brown curls popping up over the boards. Her little bottom wiggled as she carefully descended into Mama's garden and landed with a grin.

Vengeance

May 1985

Mama and I headed to the Piggly Wiggly for supplies for the Perkinses' Memorial Day cookout. Mr. and Mrs. Perkins, Sasha and Natalie's parents, were famous for their backyard parties, and everyone clambered after Mrs. Perkins' cooking whenever possible. Summer barbecues were frequent at their house, and nothing was sweeter than scoring leftovers pressed upon you after one of their shindigs.

As we turned the corner back onto Maple Street, it became apparent that something nefarious had been brewing in our absence. Fritz's pooping routine must've finally gotten the better of Nattie, and I guess bag delivery didn't cut the mustard anymore. There she was, hair frantically escaping its pins, housecoat flapping near to the point of impropriety, and slippers smacking against the sidewalk in a sharp staccato. She marched her way over to Cilla's front porch, scoop shovel in hand and caterwauling to beat the band.

"Cilla Prescott, you nasty old busybody! You keep that damn dog in your own yard, you hear me!?"

Mama pulled the car in the driveway and jumped out, ready to run interference, but she stopped short. Nattie was madder than we'd ever seen her.

"You hear me, you vile old piece of trash!?"

As Nattie stomped up the two porch steps, the front door flew wide. There stood Cilla, laughing and pointing, her mouth open like a circus barker.

I knew the instant before it happened, the whole scene suddenly fusing in my mind with the only possible conclusion taking center stage. Mama glanced at me, horrified, as she, too, had the split-second premonition. We stood there, powerless to stop it.

Nattie arced the shovel back and let fly.

With the force of a medieval catapult, Fritz's still-fresh dung heap hurtled through the air and secured its target with a sickening *whump*, plugging the erstwhile bullhorn. Startled so completely that she stood frozen to the spot, Cilla merely blinked.

Delighted, Nattie threw her head back and cackled maniacally, reveling in the satisfaction of the moment too deeply to notice when her archenemy regained her wits. Spitting out the poop, Cilla lunged across the porch, out for blood.

She hit Nattie with enough force to knock her down the shallow steps and clear onto the grass. Stunned, Nattie still managed to retain possession of the scoop shovel and desperately tried to brain her nemesis with it.

Not requiring a weapon, Cilla set into Nattie's home-hair permanent with a wrath that boiled the air.

"Hold still, you horse's ass!! *Ow!* I'll shove the rest of your face into that shit pile before—*Oof!*"

Mama and I stood helpless. Mouths agape, we wavered between shock, disgust, and a giddy panic that ran through us like a live wire. Should we try to break them up? Did the church spell out the boundaries of Christian duty for this type of thing? Had the church even *thought* of this type of thing?

The pugilists continued to duke it out. A writhing ball of lavender hair, sharp claws, flapping housecoats long past the point of impropriety, and enough cuss words to make George Carlin and Richard Pryor blush burned like a portal to hell on Cilla's front lawn.

"You've always been such a goddamn drama queen, you twit," Cilla grabbed the back of Nattie's head and yanked.

"Well, at least I always had the decency to—*OW!* Let go of my hair!"

"No!"

Neighbors began to come out of their houses and backyards to stare. I guess that was enough to shake Mama loose because she ran across our yard, followed momentarily by Mrs. Prince from across the street. They wrestled the prizefighters apart as they flailed and lunged, trying to land one last shot. Cilla tried to turn around and rage at Mama, little chunks of froth-covered turd flying from her mouth as she cussed, but Mama had a solid grip on each arm and managed to pull her back up onto the porch.

Mrs. Prince pulled Nattie across our lawn and back to her own yard, giving the abandoned shovel a wide berth. I instinctively went to pick it up but wasn't quite sure what to do from there. I certainly didn't want to go anywhere near Nattie's, and I didn't want to put it in our garage for Daddy to have to return that evening. Finally, I ran to our backyard and chucked it over the hedge like I was dumping a body and then headed back for the forgotten groceries baking in the hot car.

***

Mama came home a little while later, scratched, bruised, and exhausted, but in one piece.

"What the devil is wrong with those two?"

She plunked down at the kitchen table. Face flushed and hair mussed, she looked as if maybe she had gone a round or two with Cilla herself, a likely black eye beginning to bloom. She took a deep breath, shaking her head and staring off. I stood frozen, not knowing what to do for my battered Mama. But then she snickered.

"That woman flung a turd!"

Wide-eyed, she looked up at me. At that moment, I knew all was well. Mama and I dissolved into fits of giggles. We laughed so hard we cried, our sides aching and nearly peeing our pants. We wheezed and were like to pass out before finally pulling ourselves back together.

When Daddy walked in after work and saw Mama's black eye, he dropped his briefcase and ran over to her, worried. He was thoroughly confused when we started up again, snorting and crying and enjoying how good it felt to laugh.

***

The confrontation between Nattie and Cilla was all anyone could talk about at the Perkinses' cookout that night. Despite several tellings, people hung on every word and collapsed into hysterics at the poo-flinging part.

We gleefully reenacted the fight scene with the boys using their best Chuck Norris moves to take one another down. It was likely the first story in neighborhood history that didn't inflate with each retelling; it was simply too golden to be improved upon. Even Mama didn't mind the judgments made on Nattie and Cilla. As far as she was concerned, those two old bats had earned it.

***

"Mom, did that really happen, or are you making it up?"

"It really happened, Grace. Anger makes people do strange things some-times, things they would normally consider outlandish or ridiculous if they were thinking straight. Adults do childish things, too, on occasion."

"But wait, I want to hear more about when Cilla was a kid. Did work make her mean?"

"No, but those years were an important part of who she was and why it was so strange when things went bad."

Work

Boston, 1926

The following day, Cilla woke having slept more soundly than she remembered ever having done before. Though she was tempted to stay in bed all day marinating in peaceful luxury, she pushed the thought away in favor of getting herself set for the long-term.

Dressed for the day in her new clothes and with her face and hair done as best she could, she headed out in search of a pastry. Of course, the Omni provided breakfast at the hotel, but she was now keen to save as much money for her future as possible. A beautiful croissant from a nearby bakery seemed just the ticket, and with it in hand, she made her way to an adjacent park to think.

The park reminded her of the days before Penny died, and she missed her more than ever. While the memories were bittersweet, they instilled in Cilla a determination to succeed not only for herself but also for her little sister, who would never have the chance.

She procured a newspaper and proceeded to read it straight through, soaking up as much information about Boston as possible. Midway through, an item advertising work in Jamaica Plain caught her eye. West of downtown by about five miles, JP sat far on the other side of Back Bay.

Still, Cilla felt drawn to it somehow and decided then and there that it was where she would begin her new life.

***

The Massachusetts Public Transit Authority ran lines out to Jamaica Plain, and Cilla braved her first long solo ride. Getting off at Centre and Green Streets near the Five Cents Savings Bank, she fell instantly in love. It was the first time she had seen a working-class community and how people in it related to one another. It certainly wasn't a place her father was likely to make an appearance, anyway.

She could get to Franklin Park, an oasis amid suburban sprawl and industry, by going straight down Green Street. Peaceful and beautiful, it was rather romantic juxtaposed against the factories that made up the borough, an escape to nature right in the excitement of the city.

Businesses producing all sorts of goods hummed along, contributing to the heartbeat around her. The Continental Dye House on Brookside Avenue—which colored the brook itself various colors as a byproduct—automobile makers, print shops, bottling plants, and many more industry notables could be found within just a few blocks. Green Street alone contained barbers, florists, bakers, grocers, paint stores, dress shops, plumbers, dentists, and an auto repair garage.

The people of Jamaica Plain ranged anywhere from very poor near the tracks on Amory, to the general working class, to upper-middle-class, and their demeanor proved quite different from those in Back Bay or Beacon Hill. They appeared to have more on their minds and moved with more purpose but seemed no less happy than their counterparts in the ritzier areas of Boston.

Cilla explored the city for a while, then headed back to Bickford and Centre Streets. For what felt like the umpteenth time since she had left home the day before, she gathered her wits and courage and went to see about a job. Standing straight and trying to appear confident, she marched into the Thomas Plant Shoe Factory and crossed her fingers.

"Yes, how may I help you?" a woman asked. The desk she sat behind held a placard indicating her name was Mrs. Bennett.

"I'd like to inquire about employment, please. I've brought a copy of the newspaper advertisement if you'd like to see it." She held out the piece of paper, attempting to look mature and responsible rather than nervous and scared.

The woman looked her up and down. It hadn't occurred to Cilla that anyone might think her too posh for a job. Of course, when she'd bought the new-and-improved version of herself the day before, she hadn't foreseen factory work in Jamaica Plain.

Realizing she was staring, Mrs. Bennett quickly glanced away. It was none of her business why someone wanted work.

"Yes, well, wait here a moment, and someone will be with you shortly."

She disappeared behind a set of doors and returned with a man who greeted Cilla kindly. He introduced himself as Mr. Cobb and welcomed her like family.

Mr. Cobb wasn't at all what she had expected, nor was the factory. Asking little about her circumstances, he was more interested in evaluating her character. He explained that the founder, Mr. Thomas G. Plant, had started from the bottom himself and believed in hard work and efficiency, which continued to be the culture after he sold the factory to the United Shoe Company. Mr. Plant had also believed in making his business a place that inspired employees to do their best.

The Plant factory was well-known for several reasons. First, it employed nearly five thousand workers and paid them more than other plants in JP. But the perks didn't stop there; it provided employees with much more than a job. Because the Great War had sacrificed so many men, and women had joined the workforce in unprecedented numbers, the company had embraced the surge of female workers many years earlier. It had even gone so far as to create a daycare and kindergarten, complete with an outdoor play area, kitchen for preparing nourishing meals, medical staff, and instructive play curriculum. Mothers could be confident that their little ones were well cared for while the women were at work.

It wasn't only children and widows who benefited, however. The factory also provided a separate locker for every employee, as well as several acres of picnic area, a restaurant and dining rooms, a hall for dances and parties, a library, gymnasium, medical staff, greenhouse, swimming pool, fresh air pumped in, and cold drinking water throughout the day. It was as if Cilla would be gaining a whole new life all in one fell swoop. Not at all what she had expected.

"Ms. Dixon, we'll be pleased to have you join us," Mr. Cobb said at the end of their tour. "Please plan to begin work the day after tomorrow. Mrs. Bennett will provide you with some paperwork and any further information you require. Welcome to the Plant family!"

"Thank you, sir!" Cilla grinned.

Excited by her good fortune and not wanting to appear ungrateful, still, she pushed her luck a bit more when she returned to the secretary.

"Excuse me, Mrs. Bennett. Might you know of any places with rooms to rent?"

"Yes, of course, dear." Mrs. Bennett was much friendlier now that Cilla would be joining her as an employee. "I'll just poke my head out for a moment. You stay right there."

She called a friendly young woman named Stella from the line and introduced her. Stella knew of a boarding house some of her friends lived in not far away on Forbes Street, and they happened to be looking for another girl.

"You'll need to talk to Mrs. Morcombe. She's the house mistress. Tell her Stella Manning sent you."

***

Cilla left in a cloud of joy and disbelief. Everyone in Boston had heard about The Thomas G. Plant Shoe Factory for years, but to be a part of it was unbelievable. She made her way to the boarding house and introduced herself to the impressive Mrs. Morcombe, House Mistress, and relayed her earlier conversation with Stella.

"Yes, I know Stella quite well. Any friend of hers is welcome here. However, there are strict rules and an agreement you must sign."

"Oh, of course!" Cilla replied.

After listening to all Mrs. Morcombe laid out and signing a boarding agreement, Cilla planned to move in the next day.

As she rode back into Boston, thinking how much her life had changed in a mere thirty-six hours, her stomach wriggled with nerves. She had quite suddenly gone from a fourteen-year-old dependent shut-in to an independent woman with a job, a new home, and new possibilities laid at her feet. Still, she had never been so excited. She wished Penny were alive to come on this adventure with her.

***

Arriving back at the Omni, Cilla took some time to strategize again, though she found herself daydreaming about all she had witnessed at the factory. She would need appropriate clothing for work, though she would be given a color-coded uniform upon arrival. Sheets, a blanket, a pillow for her bed, and a bit of food to hold her over until she could determine her grocery situation at the house were the immediate needs.

She spent the remainder of the day gathering necessities and making lists of the things she would need to look into once settled. With nothing left to do, she crawled into bed to dream away her last night as a little girl from Back Bay.

The Pullman Pool

June 1985

Once summer hit, Pullman's public pool became the hot spot for kids, babysitters, and adults alike. Not your ordinary place for a dip, the land and facilities had been granted to the city by some ultra-rich old dude. Apparently, he grew up in Pullman and wanted to leave a legacy but didn't have any heirs of his own with mouths in which to shove silver spoons. So, he instructed that the city spare no expense and, therefore, we had one of the best pools in the tri-state.

Expansive enough to accommodate two slides, a diving area, lap lanes, playground, sandbox, and a zero-depth kiddie pool (or p-p-pool as we called it, because of all the "p" in it), patrons came from miles around. Our crew bought annual family passes since we lived close enough to walk and were old enough to go without an adult. So, we spent a lot of time there when we weren't playing ball.

We usually headed over around one o'clock or so, after grilled cheese, tuna salad, or PB & J at somebody's house. By then, the water was warm enough on early summer days and refreshingly cool enough on muggy mid-summer afternoons to keep us in decent spirits.

We swam for a couple of hours and maybe shared a snack from concessions if anyone had recently come into some allowance. If Pansy wasn't working at Woolworths, she and Maisy would join us. Pansy made a bit of extra pocket money by giving her mother a much-needed break from Maisy's non-stop monologue.

Once we'd had enough fun, we'd head home to carve out the rest of the afternoon. This we frequently spent either under the trees in someone's backyard until it cooled off enough to play ball or laid out on someone's living room floor, curtains shut against the heat and fans blowing directly on us. Every neighborhood mom made it her mission to close up the house first thing every morning in an attempt to keep the hot stuff out. Barring that, cool basements sufficed as final refuges, bare concrete, centipedes, and spiders being temporarily tolerated.

***

It'd been beastly hot for June. As soon as the pool opened, every kid in town turned up to stake their claim for the summer. Our usual spot sat in the grass halfway between the first guard tower of the regular pool and the bathrooms. A decent-sized willow in a neighboring yard threw shade on us by mid-afternoon, and we didn't need to wade through deck chairs, towels, and abandoned flip-flops to get to it. It took a bit more effort to get to the diving board, but that didn't bother us.

We spent a good portion of our pool time racing. Above water, underwater, single-widths, double-widths, crab walks, arms-only, legs-only, relays, tandems: you name it, we raced it. We'd all taken swimming lessons together when we were tadpoles, so our skills sized up pretty evenly. Still, I had a secret weapon.

Being the tall, skinny girl rarely ever worked in my favor. I always looked dorky in clothes petite girls looked cute in, and my sharp hip bones always bumped into things. It was mortifying if that thing happened to be human and really hurt if it was something solid. But no one ever sympathizes with a skinny girl. Adults were always telling me how great my height would be when I grew up. Still, it did exactly zero for me at eleven.

Almost every time we went to the pool, my secret weapon made an appearance. I had an unexpectedly powerful kick. Anyone who dared take me on, especially older kids and especially boys from nearby towns, thought the bean pole would be easy to beat. They forgot to factor in details like aerodynamics and egos and, therefore, leaving them wide-eyed and sucking air became my trademark. Our crew frequently enjoyed concessions earned via my win over some macho older kid who'd lost a race and a significant amount of pride.

The other upside of my hidden skill was that Garrett Hendrickson, Pansy's boyfriend, happened to be one of the lifeguards and the kind of guy that roots for the underdog. As such, he became a sort of patron of mine. He sent macho boys my way, having convinced them they could take me, which he knew they couldn't. Every time I beat one of them, I'd look up at Garrett, and he'd give me a wink. Having him on your side was the kind of thing you put in your back pocket for a rainy day.

Garrett was an all-around "good egg." Polite, helpful, wicked smart, and a fair athlete, he had baby-faced good looks that promised to be gorgeously handsome in a few years. At sixteen, he was thoroughly engaging to both kids and adults alike.

During the summer, he split his time between helping his mom with summer school in the mornings and lifeguarding in the afternoons. He was nearly perfect in most moms' eyes and dreamy in most teen girls' eyes. As such, he caused a collective swoon every time he arrived on the pool deck.

The cool thing about Garrett was that he didn't appear to notice the commotion he caused or, if he did, it didn't affect him much. Whenever he blew his whistle at some kid for running or rough-housing or generally being an idiot, he smiled and gave a casual little two-finger salute. Then he'd politely ask them to stop whatever they were doing, whether eating in the pool or nearly killing their friend playing Chicken. The other guards bossed everybody around and acted like drill sergeants just because they wore a red swimsuit and carried a life preserver. But Garrett genuinely liked people, and, as a result, people listened to him.

The Drummond girls had won Garrett's heart the year before. Well, technically, Pansy had, but everyone knew he had a Maisy-shaped cut-out in his ticker now that required filling on a regular basis. She tagged along next to him everywhere, her cute little voice narrating their journey and her squidgy hand in whichever of his wasn't holding Pansy's. Garrett never seemed to tire of her, often lifting her on his shoulders and asking what she saw from way up there. Those two could get quite philosophical over squirrels, bird's nests, or whatever else Maisy might spy from up top. Consensus was that if Garrett and Pansy ever broke up, there would be a major Maisy puddle to deal with.

***

On the first Monday after school got out, we decided a day of soaking in the sun during a cooling dip and enjoying the breeze in the shade of the willow was just the ticket. Hot and glad to finally be free for three months, no one wanted to hit the library—our other refuge due to its air conditioning throughout.

The afternoon stretched out before us, nearly perfect. The smell of hot dogs grilling wafted our way and made it seem even more like summer.

Pansy had to work until mid-afternoon, but Mrs. Drummond said she'd send her and Maisy over when she got home.

Garrett occupied the guard tower nearest us, and Jimmy and Sasha gladly provided him with unsolicited advice regarding how to handle some middle school rough-housers. He smiled to himself and took their suggestions in stride while keeping his eyes on the water.

Shortly after 3:00, Garrett's face changed, but he was no longer looking at the swimmers. I followed his gaze and saw the Drummond girls walking toward us, having just come in the gate from the pool house. Typically, this would elicit a great big grin from him, but even from my vantage point on our blanket, I could see something was wrong. Pansy looked mad. Really mad. Maisy was running to keep up with her as she stomped our way.

Arriving at our spot, Pansy threw down her bag.

"Ooh! I'm so mad I could spit."

This was not normal. She could be a bossy older sister sometimes but was pretty even-tempered. We all instinctively scooched back a smidge in case something else came flying toward our carefully constructed nest.

She shot Garrett a look of, "I'll tell you on break," and he reluctantly directed his eyes back to the pool.

"Geez, who took a dump in your Cheerios?" Jimmy asked.

"That nasty Cilla Prescott, that's who."

"What'd she do?"

Steam practically whistled out of Pansy's ears. At the mention of Cilla, we all sat up, eager to hear what sort of evil vitriol she had rained down on the populous that day.

"C'mon and sit," said Natalie. "I've got room next to me."

Maisy cuddled up to Natalie, but Pansy proceeded to pace, fists clenched, and launched into a replay of her day at Woolworth's lunch counter.

She'd started her shift at 8:00 a.m., waiting on customers with their eggs, toast, and coffee. She collected tips and listened to the same scuttlebutt heard around every small-town diner every morning of every day all across America. As usual, the police blotter was discussed at length, with corroboration and details being sought from any officer sitting at the counter, trying to pretend he wasn't interested in providing the 4-1-1.

The morning's big news was that Dicky Hickam had to tow two hot rods off of Highway P on Saturday night. Some high school kids decided drag racing out there was a smart idea. Thankfully, the only thing hurt was some pride and several rows of corn on either side of the road. While Dicky earned double-time rates for coming out on the weekend, the Monday morning coffee klatsch happily accepted the gift of idiot kids to lament.

When Cilla Prescott and her bosom marched in, everyone fell quiet, sensing blood and a show. Cilla went straight for Pansy and started in on her, cussing and frothing away.

"Miss Drummond! On Saturday past, I purchased four cinnamon rolls from this establishment. This morning, just forty-eight hours later, I awoke to find two of them moldy. I expect you will right this situation immediately and with money back!"

"Gosh, Mrs. Prescott, I'm really sorry. That must have been terribly frustrating."

"Quite. And I expect to be compensated, as I said."

"I'm afraid Mr. Wittford has stepped out for a moment, and I'm not authorized to do refunds. But if you'd like to wait a few minutes, he'll be back shortly."

At that, Cilla had laid into poor Pansy in front of everybody.

"The things that nasty old bag said were awful!" Pansy spat.

"Like what?" Sasha was eager to hear all the grimy details.

"I won't repeat them, but a lot of customers started hollering at her to lay off and give it a rest and stuff. It was so embarrassing! She kept yelling at me until Mr. Wittford came back in and hauled her out. I guess he told her not to come back."

Pansy had gone in the back for a cry and some comforting and had received larger than usual tips from several customers. But we could all see the embarrassment still burned hot inside her. We felt awful; not a single one of us would ever have been able to keep from crying while Cilla Prescott yelled at us, much less in public. Pansy, on the other hand, had held her ground until the storm passed before falling apart in private.

Garrett couldn't take his break until 3:30, so we all catered to Pansy and tried to help her feel better. Jimmy even bought her a Freezy-Pop from the concession stand, and he never parted with his money unless absolutely necessary.

***

By the time Garrett climbed down from two towers over and joined us on our blanket, Pansy was a little calmer. Maisy stood behind him and played with his chocolatey-auburn curls while he listened and comforted Pansy as she retold the story. It held more humor and incredulity and less anger this time—but she accepted Garrett's sympathies with a smile.

We swam a bit more and then packed up and headed home a little before dinner. Aside from the early-season heat, it had been a decent day for all but Pansy. If the rest of the summer went like that, it would be pretty sweet.

Incidents and Accidents

Saturday was Daddy's day to rest and take care of home and yard projects. A little recliner time to start, some grass mowing, and a baseball game on the radio, while he lay on the swing with his cap over his face, was just his speed. So, when the phone rang at eight o'clock, and Nattie began screeching in his ear, a decidedly cranky hitch cropped up in his get-along.

The man who usually mowed Nattie's lawn couldn't provide the service that week. Of course, that meant Daddy was on Christian duty. The good thing was we still had someone to do the weekend collection for us, saving me a run-in with the starter pistol.

***

With the weather already hotter than usual, Daddy headed over at nine o'clock to take care of Nattie's yard before the heat kicked in. Any earlier, and the rest of the neighborhood would be on his case, particularly Cilla. It was a tightrope walk balancing manners against a batty old bag raging at him to get a move on. I didn't envy him.

Nattie's front lawn was small and never took much time. The back was somewhat bigger but still a straightforward job. The only concern was the flower bed at the far side of the yard against the garage. Of course, Daddy was always careful and hadn't ever clipped a plant. Still, Nattie insisted on standing on her patio coaching, scolding, and criticizing the work Daddy was doing for free.

"Now, Ben, you make sure you don't run over my flowers!"

"Never hit one yet, Nattie." He started up the mower.

"Well, now, I know that, but I've seen you be a little reckless. *Watch out!*"

Daddy purposely swerved over the brick border, dangerously close to the dirt.

"Can't hear you! Mower's too loud!" he mouthed.

I giggled from our side of the hedge.

And so it went until the hungry blades had chewed off the last patch.

"There you go, Nattie. Nice and neat; no casualties. Just like you asked."

"Well, you certainly tried to give me a heart attack, Ben Walker."

"Aw, I never did. I'll put the mower back in the garage and be on my way then, shall I?"

"Yes. Put it away. But then I have another job for you."

Of course she did.

Jack had always kept his ship in tip-top shape. Since his passing, however, a few things had become a bit challenging for Nattie. Daddy helped where he could, always careful not to turn into her do-everything-at-a-finger's-snap handyman. Mama excused the caution.

"What seems to be the problem?"

"It's those god-forsaken mice. They're in my garage, again. I want you to put some poison down."

"Well, now, you know that might leave a mess when they die in there, don't you? Unless you plan on hauling out the carcasses, that is."

"I most certainly do not! And, I don't care where they die. I just don't want them in my garage alive."

"Alright, then. Where do you keep the stuff?"

"In there. Top shelf."

Daddy did as asked and tended to the hemorrhagic fate of the mice.

"You've got yourself a hole in the base where they're coming in," he said when he finished. "Oughta have your yard man fix that for you next time he's out."

"Yes, fine. Did you spread it nice and thick?"

"Sure did."

"Good. Now, do the outside, then."

"Where? Outside the garage?"

"Yes, yes, outside the garage. You said that there's a hole."

"Well, yeah, there is. But if you start spreading that stuff all over, you're gonna have a whole mess of dead critters in your yard, Nattie. Best to leave it inside for the mice."

"No, no, I want it outside, too."

"Suit yourself."

Daddy went behind the garage and spread a bit of the rat poison around the hole. No doubt he'd get called back in for graveyard duty.

"Okay, well, lots to do today, so I best be going. You have a nice day, Nattie."

"Hmph!"

***

Daddy walked in our back door, shaking his head.

"That infernal woman's gonna have a pet cemetery in her yard before she knows it. Just wait 'til she gets a 'coon or possum laid out in a pool of blood on her patio. Won't that beat all!"

"What on earth, Ben? What did she do?"

Daddy explained the rat poison situation to Mama and me, snickering when he imagined the carnage Nattie would find in a day or two.

"Annabelle, you kids be real careful if you go over there to collect balls. Give 'em a good wash with the hose, and scrub your hands with soap as soon as you're done, okay?"

"Got it."

"Good. Now, if you'll excuse me, I have our own lawn to mow."

He walked back out to our garage, giggling. Not something frequently seen after Nattie's screech has woken one up for the day.

***

Later that afternoon, as Daddy lay on the swing, chores done, a visitor crept across our back lawn. The neighborhood mole was at it again. Unbeknownst to us, he'd tunneled under the chain-link fence that ran next to the hedge. I had laid out in front of a fan in the living room reading, and Mama was running errands, so he had the place to himself. As usual, he didn't leave much of a mess, but upon further inspection, Daddy discovered it had been a two-fer kind of day.

***

Cilla charged up the steps, calling for Daddy to come quick. I popped my head up in the window and looked out. She was madder than a wet hen.

"She's done it! She's killed him!"

"Who's done it? Killed who?"

"Nattie! She's killed Fritz! She's always hated him, and now she's finally gone and done it!"

I crept out and followed them, watching through the hedge as Cilla hauled Daddy back to her kitchen doorstep and pointed. There on the patio lay Fritz, unmoving. Daddy stepped around the little dog and realized at once what had happened. Fritz's tongue lolled from his mouth, covered in blood. A red, sticky puddle pooled under his cheek. Rat poison.

"Shit."

"You're damn right, shit! She killed him! She killed my Fritz!"

"Now, Cilla, she did no such thing."

"Yes, she did! She finally got the revenge she's always wanted!"

"Damn it, Cilla! Would you shut your pie hole for one minute? Nattie did not kill Fritz! If anybody did, it was you!"

"What? How *dare* you!?"

"You let that damn dog wander and dig wherever he wanted. It's a wonder he didn't meet his maker a long time ago. I bet you dollars to doughnuts if I look in my yard, there are two tunnels, one on either side, and I can tell you exactly who put them there. If Fritz got into something in someone else's yard, that's on you and you alone."

"It wasn't someone else's yard; it was hers! I watched him!"

Daddy stared at her. She'd seen Fritz tunneling and had stood and watched as he made his merry way into Nattie's yard. Now, she was paying the price. Daddy turned and walked away, leaving Cilla fuming and calling after him.

I joined him, silent, as he passed me and headed back across our front lawn. When we reached the backyard, he got a shovel from the garage and filled in Fritz's tunnels one last time.

Life in JP

Jamaica Plain, April 1926

Cilla slept hard and woke early; her excitement was barely contained as she dressed, did her hair and makeup, and checked out of her privileged life for good. Looking the part, she hopped on the streetcar to her life in Jamaica Plain and didn't look back.

By the time she arrived at Morcombe House, the other girls were already at work. Waiting until evening to meet them suited her fine as she had things to take care of. After paying Mrs. Morcombe for the remainder of the month's rent, she settled into her room. It wasn't much, but it was hers, and she could do with it as she pleased—within reason, of course.

With move-in complete, she needed to acquaint herself with the neighborhood and purchase a few final items. Mrs. Morcombe proved helpful in that department, giving her the names and locations of many popular places the girls liked to go, including Franklin Park. However, the top of the list for Cilla was a bank in which to place some of her money, which put her even more in Mrs. Morcombe's good graces, as she appeared responsible.

Keeping back a small amount with which to buy her last necessities and make her way around the city—and a small amount simply on instinct—Cilla placed the rest in a new account. Then she stopped by a small grocery and bought lunch. Mostly finished, she headed to Franklin Park to picnic and think about all that had happened in the last two days.

While she quite enjoyed Jamaica Plain and all its differences to Back Bay, she also appreciated the memories and familiarity Franklin Park offered. Thoughts of the ducks in Boston Garden washed over her as she sat eating her lunch, and her eyes welled with tears. Poor Penny. What fantastic adventures they would've had together!

What would her life be like if Penny hadn't passed? Indeed, she wouldn't be sitting in a park in Jamaica Plain getting ready to live as an adult at only fourteen. But neither would she have felt prepared to do such a thing, which she most certainly did now.

Her mother never would've fallen apart. Or would she? Something Cilla preferred not to think about. The idea that her mother's disintegration could've been endured with Penny by her side was a rabbit hole she would not allow herself to go down as she might never come back out. One thing she knew for sure: she would never let another person hurt her the way her mother had.

***

The end of the workday neared, and Cilla put a stop to her exploring. She wanted to be prepared and not taken by surprise when the other girls arrived home.

A short while later, as she sat nervously in her nearly empty room, the front door of Morcombe house opened, and three new voices rang out down below.

"Evening, Mrs. M!" one of them called. "Is she here yet?"

"Good evening, girls. Yes, she's up—*ooh!* … stairs," she finished as all three raced past her and up the staircase.

"Oh, I can't wait!" a voice said as Cilla stood behind her bedroom door. Closing her eyes, she took a deep breath and reached for the handle.

A knock sounded as she opened the door, followed by a startled, "Oh!" as a girl snatched her hand back and burst into giggles. The tension broke instantly, and everyone was at ease.

"Hello, I'm Helen," said the lithe blond girl who had knocked. She held out her hand and confidently shook Cilla's when offered in return. "This here's Ruthie and Beth," she added, indicating the girls behind her. They reached around and offered their hands, as well.

"I'm Cilla," she answered, suddenly a bit shy. Of all that she'd had to do in the last few days, this felt like the biggest. These were people who would be part of her new life, even outside of her job.

The girls were kind and friendly, and energetic. At least, she assumed Ruthie and Beth must be to keep up with Helen. Friendships were something that Cilla didn't have a lot of experience with, having grown up as she had. It would take some getting used to, though she welcomed the change.

Still, it was more than the change itself. Friends were people who knew you better than everyone else, people who knew your secrets. She wasn't ready to share those quite yet. Up until today, her father's money had done most of the talking for her. But now, she would have to take over. She would need to take care that no one discovered her truth and tried to return her to Back Bay.

It wasn't long before the girls put her story to the test.

"So, where are you from?" Ruthie asked.

"Oh, um, from Boston."

"What brings you out to JP? You still have family in the city?"

"No. I-I used to live with my grandparents, but they both passed, so now it's just me."

"You poor thing! Well, you're in the right place. We're like family here and at the factory. How old are you, by the way?"

"Um, I'm eighteen," she lied. "Where are you all from?" It felt safer turning the attention in the other direction.

"I'm from Brookline," Helen answered. "Not so far away, I know. But I needed my own space, and I still see my family on the regular. I miss my dog, Hank, though."

"And I'm from Dorchester," Beth offered. "Not far, either, but there's lots of kids in my family. My pop tightens the screws once we turn seventeen and says if we're ever gonna rate, we'd best bounce and make a go of it for ourselves when we turn eighteen. Honestly, it's nice to finally have my own room."

"I'm from West Somerville," this from Ruthie, "even farther than you. Mama and Daddy didn't need my help at home, so I came to JP a couple of years ago. I have cousins here, and we get together a lot. You met one yesterday. Stella? She's a little older than me, twenty-two. But we always got along as kids, and she helped me get my job at the factory when I moved."

"Speaking of Plant's, you're going to love it there," Helen stepped back in. "It's like its own little town sometimes. You'll get to know so many people. And there's so much to do there, even when you're not working."

"Gosh, it feels like a whole new life!" Cilla said, inwardly chastising herself for saying such a thing out loud.

"Don't worry; we won't let you get lost." Beth smiled and put her arm around Cilla's shoulder. "Besides, you're an adult now. Time to spread those wings and fly."

They all appeared quite worldly to Cilla. Of course, anyone would, to a girl who hadn't seen much of the world at all in the last seven years. Still, it felt as if she had aged five years herself since leaving home, and she decided that whatever came her way would find her at the ready.

***

Over the following weeks and months, it became clear to Cilla that, while fate dealt her a rough hand to start, it appeared to be apologizing profusely now. She adored her housemates and Mrs. Morcombe and sensed that the feeling was mutual.

Helen, Ruthie, and Beth were significantly older, but no one noticed anything different about Cilla. Maybe she was an adept actress, or perhaps being introduced as eighteen, no one ever gave it a second thought. Either way, she fit in well and was having the time of her life. Lord knew she'd had to grow up quickly once her mother started heading downhill. She could handle almost anything life threw her way. For now, though, she was in safe hands.

The girls spent many an evening on Centre Street or at the factory that summer, simply being part of the masses and enjoying the world for what it was. They often stopped for ice cream at the parlor just down from Plant's on the walk home from work and spent many weekend afternoons in the various small parks around the city or over at Franklin Park with a larger group of friends.

While new to her repertoire, Cilla enjoyed socializing immensely and loved learning about others and where they came from. Still, she was hesitant to allow anyone too close. The pain of abandonment was etched too deeply in her soul to risk it again. She became quite skilled at turning questions about herself into questions about someone else, which everyone interpreted as her simply being a great listener and interested in other people. As a result, her social circle expanded.

As months passed, she thought less and less about her father and his world five miles further into Boston. Her time at home felt light-years away. She had all she needed in Jamaica Plain, and there was little chance he would ever look for her, a truth which saddened her, yet, at the same time, provided relief as his disinterest allowed her scars to become less prominent. This afforded her the freedom to grow into whomever she wanted. As passing months turned into passing seasons, she found she quite liked who that was.

Mr. Fix-It

Summer 1929

As spring turned to summer, Cilla walked home from work more regularly and leisurely. The warmer air and longer evenings made for an awakening in the city that she always enjoyed. Shops kept their windows and doors open later in the hopes of extra business. The community blossomed with the hope brought by fresh breezes and time spent in them, and the trials of the day felt a little less burdensome as everyone worked together to bridge increasingly difficult times.

On such a Thursday evening in June, Cilla's life once again changed forever, though she would not know for some time yet. Following her usual path down Centre Street to Forbes, she passed Schaffer's Auto Repair Shop, the same as every other day for the last three years. That afternoon, however, with the doors open wide and work visible to passersby, Cilla noticed someone she'd never seen before.

A young man, bent over the engine of a 1927 Packard in the garage's front bay, happened to stand and turn around as she walked past. His broad shoulders tapered into a trim waistline, and his head of beautiful, thick, light brown waves refused to remain tidy as strands fell forward and caressed his brow, red highlights glinting in the sunshine. His gentle eyes settled on Cilla's and accompanied the most charmingly-shy smile she'd ever seen. Her eighteen-year-old insides did a flip-flop of excitement as she smiled shyly back.

As June crept toward July, Cilla found herself looking forward to her walks and was disappointed when afternoon rains forced Schaffer's garage doors to remain shut. Any day she could see the young mechanic as she passed on the way home was a good one.

Unlike her housemates, Cilla didn't spend time stepping out with young men, not that she didn't like them. And it certainly wasn't because she didn't cause heads to turn—it was well-known that Cilla Dixon was a "looker." She simply didn't want to get too close to anyone.

Helen, Ruthie, and Beth all stepped out with particular young men on the regular, and Ruthie and her fella were quite serious. They encouraged her to accept when someone asked her to the Footlight Club or a factory dance. But, while happy to socialize with them as friends and acquaintances, she had no desire for anything more. With her parent's marriage burned into her memory, she had zero interest in pursuing anything of the sort. That being the case, why step out with anyone and give them hope that things would ever become something more?

The young man at Schaffer's was the first one to give her stomach the gollywobbles when she caught his eye. Cilla considered him a safe indulgence since she didn't even know his name, and they didn't run in the same social circles. If the garage doors stood open when she walked past with the others, she made sure to only sneak a glance at him if he was out, which he quite frequently was. Yet, despite her discretion, the other girls saw the young mechanic looking at Cilla, too.

It was Beth who had done the sleuthing amongst their friends, inquiring as to who this young fellow might be and who he ran with on the weekends. He appeared the reserved sort, not prone to discoverable outlandish behavior. Still, no one ever stayed off Beth's radar without her permission, and her social net spread wide enough to track anyone down. She managed to sniff out the shy Mr. Fix-It, unbeknownst to Cilla, and set their paths on a collision course.

***

The Morcombe House girls and their circle of friends planned to spend an early August Saturday picnicking and enjoying the day in Franklin Park. They packed baskets of sandwiches, while others packed pickles, and still others, drinks. It was a strategy they'd utilized countless times in the past, rotating who brought what, though budgets had constricted quite a bit in the last year, and the fare was nothing more than basic.

Beth mentioned that another friend of hers and her group would be joining them during the afternoon. This seemed a fine plan. As far as the girls were concerned, the more, the merrier.

Shortly after they'd finished their picnic, the newcomers came by. Much to Cilla's astonishment but, curiously, to no one else's, the young mechanic with the charming smile appeared before her. Beth, Ruthie, and Helen pretended not to notice, keeping busy with their beaus and other friends, but they made sure Cilla and the young man found themselves together.

"Hello." The young man smiled shyly and offered his hand in greeting. "I'm Marlon Prescott."

"Hello." Cilla grinned girlishly back and shook his hand, nearly forgetting to introduce herself in return. Drinking each other in for the first time up close, both turned away, suddenly bashful, only to turn right back again.

"Sure is swell to meet you proper, finally," Marlon managed.

"Yes," Cilla nodded.

The rest of the group hurried away to the Franklin Park Zoo, leaving them entirely alone. Had Cilla given a moment's attention to anything else, she would have seen Beth, Ruthie, and Helen winking conspiratorially at each other as they looked back over their shoulders.

"I, um, think your friends there," Marlon gestured toward the group, "might have had something to do with this."

"Yes." Cilla smiled up at Marlon.

He ducked his head and nervously scratched at his ear. "Well, I'll have to remember to thank them later."

That brought Cilla out of her daze, and she laughed. "Yes!"

While Beth and her machinations amused them both, neither was unhappy with the result. They chatted about Schaffer's and the Plant factory for a bit, sticking to neutral and easy topics. However, once the initial awkwardness passed, they found talking to each other quite comfortable, and they had a lot in common. Cilla was surprisingly unguarded for the first time in her semi-adult life.

"Would you like to join the others at the zoo?" Marlon asked.

"Not especially. I'd much rather walk for a while. Would you mind terribly?"

"Not at all! I was hoping you'd say that."

They meandered through the park discussing all sorts of things, from the Red Sox and their chances to the current state of the economy and how people had to sacrifice in ways not seen since the Great War. Cilla enjoyed Marlon's reserve, quickly realizing that it wasn't due so much to shyness as he simply didn't prattle on the way other men did. He was smart and thought deeply about things, never tossing out babble just to hear his own voice. When he spoke, he did so having given thought to the words and their impact.

Cilla found herself listening intently, then ruminating on what he had said when they were quiet. She also noticed herself watching him more than she had ever watched any other young man she'd encountered. Not only that, he was watching back.

Conversation ebbed and flowed easily between them. While they agreed on most things, they were interested in each other's opinions and reasoning even when they didn't, which both were unusually comfortable doing.

"You're not like other girls," he said.

"What do you mean? Not like them, how?"

"Well, you don't talk all the time, for one thing."

"Neither do you. Is that bad?"

"Gosh, no! I like watching you think. Makes me want to know what's going on in that head of yours. I've been wondering for weeks now. And you don't agree with everything just to be liked, either."

Cilla laughed. "No, I don't suppose I do." She looked up at him then, unsure. "Do you mind?"

It was Marlon's turn to chuckle. He tilted his head and looked at her, thoughtful, a lazy smile spreading slowly across his face.

"No, I don't mind at all. I find you quite fascinating, Cilla Dixon."

***

August and September passed quickly as the new couple spent much of their free time together. Walks, picnics in the park, long chats on the front stoop of Morcombe House, and shared ice cream sundaes filled their non-working hours.

Marlon became the first person to whom Cilla told the entire truth about her upbringing and flight out of Back Bay. She was eighteen, after all, and her father no longer had any claim on her. Marlon listened with interest and concern as she poured her whole heart out in the park one afternoon. Rather than judge her or her parents, he simply said how hard it must've been for them and held her as she cried. Cilla knew then what a rare man she'd found.

Though they had many things in common, the financial circumstances surrounding their respective upbringings were not one of them. Where Cilla had witnessed excess and indulgence, Marlon had lived in lack and restriction. Still, life being funny, their philosophies regarding money matched up perfectly: don't spend what you don't have to.

"My daddy took sick shortly after I was born," Marlon said. "Mother took in sewing, and we scraped by on that and goodwill from the neighbors. But then, Daddy died when I was two. Things never really got better until me and my brother, Frank, were grown enough to work at our uncle's auto repair shop, running errands and doing odd jobs. I'm not sure why he never helped us out more. Anyway, we learned the difference between wants and needs right out of the gate."

For Cilla, indulgence and unnecessary spending reminded her too much of where she had come from to want to replicate it herself. It also hadn't escaped her that had money not been saved and accessible, it would never have been at her disposal when she'd needed it most.

"You don't miss it, though? Having a lot of money, I mean."

"No. The things I want can't be bought. I like my life just the way it is." She smiled at him as he considered both Cilla and her words before leaning in and kissing her softly.

***

The wild roaring of the early to mid-1920s dulled near the end of the decade as expansion began to reach saturation and consumers learned how easy it was to purchase things on credit. Living the high life and spending the same dollar three times over, with every intention of paying it back "later," came back to bite as wages remained stagnant and the agricultural sector struggled. The party, as they say, was over.

By mid-October, things began to look bleak in the world of finance. On October 29th, the mighty gavel of the New York Stock Exchange banged out the worst day of trading in history. America and the rest of the Western industrialized world plunged into an overdue economic downturn that would last a decade. It was the deepest depression the country had ever seen.

Many of their friends lost jobs in the coming months and fell on hard times, though neither Cilla nor Marlon suffered that fate. Still, the idea that one of them might join the ranks of the ever-growing unemployment lines rattled both of them to their very teeth.

One cold evening, as they sat bundled on the stoop of Morcombe House, holding hands and discussing what the future might hold, the two most practical people in Jamaica Plain looked at each other and decided wordlessly to get married. It could have been considered the least romantic proposal ever issued. Then again, with words completely unnecessary and hearts that had known for months, it was quite romantic, indeed.

The Great Depression

C illa and Marlon married in February 1930 and spent the next several years navigating and surviving the Great Depression together. Their decision to marry had been based on love more than anything but proved advantageous, nonetheless.

Cilla managed to keep her job at the shoe factory. While he eventually lost his at Schaffer's, Marlon often found work as a skilled laborer or doing odd mechanical jobs when auto work wasn't available. He and fellow Schaffer's mechanic, Gregory Ashcroft, made a knowledgeable, dependable team that managed to find opportunities when many others didn't. They were talented mechanics and had good heads for negotiation, often brokering barter deals for their services. They were a welcome sight for those with skills to swap but no money to pay.

When Cilla left Back Bay, she'd been mindful of the fact that her father having a sizable amount of cash on hand benefited her enormously. She had learned a lot, spying from the hallway. As such, she had made a practice of keeping some of her reserves out of the bank. It proved a wise move. By no means rolling in money, the Prescotts were still much envied by their peers, many of whom frequently found extra mouths at their tables as relatives came looking for help.

Regardless of their position, Cilla grew a kitchen garden like many other families rather than spending money at the market. Not that she could find much there, anyway. Farms were failing all over, and crops were left rotting in the fields. Food wasn't wasted at anyone's table. Any leftover produce she shared with those who hadn't enough.

The years-long tradition of potluck meals with friends to help stretch everyone's budgets continued. Cilla had learned to repair her clothes when she lived at Morcombe House, and she and Marlon wore things until they nearly wore out. They tightened their belts as much as possible and found that very little was required to live.

Evenings were spent playing board games or cards with friends, with the occasional round of mini-golf sneaking into their schedule, as well. Having sprung up like an invasive species, it replaced the more expensive cinema experience, much of which withered and died.

Often faced with hostility for being a working married woman, Cilla held her ground and her job fiercely. Having determined long ago that the only one in charge of her destiny would be her, she had yet to encounter anyone who could change her mind.

Though they each experienced hardship differently growing up, it was something both she and Marlon understood intimately. They were sensitive to the needs of those struggling and often took in friends or relatives of friends who needed a meal and a place to stay. People knew that the Prescotts' door was always open. There was just the one ironclad rule Cilla refused to budge on for personal reasons, regardless of Prohibition: no booze.

Recipients of the Prescotts' benevolence found themselves back on the street on more than one occasion, having gotten the boot for imbibing on the premises. Attempting to procure refuge while under the influence was another way to get chucked. Rumor had it Cilla would toss you if you even smelled of alcohol, though no one claimed to have gotten bounced on those grounds. Marlon stayed out of it unless Cilla required backup, which she rarely did. She could hold her own, and he let her.

Occasionally, a guest would appeal to Marlon for mercy, as Charles Danthrop once tried.

"C'mon, Marlon, you know how it is," he had begged. "You gonna let a dame tell you to give a friend the bum's rush?"

"My *wife* isn't telling me anything, Charles," Marlon said in his quiet yet firm voice. "She's telling you. I'm simply waiting for you to do as she's asked."

While personally holding nothing against drinking in moderation, Marlon understood Cilla's reasons for being intolerant of alcohol altogether in their home. He'd also seen his fair share of people turn to the bottle when they had lost everything else. It never ended well.

***

President Roosevelt's New Deal provided some hope to Americans in the form of government financial aid, and after the rock-bottom year of 1933, things started to look up. Some would say it was more that they simply couldn't look any farther down without digging. Either way, the economy began to improve, which no one was about to criticize.

Marlon found full-time work again as a mechanic in the fall of 1934, and in October of 1936, Cilla quit her job at the Plant Factory, and Dorothy Prescott was born. "Teeny," they called her. Quite small at birth, she soon made up for it in energy.

Cilla doted on her little girl, reliving her own early childhood years by spending hours in the parks and the sunshine. Yet, while Teeny was well-cared for and loved to the moon and back, Cilla stood firm with discipline.

"No daughter of mine will ever be ill-equipped to put her nose to the grindstone and do as needs doing," she would say.

Two years later, baby Noah arrived, which everyone agreed was the best thing to have happened to Teeny. Having a little brother to play with and boss around kept her busy little self occupied, and the newcomer absorbed skills like a sponge as he toddled after his big sister. Their two-year age difference would again prove good timing just a few years later when the Japanese attacked Pearl Harbor, and the country plunged back into chaos.

***

When the Great War ended, Cilla had still been very young, and she didn't recall much other than the celebrations of Armistice Day. What she *did* remember quite clearly, was the aftermath as soldiers came home bringing Influenza with them, which, in her mind, had led directly to the loss of Penny. The memories remained a bitter pill to swallow, and the onset of yet another world war made the back of her neck prickle with fear, this time for her husband and children. It seemed that the world was simply unwilling to be content for long stretches at a time.

As wartime took hold of the country and its resources, Marlon began to think about the draft. The government required that he register under the Selective Training and Service Act of 1940. Most people believed the United States would get drawn into the wars in Europe and Asia at some point or another. He and Gregory Ashcroft were very aware that their skills as mechanics could prove helpful in a military setting.

"I dunno, pal," Gregory said one evening. "Going overseas to cash in my chips—or worse, come home jingle-brained—doesn't exactly sound like my idea of an exotic adventure. Lotsa guys came back with a thousand-yard stare last time."

"Maybe we wouldn't be over there. They need guys like me and you back here, too. Somebody's gotta keep all those birds in the air so the flyboys can train, and we're already aces with engines."

As it happened, it wasn't long before Marlon's draft number turned up. In the spring of 1943, he attended basic training in New Mexico and managed to land himself at the Naval Air Station in Pensacola, Florida, doing exactly as he'd predicted.

***

Being effectively single was more difficult this time around now that Cilla had young children to care for. They all missed Marlon terribly. But she had persevered many times before, and this time would be no different.

She returned to her job at the Plant factory, using the in-house child-minding and schooling services to keep Teeny and Noah up-to-speed and cared for while she earned a living. It was heartening that Marlon wasn't a combat soldier. Nonetheless, she didn't dare let her mind wander too far, having long since learned to deal with the problems of the day as they presented themselves rather than extend an invitation outright.

Letters arrived on the regular. The weather was excellent, if a little humid, and Marlon was well but homesick for her and the kids. Still, he was kept busy, so he didn't have much time to think about it. He didn't talk much about the job itself but regaled them with stories about his fellows, especially a mechanic named Jack Dennings.

Rootin'-Tootin'-Son-of-a-Gun

J ack and Marlon worked as part of a group of mechanics on base. They frequently spent their off-hours together, as they were both "shack men" who had wives at home.

Where Marlon was quiet and reserved, Jack was the center of any room; a real "rootin'-tootin'-son-of-a-gun," the boys called him. Lively, helpful, and funny as hell, he always had a genuine smile and a decent joke ready to go. It was a rare person who met him and didn't take to him instantly. Nothing seemed to please Jack more than meeting new people and learning about places he hadn't yet been.

Anytime he entered a room of equal and lesser ranking men, Jack greeted them by name, even the new guys, which put people at ease straight away. They would tell him their life story without even realizing it as it tumbled out.

"Man, how do you do that?" Marlon asked one day.

"Do what?" Jack replied. "Hey, Carl, good to see ya," he added, slapping a newbie on the back as they passed.

"That!" Marlon swiveled to look at the guy. "That kid got here yesterday, and you already remember his name. Ask anyone else in this room, and they might pull his surname, but not a one would know his first name is Carl."

"I dunno," Jack shrugged, "I just do. Names stick in my head for some reason."

Marlon gave his friend a sidelong stare. "You might be the only cat I've ever known with that affliction; you know that? And here I just thought you were a brownnose."

Jack laughed out loud. He may have been everybody's old pal right from the get-go, but he and Marlon shared a special bond. They took the mickey out of each other on the regular and in ways others couldn't. From the moment they met, they connected for life.

From the Midwest, Jack had no airs about him whatsoever. You got what you saw, and he made no apologies for it, a trait Marlon appreciated since he wasn't much of a social game-player himself. Jack would tell it to you straight, good or bad, but do it in such a way that you knew if things were bad, he'd be standing right next to you the whole time. He'd make you laugh until you cried and sit with you solid if your tears were of a different nature.

Over time, Marlon found that Jack brought a sort of emotional adventure to his life he very much needed, much like Cilla. He was the first brother Marlon had, who wasn't blood.

***

Jack had a wife back home named Natasha, and he was head-over-heels in love.

"How a guy like me snagged a dish like her is one of the Lord's great secrets," he would say. "The Big Man searched the angels themselves and found no better woman."

Natasha, or "Nattie," as Jack called her, and their young son, Parker, who was Teeny's age, had moved in with her parents while Jack was away.

"Saves money, o' course, and Nattie's parents can't get enough of their grandson. They're sure to have spoiled him rotten by the time I get home. Makes Nattie and me feel better, too, though, having her folks around. She gets a little nervous about things, and, being somewhat on the quiet side, she doesn't like to trouble people for help."

Nattie sent care packages full of Jack's favorite candy bars along with letters and news of what Parker had gotten up to. The smiles these put on her husband's face rivaled those of anyone else on base.

The kind of guy who took charge of his own destiny, Jack happily dealt with the consequences, come what may. He enjoyed being a family man, a positive force, and a paintbrush of bright color on the canvas of life. He and Marlon spent many an evening discussing their post-war options with excitement. Spinning ideas this way and that, they talked out their craziest notions and determined early on that, whatever they choose to do, they would be doing it together.

***

Both men came home at the end of 1945. By then, they had agreed on a post-war plan and had at least floated the idea to their wives. However, upon his return to Jamaica Plain, Marlon discovered that Cilla wasn't quite as eager to go along with his plan as he had hoped.

"Why would we uproot and move halfway across the country to a place neither of us has ever even seen?"

"Cilla, it'd be fine. We'd have Jack and Nattie to help us settle, and Teeny and Noah would have Parker. He's nine, like Teeny. I'm sure he knows lots of kids he could introduce them to. That's already plenty of people we'd know."

"Marlon, it's one thing to open a business and do what you've been doing for years with people you know. It's another to ask the kids and me to drop everything we know and start completely over with strangers in an unfamiliar town, and a small one at that.

"Aside from helping run the garage, I'd need to navigate a whole new life for us. Where to shop, new parents of the kids' friends, getting Teeny and Noah settled in a new school, new friends of my own. Adjusting to the Midwest, for Pete's sake! It's nothing like the east coast, you know."

"Cilla," he said, taking her hands in his, "I know." His voice was gentle as if he were quieting a wild horse. "I wouldn't ask this of you all unless I'd truly thought it out and felt it was best for our family. It's less expensive to start a business there. People know each other, and communities are closer. You can go next door to borrow a cup of sugar and know your neighbor."

"We know our neighbors here, Marlon. We've spent years making our little community of friends. I've started over before; it isn't easy. We've been through a depression and a war. Maybe we can take time to breathe for a little while."

"You weren't much older than the kids when you left home, and look how well things turned out," he argued. "Cilla, you're brilliant at making the best of hard things life throws at you. This would only be tough for a little while, and we'd all be together—nothing like a depression or a war. You're good at making friends, and so are the kids. Everyone likes them. They're friendly and helpful and polite and smart."

"Just because we're good at something doesn't mean we like it, Marlon. I'm good at sewing dresses, but I'd as soon never have to sew another one as long as I live."

"Just think about it, okay? We wouldn't do anything before spring, anyway. But Jack and I have it all planned out. The process would be pretty smooth once we have premises, and Jack knows a guy who's getting on in years and might be ready to sell his place. Chances are, we can buy his shop at a reasonable price and avoid a lot of set up costs. Promise me you'll think about it?"

The pleading look in his eyes was almost pathetic. He wanted this so badly and was so boyishly confident that she and the children would love it. He was an imminently capable man, and Cilla harbored no doubts that he would make a success of a new shop. Nor did she doubt that Teeny and Noah would adjust. Still, it was a complete upheaval, and she'd had enough of those to last a lifetime.

Marlon was right, though. It couldn't possibly be as challenging as the last twenty-six years of her life had been. Nothing could be as hard as losing Penny, running away, navigating a massive economic depression, and carrying on through a war.

"Okay," she sighed. "I'll think about it."

"Thank you." A relieved grin spread across Marlon's face.

"No promises, though! You hear me?"

He bowed his head and held his hands up in surrender. "Yes. I hear you. Absolutely." But then he squinched his face and snuck a peek at her out of one eye. Suddenly, her feet were off the floor, and she let out a *whoop!* as Marlon enveloped her in a massive hug.

"I love you, Cilla Prescott!" he shouted before planting a kiss on her lips. She couldn't help but smile.

***

For Cilla, Jamaica Plain was home. It was the place where she had found herself, where she had discovered she could rely on her wits and abilities. It was where she had felt genuinely grounded after the tornado of her childhood left her uprooted and bare. The city had embraced her, encouraged her, and validated her when she'd had nothing more than her father's money and crossed fingers. She had found her first real friends there, and those friendships continued to that day. The idea of leaving hadn't ever entered her mind.

Twenty-six years had passed since Penny died, nineteen since Cilla had left home. Truth be told, she was ready for some boring old peace and quiet. But, as the world was with peace, so was her life with quiet: never content to be so for long stretches at a time.

***

That winter in JP proved warm and dry, and Cilla often wondered what it would be like to spend it in the middle of the country. She had heard Midwest winters could be harsh, with subzero temperatures and blowing winds, not to mention a lot of snow. It wasn't as if they'd be out in the sticks, but below zero was below zero, no matter how you spun it.

Marlon was patient with her, giving her the space she needed to mull things over, though he was unsure what he would do if she said no. He wanted to move west with all his heart and itched to start a new chapter for his family in the small town of Pullman Station with Jack and Nattie, and Parker.

If she was honest with herself, Cilla had known from the moment Marlon first mentioned it that they would make the switch. He was the one person she could always be herself with. He'd accepted her, celebrated her, and validated her from the moment they'd met. Home was where he was, and she would do anything for him. Marlon knew this, of course, but gave her the courtesy of concluding it on her own. By mid-February, she had made up her mind.

***

It was a Tuesday evening, and the kids had gone to bed. The wind was howling as March posted eviction notice to the calm chill of February. Cilla and Marlon sat in the living room in front of the fireplace, each seemingly in their separate peaceful end-of-day stupor. Cilla laid her book in her lap and looked up at the fire.

"Okay."

"Mm? Okay, what?" Marlon didn't look up from his paper.

"Okay," Cilla repeated, boring a hole in him with her eyes as she gripped her book, adjusting to the fact that she had said it out loud. Marlon looked up, nonplussed.

"Okay?"

"Yes, *okay*." She widened her eyes, and it finally dawned on him.

"Okay? You mean ... like, 'okay,' okay!?"

"Yes, of course, that's what I mean. Don't be obtuse." She held up her book and pretended to read again, pushing her anxiety down.

"But ... are you sure? I mean, really sure?"

She dropped the book again and stared at him. "Well, what do you think, you twit? Yes, I'm sure. That's why I said it."

"But what about the kids and your friends and school and all that?"

"Do you want to go or not!? I can change my mind if you'd prefer."

"NO! No, it's just ... you're really okay with it? You'd really do that for me?"

"For us, Marlon. And, yes, I would. Which, by the way, you already knew months ago, and don't pretend you didn't." She gave him a sly smile.

Marlon had never been a crier, but his eyes suddenly gained an unmistakably twinkly sheen. He got up and knelt before her, taking her hands in his.

"Cilla Prescott, you are my angel, and I love you with all my heart," he whispered. At that, she leaned forward to meet his forehead with hers. Closing her eyes, she finally allowed herself to get excited.

Pullman Station Public Library

June 1985

Maisy's little bottom wiggled its way over the fence, followed by her mop of curls, which bounced as her feet hit the ground. She Maisy-skipped her way to the back door, cute as a button, flip-flops slapping against her heels.

"Look at me, Annabelle! I'm skippin'! See?"

"Good job! You're really getting the hang of it!"

"I've been practicing lots and lots. Mommy says I'll be the best skipper in the first grade next year!"

"You sure will. I bet you can skip better than Jimmy now."

"Nah. But it's okay, 'cuz big brothers are s'posed to be better at stuff."

Honestly, it looked more like she'd turned her ankle than like actual skipping, but given how proud she was of the progress she'd made, we encouraged her every chance we got.

Jimmy, Natalie, and Sasha followed a moment later. We slung our backpacks over our shoulders and set out for the library. This was our Wednesday afternoon ritual unless we were going for the air conditioning, in which case, any day but the weekend would work.

It was always a bit of a debate whether to walk or pedal our way over. Pedaling may seem like it would have been the obvious choice, what with our backpacks to secure our treasures and the trip being quicker, but despite years of suggestions, the city had yet to install a bike rack that held more than four bikes at a time, no matter how creatively arranged. So our mode of transport usually depended on the purpose of the visit. The mere check-out of a book on hold or a drop in the returns slot always called for biking. If an escape from the heat and humidity for the afternoon was our motive, bikes were risky. None of us wanted to leave our two-wheeled freedom rigs unsupervised for very long.

The problem with choosing to walk was we still had to hoof it home again afterward. After about a block, any ice built up in our veins from basking in the arctic blast of the library's HVAC system lost all utility. We'd arrive home drenched in sweat again, to lay in front of a fan blowing hot air. *Blech.*

Since the day was a scorcher, and we intended to dawdle for a while, we decided to walk and pray for a mid-afternoon thunderstorm to clear out the humidity before heading home. Storms brew up pretty fast in heat like that and, though the sky didn't look rough just then, hope springs eternal during a Pullman summer.

***

The public library was a majestic two-story building that took up an entire quarter of a block at Maple and Cross Streets. Constructed of massive white limestone blocks quarried from the surrounding hills and with a huge copper dome, it was a showstopper. An enormous stained-glass rosette window on the second story added to its stateliness. It was always a thrill to walk or pull up to it knowing you were about to enter the grandest building you'd ever set eyes on.

Inside, the captivation continued. The ground floor housed the children's section; low shelves, bean bags, beautiful dark wood floors and door frames, and lots of cubbies and hidey-holes ready to entertain the imagination of any child who dared explore. Storybook characters danced in scenes on the walls, and low-pile carpet squares littered the floor. The musty smell of old books wafted throughout, promising age-old worlds of unparalleled adventure and excitement.

Children's Hour, which was actually only forty-five minutes including storytime, was at ten and one o'clock, three days a week, for anyone who wanted to take part. The children's library was a neat place to hang out, even if we didn't want to admit it at eleven years old.

It was the second floor, however, that charmed the socks off visitors and locals alike. Upstairs housed the grownup books: encyclopedias, fiction and non-fiction, research materials, periodicals, and so forth. Part of the allure for us was that, while most of us had seen it, we weren't allowed to be up there without an adult.

A grand marble staircase, gently scuffed by the shuffling feet of thousands of adventure-seekers, scholars, and gawkers from decades past, lead up from downstairs. The thick wooden railings, dark and polished by the hands of those same patrons, curved and scrolled their way up along the sides.

At the top, the stairs opened onto a large, vaulted room showcasing a long chandelier that dangled from the center of the dome. Intricately carved, arched doorways lead to beautiful reading rooms, and the famous rosette window made it feel almost as if the fairy tales from below had crept their way upstairs.

In terms of utility, the main room contained tables for project work, card catalogs, reference books, microfiche viewers, and comfy chairs. Beyond the vaulted chamber was an area housing the stacks, and *that* was where the real intrigue lay.

Anyone who'd been in there had experienced the curious glass floors of the Pullman Station Public Library. Whispered about by children for miles around, the stacks were in low-ceilinged rooms with tightly arranged shelves containing more books than any of us had ever seen anywhere else.

Four levels, each connected by one set of narrow marble stairs on one end and one set of spiral, wrought-iron stairs on the other, were contained therein. Thick, two-foot by two-foot glass slabs held in a grid of supporting metalwork acted as both ceiling and floor between levels. This allowed patrons to view the bottoms of shoes from below and the tops of heads from above. The panes were translucent to disallow the viewing of anything of a more scandalous nature.

More than one kid had wandered off in that area as they explored, trying to see feet or magazine covers through the floors. It never failed that they ran into a tutting adult glaring at them for being understandably enchanted.

Mrs. Margaret Chisholm, Head Librarian, oversaw the whole of the library. Mrs. Chisholm was a former schoolteacher, former caretaker of the Coleman children, and close friend of the Hickam family. She had one or two assistant librarians for the adult section, but Margaret, herself, presided over the children's library.

Mrs. Chisholm was what many people would call a "good Catholic woman." She began each day by attending morning mass at Saint Mary's Church. This she followed with the recitation of a decade or two of the rosary depending on who had recently passed and might be in need of a boost from purgatory to a meet-and-greet with Saint Peter. Finally, she took a brisk walk over to the library at eight-thirty on the dot, clean of soul and clear of mind, to open things up and prepare for the ten o'clock Children's Hour.

She was a formidable woman, Mrs. Chisholm. Mid-range in stature but with a confidence that sometimes came off as a bit gruff. Still, she was kind and had a heart of gold. She made a good librarian and was at ease being in charge.

***

The last half-block of our journey was always the worst on days we chose to walk. Not even the tightrope walk along the foot-high stone walls bordering the lawn could keep our attention. The longing for the rush of cool air would prove too much, and we would break into a run despite the heat. Once we passed the majestic limestone stairs for the second-floor entrance and rounded the corner onto Cross Street, the door to the children's library came into view.

"Dibs on the door!" Jimmy always hollered.

"Nuh-uh!!" the rest of us cried in unison.

The large wooden door looked like something out of a medieval storybook. Curved at the top with old, hammered, black hardware, it made us feel like we were entering a fairy-tale, and each of us was keen to be the one to enter the castle first.

It never failed that we put on the brakes a moment too late in our frenzy to reach the cool, and that day was no different. We all slammed into it at the same time, Maisy hollering, "Wait up!" behind us.

As the door swung open, the old-ink-and-paper scent of adventure rode along on the wave of cold air attempting to flash-freeze beads of sweat to our faces. The shock was enough to stop us dead in our tracks for a moment. By the time we got moving and halfway down the outside row of books, a delicious shiver overtook our bodies as they recalibrated to the A/C.

Mrs. Chisholm knew almost every kid in town and always greeted us by name. She walked over to ask how we were and what we were looking for. It was tough to put one over on her, and we were all reasonably sure she was aware that "Um … I'm not sure yet" was code for "I'm only here for the A/C." We did our best to look academic, nonetheless.

She never once called our bluff, preferring instead to point us in the direction of a book or series she knew we hadn't read. How she kept track of who'd read what among all those kids remains one of the great Pullman Station Public Library mysteries. The woman is a legend.

"Miss Maisy. Let's see, which of the Sweet Pickles haven't you checked out yet? Ah, yes, here we go. *Zany Zebra!*"

Maisy liked a series about a bunch of animals that live in a city together and have problems just like people. She especially enjoyed *Fixed By Camel*; *Me Too, Iguana*; *Lion Is Down In The Dumps*; and *Turtle Throws a Tantrum*. Though we were older, we big kids all got a kick out of reading them to her if she asked. If pressed, though, none of us would admit we still liked them, too.

Mrs. Chisholm helped Maisy pull *Goose Goofs Off* from the shelf. Then she turned to Natalie and me. Sasha and Jimmy headed over to books about baseball before she could snag them for something more literary.

"Now, girls, come with me. I saved something special for you when they came in this morning." At her desk, she reached across and picked up two copies of *Island of the Blue Dolphins* and handed them to us.

"Gosh! Two at the same time? Thanks, Mrs. Chisholm!" I said.

We had been waiting several weeks for one copy. Two was like Christmas! Now we could read them together.

Children's Hour started in fifteen minutes. Plenty of time to use the bathroom, get a drink, and claim our seats.

***

Maisy came over with her new stash of Sweet Pickles and settled into her spot. But Sasha and Jimmy were nowhere to be seen. If nothing else, they always liked to lay claim to a couple of the good bean bags before all the little kids took them. Their absence was suspect.

Mrs. Chisholm rang the little bell on her desk to signal the time to gather in the story room, separated from the rest of the children's section by a wide archway. She walked over and sat down in her cushy armchair, smiling at everyone and noting who was in attendance.

Had I not suspected something myself, I likely wouldn't have noticed the slight narrowing of her eyes as she glanced at the bean bags. She wasn't one to miss a trick, though, and something was definitely up.

Carrying on, as usual, Mrs. Chisholm began to read from *The Adventures of Frog and Toad*. The theme for the day was "friendship," and I suddenly got the feeling two of mine were about to test the limits of solidarity.

***

Children's Hour finished without an appearance by Jimmy or Sasha. Mrs. Chisholm calmly gathered her books and chatted with the little kids as if nothing in the world was out of place. Then she casually walked to her desk and placed a four-digit call. That only ever meant one thing: upstairs.

A short while later, Ms. Crandall, one of the adult library assistants, came down the back service staircase, hauling Jimmy and Sasha each along by the arm. Of the three, she looked the healthiest. Both boys looked like they might throw up, and neither one would look at Natalie or me.

Ms. Crandall leaned over and spoke quietly to Mrs. Chisholm. The older woman's face became stony, save for her nostrils, which were flaring like bellows desperate to blow a tiny winter spark into a roaring fire. She nodded then, her face changing to a rather sly grin, and turned to the boys.

"Gentlemen, I'm told you need to call your mothers."

Her cool librarian calm sent shivers down our spines. Ms. Crandall tried to hide a smile. Jimmy and Sasha squirmed like worms on a hook. Were they sick? Did one of them throw up upstairs? That wasn't funny.

"I will let you take my phone back into the storage area to do so. Please leave the door open so Ms. Crandall may supervise."

At this, Jimmy groaned. Sasha looked at the ground and shuffled his feet.

"Mr. Perkins, your mother is not under your sneakers. I suggest you make the necessary call before I change my mind and the consequences become dire."

Consequences? Oh, geez, they weren't sick. Natalie and I were right to be suspicious. Calling someone's mom was the worst thing you could do if you'd caught them doing something wrong. But to make a kid rat on himself? That was evil genius territory.

Mrs. Chisholm handed Sasha the phone and gave him a nudge. He and Jimmy trudged back into the little storage area, trailing the cord behind them. They tried to close the door part-way, but Mrs. Chisholm reminded them to keep it open.

Ms. Crandall stood in the doorway to verify accuracy during the recalling of events. Sasha plopped down on the chair and looked at Jimmy, the fear of God in his eyes. He dialed home.

When Mrs. Perkins picked up, Sasha spoke to her as quietly as possible, not that it mattered. Once he finally managed to tell her what had happened, her voice exploded from the earpiece.

"You did *what!?* Sasha Maxwell Perkins, you should be ashamed of yourself! I will not come to pick you up! You will apologize to Mrs. Chisholm, and then you will walk home in this godforsaken heat and think about what you've done on the way. And when you get here, you had better be ready to face the consequences, young man. Wait until your father hears about this, which will come from *you*. Do you hear me!?"

Everyone heard her. Sasha sank lower and lower in the chair with each word from his mother. He was in for it, and he had to tell his dad himself. By this time, Jimmy was panting and near tears, the anticipation killing him.

When Sasha hung up, he sulkily pushed the phone toward Jimmy. But Jimmy shook his head vigorously back and forth, wringing his sweaty hands, unable to grab the receiver. Mrs. Chisholm cheerfully popped her head in.

"Your turn, Mr. Drummond." Why did adults always call us Mr. and Ms. when we were in trouble?

Jimmy whipped around as if a snake had bitten him on the behind. It was hard to tell if he was more scared of his mother or Mrs. Chisholm, but he snatched the phone from Sasha and began to dial. It took him four tries before getting his number dialed correctly without having to hang up and start again. When Mrs. Drummond picked up, he began to cry.

The conversation with Jimmy's mother didn't go any better than Sasha's had, and the result was much the same. She told him he could walk home and think about what he'd done after apologizing to Mrs. Chisholm, but then he got the dreaded 'self-punishment directive.'

He was to come up with his own punishment, with the understanding that if it were determined he had gone easy on himself, the one from his parents would be worse than if he'd come up with a doozy. That was the sharpest razor's edge a kid could walk. Get it right, and you'd likely handed yourself something more horrible than your parents would have come up with. Get it wrong, and you could kiss your summer fun goodbye.

***

There was no point in pretending Mrs. Perkins wouldn't have spoken to Mrs. Drummond by the time we got home. Sasha figured he'd better come up with his punishment, too. Once his mom found out what Mrs. Drummond had assigned, she'd be all over it like seagulls on a sandwich.

The boys 'fessed up about what they'd done in the hopes we'd assist them in navigating their manner of execution. We weren't much help, though. Truth be told, we were too stunned to do much thinking.

As it turned out, they had sneaked up to the adult stacks to conduct some "experiments" during Children's Hour. What had started out as putting their hands and magazine covers on the glass floors to see if they could see each other from below had progressed to putting their lips against the floor and puffing their cheeks out. Being 11-year-old boys, they didn't stop until they had their bare bottoms pressed against the floor. By that point, Mrs. Chisholm had called upstairs to request a search of the stacks, and they had literally been caught with their pants down.

We had no idea how to help them, and Maisy kept interrupting with questions.

"Sasha, why did you show people your bottom? We're s'posed to keep our privates to ourselves. That's important."

It was a valid question. Why they had chosen to drop their shorts and expose their nether regions in Mrs. Chisholm's library of all places was a mystery for the ages.

"I dunno, Maisy. It was just this stupid thing we were doing. And now, we're gonna pay for it big time."

Time was ticking, and the boys needed to concentrate on punishments more than explanations. Their moms were expecting them home before too long.

"Guys, I gotta stop," said Jimmy, panting. "Let's go sit by the fountain in Windham Park while we think."

To passersby, we must've made a pretty sullen-looking group. Never had anyone dipped their toes in the Windham Park fountain with such frowns and looks of concentration on their faces. We needed to come up with something good, fast.

There was some debate regarding whether the boys could get away with the same punishment plans. Ultimately, we agreed that since Ms. Crandall had caught them doing the exact same thing, it was worth the risk to assume the punishments could be identical, too. They eventually decided they would each write a formal apology to Mrs. Chisholm and Ms. Crandall, and they would volunteer to wash the glass floors on a Saturday after the library had closed.

"Geez, that's a lot of floors," said Jimmy. But they didn't want to think what their parents would come up with if they went easier on themselves.

They limped the rest of the way home behind Natalie, Maisy, and me. We, girls, hot-footed it for my house. None of us wanted to be around the Perkinses' or Drummond's place when the shit hit the fan.

Trouble

We risked running past Cilla's and into my backyard to sit and wait. We didn't want to be in the same houses as the boys when they got home, nor did we want to get too close by going through Mr. Coleman's yard lest we get detained for questioning. Still, we most definitely wanted to eavesdrop, if possible.

As we reached the board fence, predicting what the boys' respective homecomings would be like, equal parts excitement and worry filled our bellies. If things went really badly, we'd lose our playmates for a while. That would suck. However, if they managed to walk the razor's edge with skill, all would work out. Sneaking over and listening to the play-by-play from Mr. Coleman's side of the fence would no doubt be entertaining.

Natalie and Maisy climbed up and sneaked over to the other side of Mr. Coleman's yard. I followed once Maisy was clear. As I turned to get my second leg over, I saw it. Like a severed doll's head in a horror movie, a Wiffle ball lay waiting to be discovered by some poor, unsuspecting soul, striking the fear of Jason or Freddy Krueger into us. I froze.

"What? What is it?" Natalie looked back at me.

"Look." I nodded my head in the direction of the clothesline. In the grass lay the ball, or rather, what was left of it; scuffed white plastic stark against the green. It looked like a yolk-less broken egg with just the twisted membrane holding its two halves together. Beyond that lay two more.

Never had we had more than one at a time, no matter how long since the collection.

Suddenly, punishments no longer seemed like the most important problem brewing.

***

Verdicts were handed down after dinner, and I got the update Thursday morning. As expected, Mrs. Perkins talked to Mrs. Drummond, and the boys had been wise to have Sasha prepare a punishment in advance.

We hadn't heard a word from Mr. Coleman's yard, but both Jimmy and Sasha reported that things got rather uncomfortable when their fathers got home. The parents called an embarrassing group meeting to discuss what, exactly, went down in the library, aside from trousers.

Punishments were discussed, tweaked, sanctioned, and awaited final blessing by Mrs. Chisholm. The good news was they were entirely service-related and effort-intense rather than deprivation-driven, so we wouldn't lose half of our crew.

If approved, the boys would indeed write letters of apology and wash the glass floors in the stacks. However, the tweak was that they also had to help with Children's Hour once a week for a month. Not horrible as punishments go, but we knew we could count on Mrs. Chisholm to make them learn something in the bargain. And you could bet your bottom dollar, Natalie and I would bend over backward to attend and watch them squirm.

Natalie had filled Sasha in on the Wiffle situation before bed, and I did the same with Jimmy as we sat in the shade under the Perkinses' walnut tree. Sasha, unperturbed by the news, casually tossed a green walnut between his hands. As usual, Jimmy was the more doomsday of the two boys in terms of what it all meant, while Sasha enjoyed the creepiness of the whole thing.

"*Three!?*" Jimmy exclaimed. "That's bad! That's really bad!"

"What's the big deal? It's not like there was blood on them or decapitated birds laying next to them or anything. Ozzie Osbourne's done worse."

"Yeah, but Ozzie Osbourne doesn't live on our block and do weird things to our Wiffle balls."

"Man, you worry too much, you know that? We're talking about Batty Nattie; she's nuts. I'm surprised she doesn't light them on fire and throw melting grenades back over. Besides, this way we get new Wiffles. Not like *we* did anything to them, right?"

The prospect of new Wiffles pacified Jimmy for the time being. I kind of agreed with him that something was off about this particular quasi-run-in with Nattie. I just hoped it didn't signal some sort of seismic shift, warning us of worse things to come.

A Bit of a Muddle

We raced down Sanborn Street, relishing the freedom that came with two wheels, best friends, and a little spare change. Jimmy, Sasha, Natalie, and I had already made several loops through Windham Park, around Boxcar Lake, past Pullman Depot, and down around the pool. On our final loop, we stopped at Bohler's Bakery on the corner of Broadway and Sanborn next to the post office. Mama had sent me on a Christian-duty mission to buy stamps for Nattie but graciously agreed that the timeline was loose and the errand deserving of an extra pit stop or two.

As we propped our bikes against the wall outside Bohler's, inhaling slowly and deeply and thoroughly enjoying the smells of yeast and warm sugar, Nattie's gray Chevy Malibu crept down Broadway. It stopped in front of the post office, Nattie frantically gripping the wheel as if an unintended joy ride was imminent should she relinquish a moment's control.

Natalie nudged me.

"Hey, Annabelle, isn't that Nattie over there at the post office? I thought you were supposed to buy stamps for her before we go home."

"I am. Why did she ask Mama to go if she was going to do it herself? She could've at least let her know."

"But I thought she hated to drive."

"She does. I can't even remember the last time she had her car out. That's the whole reason Mama runs errands for her in the first place."

"She sure doesn't look like she should be driving. Did you see how slow she was going?"

"Guys, come on!" Jimmy urged. "I wanna get my doughnuts. Who cares about old Batty Nattie?"

My eyes stayed on Nattie's car as I walked behind my friends. Something wasn't right.

***

All curiosity vanished the moment I stepped inside Bohler's. My eyes and nose feasted upon row after row of maple long johns, raspberry Bismarck's, cake doughnuts, sprinkle doughnuts, bear claws, apple turnovers, dinner rolls, and dozens of loaves of fresh-baked bread. It was my idea of heaven on earth, and I was pretty sure the smell alone could put a body into diabetic shock. Why Cilla ever decided to buy her doughnuts from Woolworths was beyond me.

There wasn't a line this time of day. Still, we lingered over our options, dragging things out as long as possible. Of course, I always got wishy-washy over whether to get a maple long john or a raspberry Bismarck, so I wasn't entirely faking my protracted decision-making. Each option offered a completely different experience, both of which I craved.

In the end, I decided one of each was best. I'd eat one at the park and save one for after dinner. It also occurred to me that if I gave Mama and Daddy a little incentive of their own, they might not tell me to wait until tomorrow for the second one. That settled, I happily took my bag containing one maple long john, one raspberry Bismarck, one bear claw, and one apple turnover and secured it safely in my bike basket along with a blue, single-serving carton of 2% milk. Then we took off for Wind-ham Park.

***

The park takes up two entire city blocks, creating a rectangle across Broadway from the heart of downtown. Wilson, Grand, and Vander-bilt Streets bordered the remaining three sides. It's a popular place for families to go for Saturday picnics, to relax under shade trees on hot days, or throw Frisbees and balls for their dogs.

In the center stands a stone fountain and plaza area with benches all around and miniature limestone train cars situated at each corner. Little kids love to climb in the coal car, hang off the back of the caboose, or pretend to take a snooze on top of the Pullman car. The engine's tall smokestack proves a popular spot for pictures.

Spokes of sidewalk cross from the plaza to the four corners of the park, making an X, which we could see when we viewed the town from the peek-overs on top of Harriman Hill. Sidewalks also run the entire perimeter.

In the winter, the fire department floods the inside of one sidewalk triangle to form an ice rink, and the plaza benches are moved to border it. Throughout the park, old-fashioned street lamps, painted black and fitted with yellowish light bulbs to make them look the part at night, complete the picture. It's all quite charming.

Sitting at the edge of Vanderbilt Street, discussing the merits of our various purchases and arguing over which one was the best, we again spied Nattie's gray Malibu. This time, it crept around the park several times as if she was looking for something. She was hunched forward, her brow furrowed, looking back and forth through her windshield.

Eventually, she pulled over, rolled down her window, and looked in our direction.

"Excuse me, young lady."

Natalie and I stared at each other, eyes wide with shock as if one of the trees had called out to us. Neither of us wanted to answer.

"*Excuse me*, young lady."

Nattie looked right at me but appeared not to have a clue who I was. I prayed to God she didn't have her starter pistol with her as I got up and went over to her car, expecting a real tongue-lashing for stalling on the stamp mission.

"Hello, Na-, I mean, Mrs. Dennings."

"Can you tell me where to find 472 Maple Street, dear?"

Dear? This was new. And she knew darn well where to find that address. I stared at her, silent.

"Well, can you or can you not?"

"M-Mrs. Dennings, that's your house, right next to mine. One street over and down three blocks."

"What? Oh. Yes, well, of course, it is!" She sat up straighter and checked her driver's-side mirror before hitting the gas and scolding, "Of all the impertinent things!"

I stood there a moment, having not the slightest idea as to what had just happened. Natalie ran up behind me, tailed closely by Sasha and Jimmy.

"What was that all about? What did she want?"

"I dunno." I watched as Nattie's car turned out of sight. "I dunno."

***

When I walked in the back door, Mama smiled at the bag in my hand.

"You come bearing gifts, I see."

"Huh?" I looked down. "Oh, yeah, I got some for you and Daddy, too."

"Thanks, honey, that's very sweet of you." She kissed the top of my head. "Did you get the stamps?"

I thought for a minute, replaying the scenes in my mind.

"Annabelle? Did you buy the stamps?"

"Mama ... I think Nattie bought them herself."

Mama's head snapped back around. "What? How would she do that?"

"Well, she parked her car outside the post office when we were at Bohler's. It was weird, but then we saw her again at Windham Park."

I relayed the rest of the story to Mama and let her mull it over for a bit. She knew full well that Nattie hated to drive. We joked at our house that her car had probably petrified sitting in her garage. I was relieved to see Mama was just as confused as me about what had happened. The asking for her own address didn't make a lick of sense.

"Well. I'll just pay a quick visit to make sure she got them. If she didn't, I can still run yet today."

***

Mama set off for Nattie's a few minutes later, and I breathed a sigh of relief, not wanting to walk over there empty-handed only to be chewed out again. As I watched Mama go, I noticed Nattie quickly disappear from her front window perch, the sheers waving gently as they settled back into place.

Look out, Mama. She sees you coming, I thought. Mama climbed the porch steps and rang the bell.

Several moments passed before she rang it again. This time, she began speaking to someone after a moment or two and then jerked back suddenly as if they'd slammed the door in her face. She paused, turned, and headed back down the stairs, slowly making her way back to our house as she glanced back at Nattie's.

When our front door opened again, Mama came in, shut it, and stared at me, her hand still on the handle.

"Are you sure it was Nattie you saw?"

"YES, I'm *sure*, I'm sure, Mama. You can even ask Jimmy, and Sasha, and Natalie. They all saw her, too. And I talked to her, remember?"

"No, no, I believe you, honey." Mama patted my shoulder. "Only, Nattie says she's been in bed all day as she couldn't sleep last night and that I woke her up with the bell."

"But, Mama, you didn't! She was looking out her window when you went over. I saw her when she moved away from the curtains."

Mama stared at me, baffled.

"Well, I never." This more to herself than to me. "What on earth is she playing at, now? Anyway, she says she still needs stamps, so I'm going to run to the post office. And then I'm going to call Everett."

***

Mama did call Mr. Coleman after she returned. He didn't seem too concerned or offer much in the way of ideas. But Mama got the distinct impression he wasn't telling her everything.

Where There's Smoke

Thursday morning dawned warm and muggy, the sky already a steamy white and everything looking somehow ... rounder than usual, seen through the fish-eye lens of high humidity. Every breath felt more like a swallow and, by evening, we'd be rained out by a heat storm for sure. So, there we were, four innings into a morning game and play becoming intense.

It was a full house with Jimmy, Sasha, Natalie, me, and, by some stroke of fantastic luck, Garrett, Pansy, and Cliff, the Drummonds' older brother, who appeared to be enjoying himself playing with "the kids." He must've been off work for the day, though why he chose to spend it in the heat with us was beyond me.

Maisy, opting not to take ups, spent most of her time playing with ants in a mound created between two garden bricks and served as our sometimes-batgirl. Since he was the oldest and almost always hit a homer, making his placement on either team somewhat an obvious advantage, Cliff volunteered as our all-time pitcher. Jimmy, Natalie, and Pansy made up one team, and Sasha, Garrett, and I made up the other. It was about as even as possible, all things considered.

Jimmy drilled a high rocket toward the red board fence, and his team-mates cheered in pre-celebration hysterics as he scissor-skipped his way to first, whooping his arms up and hollering the type of color commentary generally reserved for the Greats.

"It's gone, folks! The crowd is on its feet! The great Jimmy D has set a new record for back fence fly-bys!! *Raaaahhhhhhhhh!!*" He cupped his hands around his mouth, imitating the roaring crowd.

His ego deflated just as dramatically when Garrett launched himself up the fence and snatched the ball out of the sky as it sailed into neighboring airspace, a legal but rare move. Stunned, Jimmy collapsed on the young pampas grass, mouth agape, staring at the sky and trying to determine how in the world that had just happened.

Sasha and I rushed Garrett as he returned to terra firma, high-fiving and back-slapping him as we trampled a good-sized patch of Mama's young petunias. A trip to Mr. Coleman's garden would be in order at the end of the ninth.

As we switched sides, alternately congratulating and consoling Jimmy for his outstanding, yet ill-fated, homer, we heard a high-pitched screech coming from parts unknown. Everyone looked around, expecting to catch someone messing with us. But something jarringly familiar about the sound put us on alert.

Then we smelled it.

A dry, acrid odor, almost like cigarettes, wafted through the backyard with a rolling cloud of dark smoke hot on its heels. Mama, who had been in the garage trying to make some sense of the chaos within, came running out. She took one look at the ominous black swirl and took off toward Nattie's house, hollering, "Call the fire department! Nattie! *Nattie!!*"

She jumped the fence, vaulted the back steps, and launched herself through Nattie's screen door.

Cliff, first to gather his wits, blasted into our kitchen to make the call. The rest of us climbed onto the chain-link fence and settled in to watch what was happening.

We could hear Mama calling to Nattie repeatedly, getting quieter and quieter as she, presumably, searched farther into the house. What we weren't hearing was a reply from Nattie. My heart thumped in my ears as we waited for something—anything—to indicate they were okay.

Finally, Mama threw open the living room windows, smoke belching out and purling toward us like an underworld demon. It seemed like an odd thing to do. Everybody and their brother learned during Fire Prevention Week that fire uses oxygen to grow.

Fire engines started to whine in the distance, and my heart fluttered a bit to think of Mama inside that house, possibly in need of rescue. Smoke continued to pour out of the windows for a minute but then, strangely, began to subside. Mama stopped hollering for Nattie, which unsettled me further. What had she been thinking running in there like that?

Neighbors gathered as they noticed the smell and commotion, and the sirens screamed from two blocks away. Mama emerged out the back door, sweating and covered in soot, supporting a violently coughing and scolding Nattie. I couldn't tell who was in worse shape since Nattie was also covered in soot.

"Susan Walker, you just let me be!"

Nearly doubled over from hacking, she was frantically swatting at Mama and trying to shove her away while chewing her out for not minding her own business. All this while Mama was literally saving the old bat's life.

For her part, Mama coughed to the point of gagging and finally sat down on the concrete, knees apart and head between them, letting Nattie flap where she pleased.

The firetrucks pulled up to the house, and firemen spilled out like an overturned colander of shelled peas. Several ran toward the front door while two ran down the driveway to Mama and Nattie, checking whether they were alright and asking if anyone else was inside.

"Everyone's out," Mama coughed. "No one's inside. The fire's out."

Everyone did a double-take, looking from Mama to the blackened windows and back in unison. The firemen were clearly questioning her sanity. Perhaps she'd gone daft from smoke inhalation.

"Ma'am, are you sure?" This from a burly gentleman helping her with oxygen.

"Yes ... I'm—" But she broke off in another fit of hacking.

A fireman emerged out the back door, having gone the length of the narrow house. He appeared to have collected a souvenir.

"We're clear," he barked into his radio, holding up a blackened and partially disfigured pot in one hand. "Looks like lunch is gonna be a little late."

Nattie swiped at the pot and resumed her cussing and chastising of Mama and now the fireman, obviously mortified. The gathering rescuers paid her no mind and persisted with the administration of first aid, oxygen, and water.

The big man took Mama aside to get a statement and then gave her permission to come home, reminding her of what to do should she start to feel ill. Nattie, on the other hand, earned herself an ambulance ride to the hospital for further observation. No one had a clue how long she'd been in the smoky house, and her general demeanor caused concern to all but those of us familiar with her usual shenanigans.

***

The excitement over, we returned to our game. Frequent mid-inning stretches occurred to rehash the chaotic scene. Jimmy and Sasha claimed foreknowledge reaching Nostradamian proportions as hindsight became 20/20.

"Aw, heck. I knew it was no big deal," said Sasha. "It didn't smell like a real fire, anyway."

"Yeah," said Jimmy. "I smelled food for sure."

"You always smell food," Cliff laughed.

Whatever. We'd all been scared out of our minds when Mama went running into that house. No one really thought much of anything other than, "FIRE!". Christian duty be damned; I didn't think I'd ever run into a burning building.

For my part, I was just glad to have Mama home safe. But something did niggle at the back of my mind: I could've sworn I had seen a pair of Prescott shoes make a rapid retreat on the other side of the hedge when we turned back to the yard. Someone had been watching.

The Cavalry

Nattie's adventure with the fire department resulted in several things happening. First, a cleaning crew came to get the smoke smell out of her house, which we kids enjoyed immensely. They came over and got a key from Mama and then proceeded to carry all kinds of furniture out and all sorts of equipment in.

Second, those of us who witnessed the incident first-hand got quite a bit of mileage out of telling others what went on. Some embellishment along the way got silly, but no one called anyone else out on it lest they get caught themselves. It became a whale of a tale, taking on mythic proportions in no time. Mama, of course, eventually filleted Moby Dick back down to a guppy.

It was the arrival of Parker Dennings, however, that made everyone sit up and take notice. He lived in Oregon and visited Nattie a couple of times a year but never brought his family. Nattie never went to stay with them, either. Word was, Parker's wife wasn't a big fan of Nattie's and Cilla's shenanigans and didn't want the grandkids witnessing them.

After the fire, we all expected Nattie to spend a day or two in the hospital. When a day or two became three, and Parker pulled up in a rental car, we knew something was definitely up.

Everybody liked Parker. Much like Jack, he was always smiling and able to make anyone feel as if they'd just spoken with him the day before. He had been a baseball star in high school and was kind of like a fun uncle for all us kids. He never turned down the opportunity to go a few innings with us.

Typically, he paid a visit to neighbors he knew growing up and always took Mr. Coleman out to dinner. So, it didn't surprise any of us to see him stroll around the corner and head in that direction shortly after his arrival. What did cause eyebrows to raise was seeing him headed up Cilla Prescott's front steps afterward, a furrowed brow worrying his face.

Years back, he would stop and chat with Cilla for a good long while when in town. More recently, their visits had been short and cordial. With Cilla and Nattie at odds, there was no wondering why.

This visit proved equally brief, and Parker left Cilla's with more of a scowl on his face than any of us had seen before. He headed back to Nattie's deep in thought and hunkered down for the next two days.

***

Nattie came home on Tuesday. Naturally, Mama stopped over with a supply of casseroles and cookies and offered to help in any way necessary. When she came back home, it was as if she'd caught whatever Parker had, her brow now furrowed, and her mind distracted.

That evening, Mama, Daddy, and Parker spent a long time out on the veranda, talking quietly. I knew better than to try to eavesdrop; it looked serious.

Parker had given Mama a lovely bouquet from Nattie's garden, and he had dressed a bit spiffier than a casual catch-up warranted. By the time they said goodnight, they'd gone through an entire pitcher of lemonade, and Daddy had brought out the Scotch. Quite serious, indeed, then.

The Penny Drops

T turned out Parker's visit really wasn't a casual catch-up. Far from it, in fact. The following day, I came down to the kitchen to find Mama sitting at the table with paperwork spread out in every direction, her reading glasses perched on her nose, which on any other day she would have been loath even to admit needing.

That much paper was usually Daddy's sort of thing at the end of the month when he sat down to pay bills and balance the checkbook. While there were some bills on the table, a lot of other stuff made up the piles, too, and I didn't see the checkbook anywhere.

"Mornin', kiddo."

"What's all that?" I took in the array of invoices, charts, and colorful graphs as I reached blindly into the cupboard for a cereal bowl.

Mama took a deep breath and glanced around at everything. She puffed her cheeks and let it out, slumping back in her chair, looking defeated.

"This," she gestured, indicating the swath of papers, "is Nattie."

"Huh?" I stopped halfway to the fridge. "What do you mean, 'It's Nattie'?"

Mama sighed and pinched the bridge of her nose.

"Annabelle, get your cereal and come sit down. I need to talk to you about something."

I got my breakfast and sat. Nothing indicated trouble for me, but something was definitely wrong.

"Is this why Parker came over last night? He didn't seem very happy."

"Yes. And, no, he wasn't, honey. These," she said, indicating one pile, "are all unpaid bills of Nattie's. And these," she pointed to the rest of the mess, "are all doctor's reports and test results from her stay in the hospital."

"Ooh-kay."

I looked expectantly from the papers to Mama. Things still weren't clicking in my head. Mama took another deep breath and put her hand over mine on the table.

"Annabelle, Nattie is sick. Not like 'she's going to die soon' sick, but sick in her head. She forgets things, gets confused. Her brain is losing its ability to allow her to function normally. It's called dementia. Sometimes she has transient ischemic attacks or TIAs. Almost like tiny mini-strokes."

I continued to stare at Mama, my spoon loaded and suspended mid-transport.

"So ... what does that mean?"

"Well, it means some of what Nattie does isn't intentional. It also means sometimes she does things to cover up what's really happening and push people away because she's embarrassed. Her doctors say this appears to have been going on for some time."

"Soo ... she's not crazy, then?"

"Well, no. And, Annabelle, that's not a nice thing to say about someone. I know she seems a little off-kilter, but her brain isn't always able to keep up as it should. Parker told us last night that the doctors spent quite some time with her doing neurological and psychological evaluations and scans. Seems Nattie's known about this for several years, maybe even since before Jack died seven years ago."

"Is that what makes her so nasty? I mean, why does she do all that scary stuff?"

"Hm. As best as the docs can figure—and Parker agrees with them—Nattie is doing a lot of things to keep people at a distance. She may be worried they'll notice something is wrong, and she doesn't want them to think her incapable. She'd rather be in control of what people think than embarrassed by what she can't help."

"Wait! Is that why she asked me where to find her house?"

"Very likely, yes. That would've been a moment when things weren't working the way they should. When she realized what was happening, she got angry and sped away. Can you imagine how embarrassing it must've been for her?

"It's also probably why she has her starter pistol and why Wiffle balls come back from her yard all cut up. She doesn't want you guys getting close. In fact, it's most likely why she watches everything so closely from behind the hedge and out her front window. Watching and eavesdropping are much easier than asking questions."

"Oh. That sounds awful."

I stared at my hands, ashamed.

"Mama? I don't think I've been very nice to Nattie." I felt bad now for having called her "Batty Nattie" and for making fun of her with the other kids. How could I ever apologize for something like that?

"Well, honey, she hasn't been very pleasant to be around. How she chooses to deal with what is happening is up to her. And the consequences are her responsibility, as well. Asking for help isn't easy. In fact, she doesn't want to now, either. I'm sure she's frightened and lonely, along with being stubborn. Regardless of how she feels, help is exactly what she needs.

"Parker asked Daddy and me if we would be willing to go over things and get an understanding of what is what. This way, we can help him find someone local who can live with Nattie and give her a hand so she doesn't need to leave her home. Her condition isn't critical yet, but it's serious enough that there are things she shouldn't do on her own."

"Oh." Then an awful thought came to mind.

"Mama!" My eyes went huge, and Mama jumped. "Mama, Cilla! She's been positively horrible to Nattie. But she doesn't know!"

Mama looked down at her lap and pursed her lips.

"What? Mama, what is it?"

"Parker visited Mr. Coleman and Cilla when he arrived. Mr. Coleman is the one who called him and said he needed to get here as quickly as possible. Cilla, however, refused to discuss anything."

"Mr. Coleman knew?"

We were all aware he was wise in more ways than he ever let on, but this was huge. He'd been in contact with Parker all this time behind the scenes.

"He knew something was off, but he didn't know it was dementia and made a promise not to tell anyone. Everett's been checking in by phone occasionally and sometimes in person over the last few years to keep an eye on how Nattie's doing. He kept his distance to prevent neighborhood gossip or trouble with Cilla. After the incident with the stove, he figured he had to say something."

"But how did he find out?"

"When Jack got sick and found out he wouldn't be around to take care of Nattie, he asked Everett to keep an eye on her but didn't mention anything specific. Everett assumed Jack was just a man looking out for his wife, and he may have been. When Everett noticed a few things that seemed peculiar, he talked to Parker. They've been in touch ever since but never suspected the cause."

"But why didn't Cilla help her? Why would she walk away from her best friend when Nattie needed her?"

"That is what we don't know. And Cilla isn't talking."

***

Parker had to return home that day, having been gone longer than intended. Mama spent most of the day making phone calls, but first, she walked over to Mr. Coleman's for a visit. Usually, she would invite him for a glass of lemonade and a plate of cookies on the veranda. This conversation didn't need to be available to Cilla or Nattie's ears, however.

When she arrived back home, she had a bit more information about Nattie and how she'd been faring recently. Well, at least up until she landed herself in the hospital. What she didn't have was an answer for why Cilla walked away. As usual, Mama sensed Mr. Coleman holding back. When it came to keeping confidences, he appeared to be the Fort Knox of Pullman Station.

By the time Daddy arrived home from work, Mama had a few good leads on live-in help for Nattie. The hospital provided for care visits over the next two weeks or until permanent arrangements were made, whichever came first.

Mama agreed to supply meals for Nattie that only required reheating in the microwave, which Mrs. Perkins and Mrs. Drummond said they would help with, as well. Of course, Nattie remained as surly as ever about the intrusion, but she did appear relieved that she didn't have to cook. The fire had at least scared her straight in that regard.

Mama arranged interviews over the next two days for long-term care providers to come and meet Nattie. Afterward, she would choose whomever she felt most comfortable with. Mama attended the visits, as well, so Nattie didn't feel quite so awkward. It also afforded Parker an accomplice who could provide an on-side account of how things went.

On Friday, Nattie grudgingly selected a young woman named Piper to be her live-in caretaker, starting the following Monday. Though, if anyone asked, Piper was her niece.

Mama called and filled Parker in on the plan. He'd spoken to Piper before the in-home visit and approved. It appeared things were, indeed, going to be in good hands.

***

After getting dinner to Nattie, Mama came home that evening and slumped in Daddy's recliner in the living room. She put her feet up, sipped a glass of cold lemonade, and soon fell sound asleep. It had been an exhausting week for Christian duty. Now, it was time to relax and enjoy the weekend, basking in the glow of a job well done.

PART TWO

The Move to Pullman

April 1946

Once they decided to move, things happened quickly. Marlon and Jack spoke twice weekly via brief telephone calls, getting things arranged and ready to go on the Pullman side. Jack's hometown acquaintance, Donley Hickam, was, indeed, amenable to retirement, knowing he was selling to two servicemen who had helped the country in its time of need. The shop would need a few updates, but nothing they couldn't take care of once the Prescotts arrived.

Cilla and Nattie exchanged letters every few days, with Nattie filling Cilla in on items she had been able to arrange for the Prescotts' new home. Cilla, grateful for help from someone who was, as yet, a stranger, had made a meticulous inventory of their possessions. Next, she arranged this into lists of what they should take, what they should sell, and what they should purchase upon arrival. Putting her faith in a stranger was new to her, but her heart was surprisingly at ease about Nattie.

Teeny and Noah were less than thrilled at the prospect of being uprooted.

"But what about my friends?" Teeny cried. "I'll never see them again!"

"Yeah, what about our friends?" Noah echoed, not nearly as despondent as his sister but eager to be included in the family drama.

"You'll be able to write to them, and you'll make new ones, I promise," Cilla coached. "Your father and I have moved many times in our lives, and look at all the good friendships we've made here. We'll make more. It will be fine; you'll see."

"But I don't want new friends. I want the ones I have." Teeny would be a tough sell.

Still, Marlon and Cilla's excitement was contagious, and both children eventually warmed to it. Teeny insisted on hoarding paper, envelopes, and stamps before leaving rather than being caught unprepared upon arrival. As for Noah, the idea of a mechanic's shop to hang out in sounded like nothing short of paradise. Thus, his objections soon faded, as well. The whole family became enchanted by the romantic notion of moving across the country by rail.

***

Things appeared to be going swimmingly, with everyone starting to look forward to Pullman Station. On April 25, however, a high-speed, inter-city train named the *Advance Flyer* was traveling on the Chicago, Burlington, and Quincy railway line in Naperville, Illinois, when its cohort, the *Exposition Flyer*, rammed into it. The *Exposition* was traveling just two minutes behind its fellow at eighty miles an hour when the *Advance* made an unexpected stop for maintenance. The *Exposition's* engineer hadn't enough time to slow down after seeing the first yellow warning flag and was still traveling over forty-five miles per hour at the time of impact. Dozens of people died, and many more were injured. As the news hit papers, suddenly, the idea of hurtling through the countryside to a new home went from romantic adventure to terrifying risk for the Prescott family, and one nine-year-old in particular.

"Teeny, those were high-speed inter-city trains. Lots of traffic and confusion. Only minutes apart. Not at all like what we'll be taking to Pullman Station," Marlon explained. "Think of all the trains that run every day, and we never hear a thing about them."

"But, Dad, people died!"

"Well, yes, but people die in car accidents, too, honey. Driving that far would give us much more time on the road to get hurt or break down. Would you rather have car trouble in the middle of nowhere or be stranded on a train with people to help?"

"We could get stranded!?"

"Marlon," said Cilla, "that's not helping. Why don't you go work on packing, and Teeny and I will go for a walk."

Marlon did as told. Though even-keeled, his desire for the family to be as excited as him sometimes got in the way. Cilla would talk Teeny around in her matter-of-fact yet, soothing, motherly way, and things would be fine. She understood nine-year-old drama and fear much better than he. Still, it would be a trick getting their daughter on that train.

"It's just an outlet for all her nerves, Marlon," Cilla explained later that evening. "She's anxious about all the change and doesn't have a good way to deal with it. Being a kid is tough when you don't have any control over your life."

"But we do have control."

"*You* have control, Marlon. Teeny only sees that she's saying goodbye to nearly everything and everyone she knows. Believe me; it's a scary place for a young girl to be."

"I suppose. I wish I could show her that it will all be alright. I just want her to be happy."

"I know. And she will be. Her timeline is just a little different than yours."

***

In mid-May, Marlon boarded a train to head west ahead of the others and secure a house. Teeny cried as she hugged her father goodbye.

"Please, Daddy," she wailed. "Send a telegram directly when you get there!"

Cilla, pulling her daughter off Marlon, silently wished for the same thing. Though she knew that anything like the Naperville accident was unlikely to happen again after such a tragedy, she didn't relish the idea of not knowing immediately after her husband had arrived undamaged.

As she watched the train pull out of the station, Cilla knew her life was about to change again in a big way. What she didn't realize was just how much those on the other end would come to mean to her.

***

One month after Marlon's safe arrival in Pullman Station, Cilla and the children joined him. The goodbyes were hard, of course, but the most difficult one came as a surprise.

They could write to friends and receive letters in return, but saying farewell to the place where she had found herself proved most heartrending for Cilla. Unsure whether she'd ever be back, it hit her that she may never walk past the Plant factory or wander through Franklin Park again. She may never have memories knocked loose by these landmarks or the sounds and smells specific to Jamaica Plain. She may never be this close to her memories with Penny again, and it felt almost like its own sort of death.

She had been so busy reassuring the children and getting things ready that she'd neglected to check on herself. Her goodbye hadn't been gradual, and their departure left her breathless.

Upon their arrival in Pullman Station, a deliriously happy Marlon greeted them.

"Hiya, kids!" he called before lifting them in a bear hug, his delight palpable.

"And, hello, my love," he smiled broadly, taking Cilla's face in his hands and pressing his forehead to hers. She could feel him soaking in the relief of her presence and transferring his joy to her heart. When he kissed her then, she knew that they had made the right choice.

Jack stood beside Marlon on the platform, wearing a smile of equal wattage and radiating energy that soothed any remaining fears. He offered his hand.

"Name's Jack Dennings, ma'am. Welcome to Minnesota. I can't tell you how tickled we are that you're here."

"Hello, Jack. It's nice to finally meet you in person. And this must be Nattie."

Nattie stepped forward and embraced Cilla fondly.

"Gosh, I feel like I've known you forever, already," she said. "Welcome home."

"Thank you, Nattie. We're glad to be here."

"I'm Parker," said a precocious young boy behind Nattie, offering his hand as his father had.

"Nice to meet you, Parker. I'm Mrs. Prescott, and these two are Teeny and Noah. I hear you have lots planned for them already."

"Oh, yeah! Come on; I'll tell you all about Pullman Station!" He grabbed Noah by the hand and gestured for Teeny to follow.

"Was the train ride long? Did you talk to the engineer?" He led on ahead, peppering them with questions about rail travel and news of his plans for their future. An only child, he was positively vibrating with the notion of two new, ready playmates his age, with whom to seek adventure.

The adults followed at a slower pace, chatting while they waited for the luggage. As they gathered belongings and headed toward the cars, Cilla's shoulders relaxed. They had done it. They had landed on new soil, hopes in hand, and found the ground solid and the atmosphere welcoming. Marlon had been right: it would be just fine.

***

Though more reserved than herself, Cilla discovered Nattie to be a tremendous help, and the two were quickly inseparable. Cilla had endured and defeated many challenges in her life that would have seemed impossible to others, but she wasn't at all sure she could have done this without Nattie. Her kindness, patience, and organization were a perfect complement to Cilla's drive, independence, and head-on personality. It quickly became evident that, like their husbands, there wasn't much the two of them couldn't accomplish together.

The kids immediately took to the enchantment of a new place to explore. Parker was thrilled to be their tour guide and event coordinator, and the three of them were fast friends.

Parker introduced Teeny and Noah to the Coleman children, Beatrice, or "Bea," as everyone called her, and Marty. Everett Coleman was a friend of Jack's, and the men had hired him to help on evenings and weekends.

He was a kind man who had lost his wife shortly after Marty's birth and was happy for any sort of work that gave him flexibility during the week, which fit with Jack and Marlon's plan perfectly.

Thick as thieves, the children ran together non-stop. Where you found one, you could usually expect to see the rest. Noah dismissed his reservations regarding the move, and even Teeny had to admit that she was happy in their new home.

Traditions

May 1950

E ven though they worked together, the Prescott, Dennings, and Coleman families played together, too. They were a rowdy bunch that loved to have fun, especially outside. Hillman Park, located ten miles from Pullman Station, provided just the outlet needed and brought out the kid in everyone.

In 1948, they began an annual tradition of a Saturday picnic in late May to celebrate the end of the school year and ring in summer. They also invited Donley Hickam's son, Dicky, and his family—Marlon and Jack had purchased the garage from Donley—and went rain or shine.

**

The park sat between the bluffs and off the highway—one of the hidden gems tucked in among the sleeping giants. It was long and narrow, carved out by spring-fed Hillman Creek, which began its journey far back in the hills and ran through the park along one side. It meandered here and there, deeper and shallower, finally finding its way down to Pullman via the highway ditches.

The grounds contained picnic tables, swings, merry-go-rounds, slides, campsites, fire pits, two stone pavilions along with some wood-and-metal ones, and a few creepy outhouse buildings. The stone pavilions were more protected up against the hillside than the flimsier ones out in the open, which did nothing to block the wind. More than one celebration Saturday was spent soaked to the gills in a mix of sweat, sideways rain, and orange Cheeto paste.

Most years, they managed to snag the biggest one, everyone's favorite. Made of limestone blocks and tucked up against the hill, it offered refuge from storms while still letting air through. Stairs led up inside, with pillars at all four corners, a vaulted roof, and a half-wall all around. Being up high allowed for a fantastic view of the park, and the walls made perfect launching pads for daring jumps to the earth below. A small bridge crossed Hillman Creek there, which made everything feel all the more private and secluded, away from anyone else trying to nose in on their fun.

Down from the pavilion stood a set of high swings perfect for under ducks and flying leaps from great heights. A teeter-totter, metal slide, and a merry-go-round rounded out the gauntlet of equipment that likely should have broken someone's neck. Past that was one of the outhouse buildings. It smelled terrible, and timing was key, especially on hot days. The ability to hold your breath for a while didn't hurt, either.

Trickling along beyond the bridge, Hillman Creek bubbled and gurgled, tripping over rocks, fanning out the watercress, and whispering temptation to children with its playful voice. Past the bathrooms, it hung a left and headed back to an out-of-the-way little pit-stop pond tucked up against the hill where the bottom fell out for a bit before the water rushed merrily on its way again. That makeshift pool was kid kryptonite.

First to get wet was always a hot bet, though no one was ever in doubt about who it would be. Everyone packed extra clothes for the day, but

Cilla always sneaked in a few additional changes for Noah. It was as if he gained divining ability as he crossed through the park gate. Wherever water trickled or rushed, he found it; almost like a superpower, save that it nearly froze his bits and pieces off a couple of times.

Hillman Creek, being spring-fed, was mighty cold. Some people would say it "wasn't bad." Those were people who wanted to see you cannonball into the pond and bob to the surface as an ice cube. There was no truthful way to put it than to say it was absolutely freezing. Deep or shallow, you'd likely pee yourself a little when your feet first hit the water. But once they went numb and the pain went away, you were free to play all you wanted. If the sun was out and the day hot, so much the better for cycling between freeze and thaw. If it was cold and rainy, deliberation was strongly encouraged.

Every single year, regardless of the weather, the kids built a dam in the creek. It occupied them for hours while giving the grown-ups some quiet time to chat and relax.

Noah usually found the water shortly after they arrived, though most others waited until bellies were full. Dunking before food meant they had to come out to eat, start to dry, and then acclimate to the cold and wet again afterward. Not the wisest approach. If they held off until after lunch, they only had to adjust once, when their stomachs were full of extra fuel for body heat, something Noah never seemed to cotton onto. Everyone else would run up and down the teeter-totters, almost puke on the merry-go-round, burn their legs on the metal slide and give each other under ducks on the swings until they'd worked up a roaring appetite. Then they went hunting and gathering in the picnic baskets.

***

Celebration Saturday in 1950 was no different. No sooner had they gotten their things out of the car than Noah decided to do a rock walk instead of using the bridge. *Ker-plunk!* Screams rocketed out of his throat as he dragged himself out, arms aloft and walking like he'd dropped a load in his pants.

As it happened, the forecast called for a relatively warm afternoon, lucky for the damming efforts. Everyone worked up appetites on the playground gear, inhaling the smells wafting over from various grills around the park. Noah sat in the middle of the merry-go-round, as usual, while everybody else, save Jamie Hickam, hung themselves off the edges.

Jamie acted as the propeller. His long legs and strong arms whipped them around at a pretty good clip as they hung on for dear life, trying to pull their heads back in. Once in a while, someone would go flying off, having lost their grip, and come to a rolling stop in the grass. Noah simply went cross-eyed in the middle. When things came to a halt, he staggered off to try and walk a straight line while everyone else rested their arms and necks.

When they'd had enough, they moved on to the swings and teeter-totter. Both Bea and Marty Coleman were daredevils. They took to the teeter-totter, crouching one-legged on opposite ends with their free legs hanging off to pump. On the agreed upswing, one of them would stand up and fly off. Smart enough not to go full bore, they still impressed the rest of the gang and freaked all of the parents out, save for their father, who was tough to rattle.

They had learned over the years that the only thing worth doing on a metal slide sitting in the sun was to run up it. Clanging up the front, they slid down the railing side before heading to the swings.

Jamie held the title as the best under ducker, while Marty held the "flying" title. He always got higher than anyone else dared and would go shooting off time and again to "oohs" and "aahs" from those watching and egging him on. Luckily—or unluckily if you happen to be Marty—he had broken his arm doing that very thing at Boxcar Lake one year, so he didn't take too many uncalculated risks. He had it mastered.

***

After a lunch of grilled burgers and hot dogs, along with Cheetos, potato chips, potato salad, pickles, fruit salad in a watermelon boat carved by Mrs. Hickam, Cilla's famous peach cobbler, and way too much Coca-Cola, they headed for the creek. The sun was blazing down, and they were ready to get to work. Still, the process of actually getting in the water was always intimidating.

The worst part of it was the pain. Everyone had on their old clothes and creek-walkers, so it wasn't a matter of keeping clean or not ripping any clothes or destroying shoes. The hesitation was purely instinct. No one should have willingly gone into a creek that cold and enjoyed it. But, having done it many times before and having had the time of their lives, they always knew it would be fine if they just bit the bullet and got in—instinct overridden.

Bea and Teeny were "dippers." They'd walk along in the shallows until the pain stopped, and they couldn't feel their feet anymore. Once accomplished, the rest came easier. Nothing more than their feet, hands, and lower arms actually needed to get dunked to move rocks and sticks and build something functional. Sure, their torsos got wet carrying things, but they wouldn't be submerged, and that was always a huge consideration in water that cold.

The rocks, however, were slick and the watercress misleading. Place a foot wrong, and they might go butt-over-tea kettle simply because water hit a part of their leg they didn't expect, and the shock set them off balance.

The boys didn't much care how they got in, and it usually proved wise to give them plenty of space to let some energy out before trying to approach the area with them in it. By the time the girls reached them, the boys would be soaked through.

The key to making a decent dam was a careful harmony between large and small. A solid foundation that wouldn't float away was need- ed, along with a netting of smaller materials that would allow it to build upon itself as debris came by. Some people looked scornfully at the activity, saying they were altering nature's course for the creek. But the dams weren't permanent. As soon as a good gully-washer came through, it would blow the whole thing to smithereens, and Mother Nature would have her way again. After all, they were keen builders but weren't the Army Corps of engineers.

***

They had gotten a fairly decent start when Nattie and Cilla stopped by to evaluate their progress. The best thing about building at the bottom of a limestone bluff was that many small boulders they could use for a solid foundation got washed down over time. The biggest problem was lifting them. They usually found a downed tree branch and used it as a lever, working together to move the rocks into the right spot.

It was tricky, wet work, but the satisfying sound of a large boulder plunging into a pool of water was not to be missed. A full-bodied, soul-filling *GLUNK!* was a thing to behold. Frequently followed by triumphant ululations, it served as a signal to the adults that all was well.

Just that sort of celebration is what brought Nattie and Cilla over to the mini excavation camp to assess progress. Looking like a bunch of gleeful, muddy backhoes, everyone grinned at Nattie on the bank while she snapped away with her camera. Even the girls stood soaked through, though, not quite as sopping as the boys.

Cilla, always adventurous, edged her way over to a fallen log to get a better look at what they had accomplished, which wasn't insignificant. As she peered over the water, Noah and Parker saw an opportunity fit for seizing. They each grabbed a smallish boulder from near the far bank of the pond and heaved them toward the log. They hit right on target with an achingly satisfying double-*GLUNK!*, surprising Cilla as the water rebounded into her face. She lost her balance, spinning around, arms and legs pinwheeling like a drunken marionette, and completed the display by doing a beautiful fade smack into the pond with an almighty splash.

You'd have thought someone was murdering a screech owl. At first, Cilla was so shocked by the cold that the air left her lungs in a reflexive, high-pitched banshee scream, followed by silence as her body seized up, too stunned to reverse and inhale.

"Cilla!" Nattie scrambled at the edge of the pond. "Cilla, are you alright!?"

Meanwhile, the kids couldn't breathe, either. Of course, their problem was that they were laughing almost to the point of passing out.

"HOLY COW!!" Cilla screamed at the top of her lungs, finally gaining her breath again. "Oh, my word! Oh, my word! Oh, it's so cold! Oh, my goodness!"

"Cilla, give me your hand," Nattie called, setting her camera out of harm's way and reaching out. Cilla flailed around, trying to figure out which way was which while Nattie inched toward the muddy landing they used as the access point to the water.

"Cilla, over here!" Nattie leveraged her weight with one foot forward as she reached out.

Finally understanding, Cilla made her way through the icy water as it sliced through her nerves. She gained purchase on the rocky bottom and stretched up toward Nattie. They grasped hands, and Nattie pulled, shooting a glance at Noah and Parker as if warning them that if they expected a head start, now would be an excellent time to run.

Marlon, Jack, Mrs. Hickam, and Mr. Coleman all came running around the bend just in time to see Nattie lose her footing in the slippery mud. She gave a whoop, wind-milled, and pitched face-first into the pond next to Cilla. The other grown-ups stopped abruptly, eyes huge as they tried to process the scene playing out in front of them: two screaming women, six frenzied kids, and a cheerfully bubbling creek made for quite a sight.

Jack lost it first. He collapsed on the ground in a fit of hysterical laughter, quickly followed by Marlon as the two of them made absolute ninnies of themselves. They rolled around clutching their stomachs while their wives flapped about, freezing their butts off in the ice-cold drink.

Mrs. Hickam, however, rushed over and began looking for a branch to use to fish her two friends out. Soon, she, too, was nearly hysterical with laughter and unable to be of much assistance as she doubled over and crossed her legs so as not to wet her pants.

Cilla and Nattie finally made their way out of the pond with Mr. Coleman's help, but not before Jack had pulled himself together and grabbed Nattie's camera. Both women stood shivering, their teeth chattering as they scolded their husbands for not helping. Then they turned on Noah and Parker, pointing fingers. The boys grinned and waved from the other side of the pond. Already soaked through, what could anyone possibly do to them now?

As the grown-ups made their way back to camp, the kids continued construction on the dam. When finished, they climbed out, proud, exhausted, and hungry again. They walked the creek back to the little bridge and squelched up the path to the pavilion for food, clothes, and heat. Someone had set up a tent of quilts, so changing didn't need to occur in the bathrooms, thank goodness. They warmed their dry, clothed bodies in the sunshine and settled in for a second lunch, content and happy.

***

At the end of the day, six exhausted kids and seven weary parents packed up the cars and headed home. These were the halcyon days Marlon and Cilla had so hoped for when they decided to move to Pullman Station.

Things had worked out beautifully. They had made new friends, as had Teeny and Noah, and established new traditions. Life was good. Cilla looked at Marlon as they pulled in the driveway, a smile spread across her face. This was, indeed, home.

Pullman Days

June 29, 1985

Every summer, the city held a "Pullman Days" carnival in Windham Park to celebrate the town's history. The fun included a bake-off, craft sales, balloon stand, concessions, and a raffle. A railroad-themed soapbox derby took place around the plaza for anyone under thirteen. Sack and three-legged races, Bingo, a carousel, and face painting were all available in various locations around the park. Firetruck displays, water fights, and a dunk tank were always popular, and fireworks over Boxcar Lake in the evening always topped things off. It was *the* summer event, and few people missed it.

Our parents decided to let us older kids wander around without them for the first time as long as we stuck together. Two blocks may not seem like a lot of freedom, but with everything going on, we felt like we were miles away.

We'd each taken five dollars out of our saved allowance and now stood in a huddle trying to decide how best to spend it.

"How about we each pick something that we want to do while the others wait for us? Then we can use the rest for anything else we want as a group," said Natalie.

"That sounds fair," said Jimmy.

"Dude, I'm so doing the dunk tank while Dad's in it!" Sasha rubbed his hands together. He was giddy with anticipation of dunking his old man.

"I think I'm going to do the face painting," Natalie announced.

"Me, too," I said.

"I dunno," said Jimmy. "I really wanna dunk Mr. Perkins, but the water fights were super fun last year."

We agreed that we would all ride the carousel once because we'd done it together every year since we started going to the carnival, and it was a tradition we weren't quite ready to give up.

Jimmy finally decided to join Sasha at the dunk tank.

"If we team up, we're sure to get him good at least once. If we miss with all six shots, we're pathetic, and I'm never playing ball again."

The odds were in their favor. Both were pretty accurate when it came to pitching, even if Jimmy blamed Sasha for bad pitches when he fouled a Wiffle into Nattie's yard. Their biggest challenge would be to stop laughing long enough to throw.

***

We headed to the dunk tank first since Mr. Perkins was on an early afternoon shift. Lucky for him, the sun was shining and the day plenty warm. Jimmy and Sasha joined the line while Natalie and I stood to the side discussing what to have drawn on our faces.

Mr. Perkins was still dry, something that both boys hoped to be the first to rectify. The closer they got to the front, the more they danced in place. Mr. Perkins playfully begged everybody to please dunk him before his son did.

As other contestants got close with their throws—one nicking the target lever on the side, though not hard enough to trigger the seat—Sasha and Jimmy pumped their fists and jumped up and down, whooping and hollering.

"We're coming for you, Mr. Perkins! Get your nose plug ready!"

"Yeah! Hope you brought dry clothes, old man!"

Mr. Perkins laughed and pointed a warning finger at Sasha for the "old man" dig.

One kid hit the Plexiglas with a wild pitch, nearly causing Mr. Perkins to fall off the narrow seat as he instinctively ducked. That sent everyone into fits of laughter.

Then it was finally Sasha's turn. He and Jimmy walked over to the guy in charge and whispered something. The man looked at Mr. Perkins, shrugged his shoulders, and handed them three balls each.

Sasha made a big show of trash-talking his dad before he hurled his first pitch; a near-miss met with groans from the crowd and hung heads from the boys.

"It's okay, s'alright. He's just warmin' up, folks. We got this!" Jimmy hollered.

Then, rather than throwing his second, Sasha stepped aside for Jimmy to take a turn. Another miss. The boys conferred and swapped again, this time with Jimmy standing behind the lever. Sasha focused hard for a moment, bending into his stance. He shook his head as Jimmy signaled pitches.

"Nuh-uh ... nope ... nope ... yep, that's the one!"

Jimmy backed out of the way as Sasha did a slow wind-up. He let fly with a massive pitch that hit the target with a *CLANG!*, sending Mr. Perkins into the water and the boys into hysterics.

"OH, MY GOSH!! Did you see that!? He totally threw a heater! He nailed it! He got 'im!"

They jumped up and down, hugging and high-fiving each other and anyone else nearby. They banged on the Plexiglas and flexed their bare-ly-there muscles at Mr. Perkins, who was laughing too hard to climb back on the seat. The crowd whistled and cheered at the first dunk coming from his own kid, and they began to chant as Jimmy took position for his second turn.

"Take him down! Take him down! Take him down!"

Again, the theatrics of pitch selection played out, this time with Sasha behind the lever. Ecstatic whoops went up as Jimmy, too, managed to submarine Mr. Perkins with flair.

"Yee-haa!! That's two! Might as well stay in the water, 'cuz we're not lettin' up!"

***

All in all, the boys tallied three dunks in six turns between them. The re-plays were on a continuous loop for the next fifteen minutes while Natalie and I got our faces done. We then decided a full lap around the park was in order to assess the other attractions and see what else might live up to the dunk tank excitement.

The tastes and smells of the carnival created a pleasant fug, something I always looked forward to. Fresh lemonade, ice cream, salt, warm sugar, and various fried and baked foods, overlaid with a subtle cigarette smoke finish, perfumed the air. While I usually hated the smell of cigarettes and considered it a disgusting habit, there was something very "carnival" about tobacco on the breeze that would have seemed wrong in absence.

We lapped the park several times, stopping to cheer on a couple of derby heats, as well as a few water fights. Walking around with my friends and no parents felt like the most grown-up thing I'd ever done. It was a decent contender for the best day ever. Near perfection, in fact. The fireworks that night would put the cherry on top.

We spotted Garrett and Pansy by the carousel several times as Maisy rode to her heart's content. Face sticky with ice cream, she would likely crash soon. She'd never been able to stay awake late enough for the fireworks, but at nearly six years old, she was growing up faster than any of us cared to acknowledge. She'd been chattering about seeing 'the sky full of sparkles' all week. It would be a night to remember as she giggled and squealed at all the colors and sounds, and we were all just as excited to watch her as we were for the show.

***

At five o'clock, we met up with our parents at the carousel and headed home. We ate, gathered blankets and coolers, and lathered up with bug spray before driving over to Boxcar Lake.

The park around the lake was filling up quickly. People had laid out their blankets and set up chairs earlier in the day to save spots or have dinner along the shore. Parking got tricky, but we all managed to find places near enough to allow us to run back and forth between blankets.

As predicted, Maisy had crashed for a nap when she got home and was now beside herself with excitement and energy as the sun began its descent. Pansy and Garrett had their own blanket not far from us, and Maisy planned to join them for the actual show.

In the meantime, she entertained the general vicinity by stopping to ask random strangers if they'd ever seen fireworks before and telling them this was her first time. As if they hadn't heard her say it to the person five feet away, thirty seconds earlier.

Jimmy, Sasha, Natalie, and I brought a blanket to sit together on, and we hauled snacks from our parents' blankets over to our own, which was about as far away as they would allow, being that it would be full dark when we regrouped. Each of us had a large baggie of popcorn, a couple of ropes of red licorice to use as straws, and a can of orange pop, a rare treat for everyone.

The day had cooled off nicely. A gentle breeze was blowing, carrying the scent of burning sparklers and keeping the mosquitos at bay. Crickets had started to sing, and conversations floated around us as voices grew quieter with the waning light. There was no other place I wanted to be. The perfect summer day was turning into the perfect summer night.

***

Traffic snaked slowly around the lake, packed, as people continued to jockey for parking spots, hoping that someone would call it quits before the show and pull out, so they could swoop in. Some would even drive around during the show to get out and home quickly once it was over. Headlights flashed here and there between parked cars. The sounds of laughter, coolers being wheeled past, cans cracking open, and tires squealing as drivers got irritated and hit the gas punctuated the evening air.

Maisy ran over as we sat on our blanket, debating whether to open our pops right away or wait until the show started.

"Look at my pinwheel! I won it at the ring toss." She twirled around, making it spin. Her adorable ringlets bounced as if powered by the whirling plastic, and her smile lit the evening around us as folks watched and nostalgically relived their own first fireworks.

A piercing bark came from a nearby blanket, followed by the jingle of dog tags and a deep-voiced reprimand. Maisy stopped cold, her eyes instantly wide with fear. She shot off in the opposite direction, her pinwheel flapping and her ears deaf to our shouts as she screamed at the top of her lungs.

The little pup bolted from its owner's blanket, enticed by the running child and flashy plastic. It followed in hot pursuit as its owner swore and stumbled after it.

Maisy wove between blankets, her little sandals slapping the grass with urgency as she shrieked and cried. Blinded by fear and with no sense of direction, she tried to make her way back to her parents. She hooked an abrupt left between two parked cars. In the twilight and confusion, no one was able to grab her.

The squeal of tires was followed by deafening silence as Maisy's terror was knocked from her throat. Her tiny body flew through the air. She hit the ground with a sickening thud, and the night shattered into a million tiny shards as Mrs. Drummond screamed for her baby.

Devastation

Maisy's tiny body lay in the street, injured and badly broken. Daddy and Mr. Perkins pushed us back and made sure we weren't allowed close enough to see. Mr. Perkins held Jimmy in a bear hug as he kicked and screamed, trying to break loose and run to his little sister.

Garrett grabbed Pansy, and the two of them ran to the street, though he didn't allow her to look. They were both in tears, Pansy hysterical and Garrett wanting desperately to comfort her and go to Maisy at the same time. He suddenly looked like a frightened boy of eight rather than the steady-as-he-goes lifeguard we all relied on.

Two volunteer firemen were on blankets nearby, and they ran to render aid and do whatever possible to save Maisy. A lake neighbor called 9-1-1, and sirens began to wail in the distance.

The driver of the car got out and tried to help but was frantic and had to be subdued by bystanders. The car's headlights shone on the pavement where Maisy lay, simultaneously aiding the firemen's efforts and grotesquely exposing the horrific scene.

Mr. and Mrs. Drummond sat hunched near their baby, Mrs. Drummond rocking back and forth, begging Maisy to be alright. The beautiful and perfect night had exploded into chaos, the night air torn open by sirens instead of sparkles.

***

The ambulance pulled up, and the firemen filled their colleagues in. Maisy was badly hurt but conscious. The paramedics stabilized her as best they could and moved her to a gurney.

"You're going to be okay, sweetie. Alright? Can you tell me your name?"

A paramedic named Mac tried to keep Maisy engaged while his partner, Jeannie, continued to monitor her vitals.

"I need you to hold real still, okay? I know it hurts. We've got some nice people who are going to make you feel a whole lot better."

"Respiration is slowed."

The ride to the hospital was only a few short blocks. Mr. Perkins took Mr. Drummond's keys and drove Mr. and Mrs. Drummond over. Mrs. Perkins, Sasha, and Natalie followed behind.

The ambulance pulled up outside the emergency room. Staff was waiting to meet them and take over. Mr. Perkin's pulled up a short distance behind, allowing them plenty of room to work.

As they brought Maisy out of the back, she threw up.

"Hang on, hang on, hang on..." Jeannie stopped abruptly. She rechecked Maisy's pupils, glanced at Mac, who nodded, and then hollered up to the driver. "Radio Mike's and tell them we're coming in with a pediatric head trauma!"

Mrs. Drummond tried frantically to get to Maisy.

All hell broke loose as they reversed back into the ambulance. Mac shouted to Mr. Perkins, one hand ready to close the back door. "Can you bring them to St. Michael's in the city?"

"Yes!"

The ambulance door slammed shut, and they sped away, siren screaming and lights shattering the sky with urgent warning.

A nurse took Mrs. Drummond by the arm and led her forcefully toward the car. "I'm sorry, ma'am. You can't go with them. Meet them at St. Mike's ER. Go! *Now!*"

***

Mama and Daddy gathered Jimmy, Pansy, and Garrett; then, we rode to their houses to collect some things before heading to our house. We made up beds and sleeping bags, but no one was going to sleep.

Garrett asked his parents' permission to stay overnight, and he and Pansy sat huddled together on the couch. Cliff had called our house, frantic when he heard that Maisy had been hurt, and no one answered at home. His friend dropped him off, and he sat hunched in the corner, knees pulled up, arms creating a protective cocoon around his head.

I cuddled up to Mama while she caressed my hair. Across the room, Daddy sat in the oversized recliner watching Jimmy, who was pacing back and forth, wringing his hands and trying to be brave. Eventually, Daddy gently reached a hand out to stop him, and he collapsed into Daddy's arms, sobbing. When he finally quieted, we all prayed together.

***

The phone rang a few minutes before midnight. It was Mr. Perkins calling to let us know that Maisy was at St. Michael's as they were better equipped to deal with the degree of trauma she had suffered. Her slowed breathing and subsequent vomiting had tipped the paramedics to swelling in her brain. Her skull was fractured—a small blessing in that it allowed a bit of grace for the swelling—but small boreholes were still necessary to ensure the relief was adequate.

She'd lost consciousness in the ambulance shortly before arriving at St. Michael's, a result not of the head trauma but a ruptured spleen. A CT scan confirmed it, and they rushed her into emergency surgery to remove it and stop the bleeding.

Her left femur and pelvis were broken. She was a mess.

***

A short while later, Mr. Drummond called. He spoke briefly to Cliff, Pansy, and Jimmy, telling them that he and Mrs. Drummond loved them and to keep praying; the doctors and nurses were doing everything possible for Maisy. He promised to call again when they knew more.

Cliff kept a stiff upper lip as he listened, his jaw clenching and un-clenching on a loop. When it was her turn, Pansy's head nodded, and tears streamed down her face, but she didn't make a sound.

"Dad?" Jimmy's voice broke. *"Dad?"* It was all he could manage until, "Okay, I love you, too," and he hung up.

Cliff grabbed his siblings and hugged them hard. Finally, as if wounded, his façade cracked, and he let out a sob.

Whammy

After a long, sleepless night, Mama made scrambled eggs, bacon, and toast with cinnamon sugar for breakfast, but none of us ate very much. The ticking clock above the stove replaced our usual chatter, and the breeze through the open window whispered anxious nothings in our ears. It was as if someone stood in the kitchen doorway with a huge pair of cymbals, and we were all waiting for them to crash together. We turned at every bang or rustle to check who was coming, but no one did.

We took it in turns to have a quick shower and at least scrub off the bug spray and salty tear tracks from the night before. Everyone's pounding heads felt full of cotton, our eyes full of sand. But, for the moment, we were cried out and just sat in the crushing silence, stunned. Mama finally convinced us to go outside and get some fresh air and sit in the shade. She promised to let us know as soon as anyone called with any news.

None of us saw the accident directly. No one but Garrett had seen Maisy lying in the street, and that hadn't been up close. We didn't know just how bad it was. Nobody told us what Maisy had looked like. Mama and Daddy had seen her, but they didn't say much. Surely, someone would have called by now if she had died during the night, right?

***

The phone rang around ten o'clock, and we ran to the screen door to listen, not even realizing that we were all holding our breath. Mama gave Daddy a wary glance before she picked up.

"Hello, Walker residence."

After a moment, she handed it to Daddy, and we all deflated and headed back to whatever we'd been pretending to be doing. It was only a business acquaintance calling to see if he wanted to join them for a round of golf. He politely declined.

At 10:17, Mrs. Perkins called to ask if they could come over. Mama spoke quietly for a minute and then hung up, staring off somewhere in her mind's eye. The Perkinses joined us a few minutes later, and we all waited together.

At 10:24, a Red Cross volunteer called, asking for Mama to schedule her regular blood donation. Yes, thank you, she'd take care of it.

When the ringer clanged again at 10:36, it was like a 'Press Your Luck' button had been installed on the kitchen wall. We were all waiting to see which call would be the Whammy.

Again, we ran to the back door. Then, as Mama picked up the receiver, time stood still.

She listened for what felt like forever—motionless, save for the ripples of fear that visibly pulsed from her and the slight twitch in her nose.

"Okay," she whispered. "We're praying hard."

She hung up the phone gently, and a shaking hand went to her mouth. Daddy had gotten up and waited behind her. He pulled her around the corner into the living room, where she dissolved.

Daddy held Mama close, not saying a word. He reached back around the corner for the tissue box and grabbed one for each of them. I don't think I'd ever seen Daddy cry before, and it scared me more than anything.

Mr. and Mrs. Perkins joined them. Cliff, Pansy, Jimmy, Garrett, Natalie, Sasha, and I stood still as statues, peering through the screen door, terrified. Finally, Daddy looked up and saw us and nudged Mama, who came rushing over, arms outstretched, flapping her hands for us to come in. She gathered us and held on while Mrs. Perkins joined in and squeezed Natalie and Sasha.

"Is Maisy dead?" Jimmy asked faintly as he pulled back, as scared of Mama's reaction to the call as to anything else he could have imagined had happened to Maisy.

Hearing the thought put into words jerked my belly button back against my spine. Noise rushed in my ears, and my face got hot. Maisy wasn't my little sister, but she was as close as I'd ever get to having one. Besides, she was a little kid. Kids weren't supposed to die. Ever.

"No, honey. She made it through surgery." Mama cleared her choked throat. "Your uncle Stewart and aunt Nicole are on their way to fill us in."

"Is she gonna be alright?" Pansy's voice sounded like that of a frightened six-year-old rather than a confident teen.

Mama's face wavered, and she pressed her lips together. She squeezed Pansy's shoulder, and Jimmy grabbed his sister's hand.

"Your aunt and uncle will tell us more, sweetie."

***

A car door slammed outside, and the top of Stewart's head slid past the window. When he walked in the back door, face utterly broken and eyes shot with blood, the roar came back to my ears, and my eyes started to sting.

Whammy.

I never wanted the phone to ring again.

Reckoning

Maisy spent a long time in surgery after she arrived at St. Michael's. Stewart ran through her injuries for us again: fractured skull, ruptured spleen, cracked pelvis, broken left femur. It was strange to think about, but he told us the doctors had said she was lucky. Children's bones are softer and take a hit better than older ones that have calcified more. It could've been much worse. Unfortunately, because of her height, her midsection took the brunt of the impact.

It felt like Maisy was right there, in my chest somehow, grinning her dimpled grin at me, curls bouncing. I mean, I knew she was dreadfully hurt, but I guess my brain forgot to tell my heart, and so it just kept expecting her to climb into the backyard and show me some neat rock she'd found or ask me to bring my old roller skates out. I could still feel her somewhere, warm, sweet-smelling, and adorable. She couldn't die.

Later that afternoon, we all should've been playing ball or going for a bike ride. Mama should have been making something to take to the Perkinses' for a barbecue to celebrate the end of Pullman Days. Instead, she was at the Drummonds' house, organizing, answering calls and the doorbell, and making sure they had something to eat. Sasha and Natalie were home helping their mother get groceries and make freezer meals for the Drummonds for the next few weeks.

***

Daddy stayed home with me, sticking close. We'd been running errands for Mama when she called with a need, and it wasn't until evening that I sat down next to him on the davenport and laid my head on his shoulder. Confusion had sapped what little energy I'd had earlier in the day.

Daddy put his arm around me and pulled me close, kissing my forehead. I curled into him, safe.

"What's up, kiddo?"

Suddenly, the tears rushed forward again, and a million questions jockeyed for position in my head, but I couldn't ask a single one. My voice only sobbed, sometimes a squeak, sometimes blowing, sometimes entirely silent and gnawing.

"Why?" was all I managed.

It seemed like the lynchpin question. If I knew the answer to that, I could reason my way back and change it somehow.

Daddy took a long, deep breath, pausing before letting it out.

"I don't know, honey. I don't know." He stared into nowhere and shook his head.

But he was supposed to know! He was a grownup! Doctors explained things to grownups, and then grownups explained them to kids and answered all their questions. They *always* knew.

"But Maisy's a little kid. Kids aren't supposed to get hurt like that or die. They have grownups and brothers and sisters to look out for them."

"Annabelle." I realized he was crying, too. "Annabelle, sometimes bad things happen to good people, and there isn't a reason or a why to be found. Sometimes, no matter how many people a person has looking out for them, or how innocent and perfect they are, bad things happen in the blink of an eye."

I thought about that.

"But, Mrs. Chisholm always says God won't give us more than we can handle, and I don't think Jimmy or Pansy or Cliff or Mr. and Mrs. Drummond can handle this."

I wiped tears and snot on my shoulder.

"Honey, I don't think Mrs. Chisholm gets that one quite right."

That surprised me into momentary stillness.

"God didn't do this to Maisy. He loves her very much, and he loves Cliff and Pansy and Jimmy and Mr. and Mrs. Drummond and *all* of us. He doesn't want his children to hurt."

"Then who did?"

"Some would say, 'Satan.' Others would say, 'life.' Still others would say, 'chance.' But, Annabelle, God *will* help us all cope with this if we ask Him to. We *must* ask Him to."

I thought about that, too, for a minute. This wasn't territory I was terribly surefooted in. God was supposed to be in charge, not Satan, or life or chance. We were supposed to trust that everything would be alright, that He had a plan, and He would protect us; that's how it worked. How had anything else gotten the upper hand?

"Daddy, why wasn't God strong enough to knock the other thing out?"

He stared at the curtains. I started to think he was mad at me for asking or doubting God. Finally, he cleared his throat and shifted, turning to face me, taking my hands in his.

"Annabelle, when your mama and I got married, we wanted children very, very much. We thought it would happen right away because that's how it was supposed to work. Look at Mama's family; they have a bunch of kids. But it didn't materialize for us until you came along, and we lost several pregnancies before you.

"Mama and I were angry, heartbroken, shattered for a long time. We loved those babies more than anything in this world and wanted them with us. We didn't know why God kept giving and then taking away or understand what we had done to deserve it.

"But, God wasn't taking away, honey. He was simply allowing life to happen. He hurt right along with us and waited for us to trust Him and ask for His help in coping. We did, and eventually, we learned how to cope with the losses. After a time, we were fortunate enough to have you, and you completed our family. But God continues to get us through the rest.

"Some people say everything happens for a reason, but I'm not so sure. What I do know is that in everything we do and in everything we experience, we can learn love. We can give and receive compassion. Hurting stinks and feels unfair, and grief can be torment beyond measure, but we can learn to love through pain. We can learn to heal through compassion, and we can learn God's ways by walking with others through their trials. We must learn to give of ourselves to grow, and that lesson is frequently best studied through hardship. It's how we learn to accept our Christian duty."

I'd never thought about Christian duty that way before. I swished it around in my brain, mentally sampling the theory.

"So, Maisy's family is supposed to help other people whose kid gets hurt?"

"I don't know, honey. Maybe someday. Right now, they need to lean on others who love them. They may be quite angry at God for a long time. It might be a very long while before they are able to do anything but survive."

***

I fell asleep on the couch next to Daddy, tear stains drying on my face. He eventually carried me up to my bed.

I woke in the middle of the night. Mama was lying next to me, her arm over my stomach. She was still in her clothes.

More Muddle

Monday morning dawned bright and cheery as if nothing at all was wrong with the world. But nasty bits of weather brewed on either side of our house.

The headline above the front-page fold of the Pullman Gazette referenced Saturday evening's accident. Pullman being a small town, and most townsfolk having been at the fireworks, there wasn't any point in trying to keep Maisy's name quiet. Word would have spread quickly, regardless.

Instead, the article concluded with information regarding the collaboration of several churches on a prayer chain and a meal train. Mrs. Chisholm headed up the St. Mary's contingent while Mrs. Hickam led First Congregational's crew. Between the two of them, they would make sure that the Drummonds were taken care of.

Mama dragged herself out of bed at 7:00 a.m. when Daddy left for work. She planned to be at Nattie's and, hopefully, of some help when Piper arrived at 8:00 to begin her residency as doting "niece."

Being none-too-pleased about the whole affair, Nattie bossed Mama around, slapping her hand whenever she tried to assist Piper. Frankly, she pushed the limits of Mama's Christian duty. Tough to do, but Mama hadn't gotten much sleep in the past forty-eight hours. Even her reserves were running on fumes.

Nattie made a loud show of things outside the house to avoid any questions regarding Piper's identity. As far as she was concerned, anyone within earshot would know from the get-go that her long-lost niece had come to stay for a spell. Mama didn't bother mentioning Maisy.

***

Just before noon, Cilla came stomping up the front steps and rang our doorbell. Mama and I had finished our grilled cheese and tomato soup and were getting ready to head over to the Drummonds' again. Mrs. Perkins had spent Sunday night in their guest room to be there for Cliff, Pansy, and Jimmy since Mama needed to be next door so early on Monday morning. She and Mama planned to switch off for the next several days.

Cilla stormed past Mama as soon as she opened the door.

"What in the *hell* is going on around here?"

She had, of course, seen the goings-on at Nattie's earlier along with the increased traffic as people turned her corner on the way to the Drummonds' to drop off cards and meals. What she hadn't done was read the paper.

Not being one to attend the fireworks or church, Cilla hadn't been present at the time of the accident, nor had she been part of the various congregational buzzings on Sunday morning. Having declined to consult anything as authoritative as the Pullman Gazette, she remained grossly uninformed, something which seemed almost impossible after all we'd been through in the last forty or so hours.

Mama politely invited Cilla to sit, which she resolutely refused to do. Instead, she positioned her bulwark of a bosom front and center over crossed arms as if it could somehow command more attention than her obnoxious personality. She wouldn't move until someone told her precisely what was going on.

Mama calmly explained that Nattie's niece, Piper, had come to visit for a while. She volunteered no further information.

"Nattie doesn't have a niece named Piper. After all, I should know," Cilla scolded.

Mama didn't budge, pursing her lips in an attempt to keep from telling Cilla exactly what she thought of her for abandoning her friend.

Mama next explained about Saturday evening, ignoring all protests about the validity of Nattie's story and maintaining a rather impressive—albeit tenuous—hold on her patience.

"Maisy is at St. Michael's in the city. Her prognosis is quite precarious at the moment." Mama's grip was loosening, her volume increasing with every word.

"The next few days will be crucial if Maisy is going to survive. If you would be so kind as to pull your horns in and consider someone other than yourself for a moment, a card, some prayers, and an attitude adjustment would certainly be in order and more than welcome!"

Oh, boy.

If Mama surprised herself with her candor, it didn't show. She stared Cilla down, silently daring her to twitch even a single hair out of place. As for me, I stood stock still, my eyes darting between Mama and Cilla, waiting to see who would explode or back down first.

Whatever Cilla had been expecting to hear, it wasn't that. Though she didn't move, her entire demeanor changed. Her face lost all color and malice and morphed suddenly into a childlike mask of what looked like fear.

She began gulping air, eyes wide and brow instantly damp. It was incredibly unnerving as Mama and I stared at her, wondering if she was having some sort of fit and was about to hit the deck or vomit on the living room carpet. Though we likely should have been spurred into action by the practically apoplectic woman in front of us, we didn't move. Cilla turned on her heel, snatched the door open, and bolted out, bashing her shoulder on the door frame, quite unsteady on her pins.

My eyes met Mama's. She was thoroughly exhausted and just didn't have any shits left to give. She waved Cilla off, shaking her head as she headed back to the kitchen.

***

Cilla stumbled back to her front porch, doubling over and leaning heavily on the railing for support. She felt sure that anyone watching could see her heart slowly bleeding out onto the two shallow steps, the blood gently cascading down her walkway. Her vision blurred, and she couldn't seem to get enough air, alternately gasping and groaning. Her head ached, and noise rushed all around her. *Please, God! Someone make it stop.*

In her mind's eye, she saw Maisy climbing over the red board fence, curls bouncing as her feet hit the dirt, and she happily Maisy-skipped her way to the patio.

"Look, Annabelle, I'm doin' it!"

Her mind lurched cruelly back to Boston Public Garden and the Duck Boats.

"Look, Prissy! I'm feedin' the ducks!"

Of course, Maisy hadn't known Cilla was watching her; Cilla had made sure of that. She hadn't wanted to frighten the girl. Maisy's sweet little voice and constant monologue of questions played in Cilla's ears as she pulled herself to the front door and stumbled in. Making her way to the dining room table, she collapsed onto a chair and proceeded to fall entirely to pieces.

St. Michael's

Over the next few days, Mama and Mrs. Perkins organized and sorted all the meals coming in from friends, neighbors, and the church pipelines. Thankfully, the Drummonds' chest freezer had room for most of it, and Mama and Mrs. Perkins could store the overflow. They also each spent a couple of nights at the house while Mr. and Mrs. Drummond stayed at the hospital.

News from the ICU was slow and cautious. Every hour, every day Maisy didn't backslide was good, but the waiting and uncertainty wore on everyone's nerves. She would be in the Intensive Care Unit for a while, and Cliff, Pansy, and Jimmy had yet to see her.

They all looked terrible, faces drawn and with dark circles under their eyes. People volunteered for Garrett's shifts at the pool so he could be with Pansy, but he wasn't in much better shape than she was.

***

News finally came early Wednesday morning. Maisy was stable enough for another operation later in the day to stabilize her pelvis and place screws in her femur. Her skull fracture continued to be a blessing, and things in that area looked better than initially expected. The doctors said once this surgery was complete, her siblings would be allowed to see her.

The day was humid and miserable and would have been perfect for our crew to head to the pool. Instead, we gathered at the Drummonds' again. Cliff, Pansy, Jimmy, Garrett, Sasha, Natalie, and I sat in the dark, shaded living room in front of fans, trying to color Get Well cards; not an easy feat considering the fans were blowing at full blast, but it kept us occupied and, for that, we were grateful.

We hesitantly discussed what everyone thought the Drummonds might see when they visited.

"What do you think she'll look like?" I asked Cliff.

"I dunno. Probably pretty beat up."

"Do you think she'll have a lot of blood on her still?" asked Sasha.

"No, they probably cleaned that up when she got there," Pansy answered. "I bet there will be lots of machines and stuff, though, like on that show *St. Elsewhere*."

"Just bruises, then?" asked Jimmy.

"Yeah. And maybe stitches and a cast or something. It's been four days already." Cliff picked at his cuticles, clearly uncomfortable picturing his baby sister beaten and broken.

But none of us wanted to talk about the fact that Maisy would likely be asleep and unresponsive, that she might look dead. It was too close to things we didn't want to think about.

***

Cliff, Pansy, Jimmy, and I were all ready to go the moment we got word Maisy was out of surgery. Mama and I would drive them over, though the two of us wouldn't be allowed in the Intensive Care Unit. I just wanted to be near to where Maisy was, and Mama agreed to let me go.

At around three o'clock, Mr. Drummond called to say they'd spoken with Maisy's doctors, and she'd come through the surgery better than expected, though she was still in bad shape. She would spend some time in post-op recovery, but her siblings would be allowed to visit her briefly by evening. He asked Mama to caution them that she wouldn't look much like how they remembered her, and, as expected, she likely wouldn't be awake.

We grabbed our things, including other cards which had come in from neighbors, friends, and relatives, and a cooler we packed with sandwiches, drinks, and snacks since we weren't sure how long we would be at the hospital. We set off, waving to the others as we pulled away.

***

The drive to the city usually took about twenty minutes, but it had never dragged on so before. Everyone was quiet. While we'd spent the morning speculating about what it would be like for the Drummond kids to see Maisy again, staring the actual thing in the face brought a trepidation that painted them with broad strokes of anxiety. Their faces said they wanted desperately to run to her and away from her at the same time.

Pansy chewed her lip and stared out the window while Cliff bounced his knee and examined his hands. Jimmy sorted the cards over and over. Mama didn't force any conversation other than to relay what Mr. Drummond had said about preparing them for Maisy looking different.

Once she pulled into a parking spot, she turned to them.

"Okay. You ready, or do you need a minute yet?"

Cliff put his hand out for Pansy and Jimmy to grab and blew out a deep breath, searching their faces.

He met Mama's eye, trying to appear more confident than he felt. "We're ready."

***

At the front desk, Mama told the receptionist where we were headed, and she called up to the ICU to say we'd arrived. She gave us directions to where Mr. Drummond would meet us, the farthest Mama and I would be allowed to go.

One elevator ride, three turns, and two long hallways later, we saw Mr. Drummond heading toward us. His kids ran toward him, instantly tangling into a giant knot of arms upon contact.

They hugged for a long time before Mr. Drummond pulled back to greet Mama and me as we reached them. He gave us both a big hug and thanked us for bringing everyone over. His voice broke, and he held back tears, exhaustion seeping out of him.

Clearing his throat, he pointed to an area for us to sit down. Mama and I would wait while he took Cliff, Pansy, and Jimmy into the unit one at a time. They wouldn't be allowed in for more than a couple of minutes each, but he and Mrs. Drummond would come back out with them again when they were all finished, and we could chat. Then, taking a deep breath, he turned to his kids.

"I know Mrs. Walker has told you, but I want you to understand Maisy doesn't look like herself right now, and she can't talk to you." He put his hands on Pansy's and Jimmy's shoulders. "She's bruised and swollen and has bandages around her head and scrapes and stitches on her face and arms. There are a lot of machines and wires and sounds around her bed.

Lots of tubes and things are going in and out of her. I want you to know that before you go in. She may be tough to look at."

"Can we talk to her? Will she hear us?"

"She might, son," Mr. Drummond answered, moving a hand to Cliff's shoulder. "She's sedated, but I think it would be great if you talked to her. The doctors say they don't always know what patients can hear or process at the moment. It doesn't hurt to try and, if she can hear you, so much the better." He squeezed Cliff's shoulder and smiled weakly.

"Can we touch her?" Pansy asked.

"We'll ask the nurse. You might be able to hold her hand."

Pansy nodded quickly. Jimmy stared anxiously up at his dad, licking his lips and gripping the bag of cards tight. Mr. Drummond cupped his hand around Jimmy's cheek and winked.

"Cliff will go in first. You have to go one at a time, but I'll be with you, and Mom is in there already. Does that sound alright?"

All three terrified Drummond kids nodded.

"Okay." He glanced up at Mama, putting his hand behind Cliff. "Here we go."

Scared

Mr. Drummond led Cliff to the entrance of the ICU, keeping a close eye on him as the doors opened. They walked through together, his hand still on his son's back.

Pansy and Jimmy stared at the doors as they closed again, leaving them separated from those they loved.

"Come on and sit, guys. They'll be back before you know it," said Mama.

Pansy stepped slowly backward, the backs of her knees hitting the chair, and she gently sat, still watching the doors. Jimmy remained where he was, unhearing, as if he were standing guard, ready to challenge any bad news Cliff might bring back out.

The second hand on the electric wall clock made its smooth, lazy journey toward the next minute, like honey at the bottom of the little plastic bear oozing its way toward the nozzle. Two trips around seemed like hours, though Jimmy still hadn't moved save to shift his feet a bit, and Pansy's eyes remained glued to the last place she had seen her father and brother. I could only imagine what was going through their minds as they waited for their turns and proof that Maisy was still with us.

After two minutes, the doors opened again, and Cliff and Mr. Drummond walked out. Pansy jumped up but didn't move toward them. Jimmy stalked right up to Cliff as if he could somehow shake news from his stricken brother. Locking eyes with Pansy, Cliff didn't say a word. Pansy's lip trembled, but she stood firm.

"Pansy?" Mr. Drummond held out his arm in invitation.

I saw him sneak a meaningful glance at Mama. She nodded, gesturing for them to go. She would watch over Cliff, who had sat down and was now staring silently at the floor.

Pansy looked at her dad, then Cliff, and back at her dad again, hesitating.

"It's okay, honey." Mr. Drummond put his arm around her as she joined him. Leaning in, she shot another glance back at her brother before disappearing through the doors.

Jimmy sat right next to Cliff, staring at him, brow furrowed and still clutching the bag of cards, now somewhat rumpled and sweaty. Mama and I watched, too, waiting for Cliff to come back to the moment. He didn't look up.

"Did she die?" Tears teetered threateningly on Jimmy's lower lids. Cliff's head snapped up.

"Huh? What? No!" he stammered, coming back to us. "No ... no, she didn't ... she didn't die, buddy." He wiped an eye with the back of his hand and sniffed. Clearing his throat, he turned to Jimmy.

"Um, no, she's um ... she's pretty beat up. She's ... sleeping and healing and stuff."

"Is there any blood?"

"No, man. No blood. Lots of bruises and stitches and bandages, though. And she, um ... she kinda looks a little like a robot 'cause she's got a lot of wires and tubes and shi—um ... I mean, stuff coming out of her." He glanced at Mama, who gave a sympathetic smile and let the cuss word pass.

"Okay," Jimmy nodded quickly. He stared at his hands and a few moments passed in silence.

"Cliff?"

"Yeah, buddy?" Poor Cliff sounded exhausted.

"Are you scared?"

He drew a deep breath and considered Jimmy's question, evidently deciding his little brother deserved the truth.

"Yeah, man, I am. She's in real bad shape, buddy." He put his arm around Jimmy, pressing his lips to the top of his head, hoping his little brother wouldn't see his tears.

The doors opened again, and Pansy came out, wet tracks running down her cheeks. Jimmy jumped up, terrified.

Directing Pansy to Mama, Mr. Drummond held out his arm for his younger son. Jimmy licked his lips, crumpled the top of the card bag for the millionth time, and walked to his dad.

Then they went in.

Jimmy

Jimmy stuck to his dad like lint to Velcro, looking this way and that as if something might take him by surprise. Mrs. Drummond met them inside the doors, giving Jimmy a big hug and running her hand through his hair. She smiled reassuringly. They completed the short walk to the nurse's station, where Jimmy gowned up, then they entered Maisy's room together.

It surprised him that the room didn't have a regular door. The entire wall was glass with an extra-large automatic door and curtains. If anyone needed to keep an eye on things from the hallway, they could leave the curtains open. The doorway was wide enough for huge rolling beds to go in and out. There were lots of machines and equipment, but it wasn't at all cluttered. In fact, it was about the cleanest room he had ever seen—nothing on the floor and plenty of room to walk around the bed.

Sights, sounds, and smells inundated him. Lights blinked, and screens flashed. A whooshing sound like Darth Vader's breathing came from somewhere near the head of the bed. Beeping. It smelled harsh and forbidding and not at all like home. Wires and tubes hung from the ceiling and walls, and everything had wheels. A single modest vinyl chair sat in the corner. The bed had sides that could be up or down, and the bed itself could adjust from laying to sitting.

In the middle of it lay Maisy. She looked so small. Completely still, save for her little chest, which was moving gently up and down in time with Vader.

They'd wrapped her head so that he couldn't see her curls. A large tube coming out of her neck, and another out of her mouth, were startling. Her face, what he could see of it, was bruised and swollen, and her cheek had a line of black tracks stitched into it. Coming from under the covers was yet another tube, which brought the first question to his lips.

"What if she has to go to the bathroom? How will she tell anybody? She *hates* wetting her pants."

His parents smiled.

"It's okay, buddy. Special tubes take care of all that for her. She doesn't have to do anything but heal right now. That's her one job." Mr. Drummond pointed to Vader. "That machine over there is even breathing for her."

Jimmy stood, watching. He hadn't gotten too close yet and didn't know if it would be okay. Everything looked so delicate—as if he might mess it all up just by blinking wrong.

"Do you want to say hello?" Mrs. Drummond had been standing right behind him, and now he felt her hand on his shoulder. "You can walk up next to her if you'd like. We'll be right here."

Jimmy glanced at the nurse, who he hadn't noticed before, near Maisy's head. She smiled at him behind her mask. At least, he thought she did. She fiddled with a tube dripping liquid from a bag and moved back to give him room.

Sucking his lip, he slowly took a cautious step forward. Then another. He looked back for reassurance, and his parents stepped up with him.

"Hi, Maisy. It's me."

He glanced back at his mom, and she nodded. He tried again.

"Um ... I brought you a whole bunch of cards from people. They're real nice ones. Me and Pansy and Cliff, and Garrett and Sasha, and Natalie and Annabelle all made some, too. We tried to draw your favorites."

He stopped, not sure what else to say. As he looked at his baby sister, tears welled in his eyes, and his throat closed painfully.

"Maisy?"

The machines continued to whir as Maisy lay eerily still. Mr. Drummond squeezed his shoulder.

"It's okay, buddy. She's in there."

Jimmy nodded quickly. The nurse stepped forward again and gently touched Mr. Drummond's arm. Time to go.

"Can I give her a kiss?"

"I'm afraid not," said the nurse. "But you can blow her one, and it will land right on her heart, I promise."

Jimmy's head bobbed again, and he stared at his baby sister.

"Goodnight, Maisy. I love you." He blew her the softest kiss.

The three Drummonds left the room and walked down the hall to the double doors. Stepping through, they joined us in the world where time hadn't stopped.

The Silent Treatment

The ride home from St. Michael's was as quiet as the one there had been. Mr. and Mrs. Drummond had spent time with us in the lobby talking about what the doctors said and what would happen next. I didn't understand much of it, but if things went well and Maisy continued to improve—or at least not backslide—Mr. and Mrs. Drummond would start trading off days and nights over the weekend. They both appeared utterly drained, like no amount of sleep would fill them back up. Still, it would be good for Cliff, Pansy, and Jimmy to have their mom and dad back, even if it wasn't at the same time.

As we drove through the twilight, my mind raced. I wished I could have seen Maisy if only to witness for myself that she was still alive. The looks the Drummond kids had given each other scared me. Jimmy hadn't said a word after he came out of the ICU, and he wouldn't look at me at all. He seemed really messed up. I couldn't tell if he was sad or mad or what. Usually, I could read him like a book. Now, he was just a page of scribbles.

I wanted to cry but didn't want anyone else to notice. Mama would understand, but the Drummond kids might not. Maisy felt like my little sister, too, though. Same for Garrett and Sasha, and Natalie. I wondered how long it would be before we got to visit her.

Then I remembered that we might never get to if she died, and it was like someone banged a gong in my stomach. My whole body got hot. Tears stung my eyes, and I could feel them running down the inside of my nose.

I would either have to sniffle or use a Kleenex. I opted for my short sleeve so no one would see or hear. At least it was almost dark out.

***

Mama dropped me off at our house before taking the Drummond kids home and staying the night. She called Daddy and gave him the update on Maisy while he and I cuddled on the couch in front of the TV. The news was on, and reporters talked about things as if they were as important as Maisy being hurt. They weren't.

Daddy hadn't been paying attention. He was cuddling me and staring off. When he started hugging too tight, and I squirmed, he apologized, lying on his side on the couch and tucking me under his arm next to him. I felt safe.

Our house smelled so much better and more comforting than the hospital had, and I wondered if Maisy could smell anything while she was in the medicine sleep.

"Maisy has metal in her now."

"Does she? Do you suppose that makes her like the Bionic Woman?"

I smiled a little. "No, she's too small for that. Pansy said she has big tubes going in and out of her, too. One even pees for her since she can't do it herself. It's good, though, because Maisy hates peeing her pants."

"Oh, that is nice, then. Did they tell you anything else about what they saw?"

"A little. She has a railroad track on her cheek and a bunch of scratches and scabs, too. I guess there were a lot of machines around her. One sounded like Darth Vader, Cliff said."

"Mm." Daddy thought a moment. "It was probably a ventilator to breathe for her while she sleeps from all the medicine. They do sound a bit like Darth Vader."

"Cliff said they couldn't see much of her because of the bandages on her head. She just looked really little."

"Mm. And what did Jimmy say?"

"Nothing. Daddy, I think something might be wrong with Jimmy."

"Oh? What makes you think that?"

"Well, usually, I can tell what he's thinking. And he talks a lot when he's scared. Cliff even said *he's* scared. But Jimmy didn't say anything at all when he came back out from Maisy's room. Not even on the way home. He didn't even look at me."

Daddy thought for a while before he spoke.

"Annabelle, I think it's possible Jimmy isn't sure what he thinks or feels yet about what he saw. Maisy probably doesn't look much like the little sister he remembers right now, and he may not know how to handle that. He might be angry, or sad, or confused, or scared. Possibly all of those things. Maybe even a little embarrassed. Boys his age don't like to let people see when they get emotional. Especially girls."

"Yeah, his eyes were all red and wet when he came out. But he didn't mind us seeing him cry when he got in trouble at the library."

Daddy laughed. "Well, that's a little different. See, boys tend to get either really quiet or really irritable when they aren't sure how they feel about something. It can feel a bit like they've lost control on the inside, and I don't know too many guys who like that feeling."

"Oh. I guess I know how that feels. But what if he doesn't ever talk to me again? He didn't even look at me, remember?"

"I think the best you can do right now is to be there to listen if he does, and if he doesn't, be his friend, anyway. I think he will, though, when he's ready. For now, Pansy and Cliff and his parents will be the ones he turns to."

"I guess. Daddy?"

"Yeah, kiddo?"

"I don't like what chance does to people."

"Me, neither, sweetie. Me, neither."

Dude, What is Your Deal?

Maisy continued to improve in the ICU, albeit not without sustained anxiety back home. Mama and Mrs. Perkins continued to switch off at the Drummond house, encouraging Cliff, Pansy, and Jimmy to go outside and play or hang out with friends.

Garrett was there for Pansy along with her girlfriends, and Cliff's buddies would stop by, but Jimmy mainly kept to himself, despite all our attempts to the contrary. Toward our little crew, he remained uncharacteristically distant.

***

Back on our side of the block, Nattie and her "niece" were settling into a routine. It wasn't exactly civil yet, but Piper had the patience of a saint and the determination of a badger, so it was possible that Nattie had met her match. Mama checked in on them at the end of the week and came home with a sly grin on her face, secretly pleased that Nattie was getting some healthy push-back.

Cilla had been oddly absent from the front walk since the altercation in our living room. Indeed, with the arrival of Piper, she should have been on frequent promenade, snooping to gather whatever tidbits she could use in her arsenal against Nattie. The minor detail of Fritz no longer requiring a walkabout didn't seem the type of thing to slow her down. But we saw neither hide nor hair of her save for poking her head out to get the mail. Mama didn't have time to check on her more than that but remained satisfied that she was at least upright and above ground.

Sasha, Natalie, and I spent our usual time together, though it felt strange without Jimmy. We all missed him but didn't know what to do about it. I thought a lot about what Daddy said about being there for him one way or the other, but we couldn't exactly do that if he didn't want us around. Still, Mama and Mrs. Perkins kept an eye on him, and Mr. and Mrs. Drummond would start switching off at home soon. We continued to see if he would come out and play ball, but it looked like he would have to make the first move.

***

Monday slid in on a wave of heat, reminding us all that we still lived in Pullman Station and life carried on around us regardless of whether we chose to keep pace. Maisy's doctors were optimistic but still with an abundance of caution. Jimmy's reclusiveness persisted, but he was forced to go over to Sasha and Natalie's for the day since both Mr. and Mrs. Drummond needed to be at the hospital that morning, and Cliff and Pansy were going back to work. I joined everyone at the Perkinses' for an awkward morning of *"Let's Try To Get Jimmy To Talk"* while Mama crawled back into bed to try and sleep enough to feel human again.

Jimmy still wouldn't look at anyone, not even Sasha. We asked him a few questions but got only shrugs in return. Sasha tried to get him to play *Battleship*, going so far as to close his eyes and blindly set Jimmy's ship grid up and hand it to him, but it was like talking to a wall. We all felt weird sitting and doing nothing until, finally, Mrs. Perkins said we could turn on

The Price Is Right as long as the TV went off before *The Young and the Restless* came on.

We sat and watched as Bob Barker flirted with the female contestants and models, reminded everyone to control the pet population, and poked fun at several of the male contestants' bids. Cars, vacations, exercise bikes, washing machines, whirlpools, and all sorts of shiny prizes rolled past as people played *Cliff Hangers, Squeeze Play, Hi-Lo, Plinko*, and other games we loved. We yelled and advised them about their ridiculous calculations and leaned forward in giddy anticipation when they took their turns on the Big Wheel. Every kid we knew dreamed of giving that thing a spin.

As the *Showcase Showdown* played out, everyone sat riveted; everyone, that is, except Jimmy. He sat in the recliner, not bothering to get in on the excitement of forbidden weekday morning TV. When Sasha finally turned it off, he'd had enough.

"Jimmy, man. Let's go play ball or somethin', huh? I don't wanna keep sitting here."

Natalie and I watched Jimmy closely, but he didn't move or say a word.

"Dude! What is your deal? Why won't you talk to us? It's not like we put Maisy in the stupid hospital."

That did it. Jimmy glared up at Sasha.

"Shut *UP!*" he roared as he launched himself out of the recliner and cannoned into his best friend. Physically, Jimmy was the more solid of the two. He hit Sasha right in the numbers, knocking them both onto the sofa, where he began punching and screaming.

"It was an accident, asshole! I couldn't catch the stupid dog, okay? I couldn't catch it!"

Jimmy was crying, dripping tears and snot on a stunned Sasha who couldn't do much other than shield his face with his arms and try to hold Jimmy off with his knee.

"Dude! What the heck!?"

Mrs. Perkins came running in and tried to pull Jimmy off. Natalie and I suddenly hopped to and gave her a hand. We pried Jimmy away, and he sat puddled on the floor, sobbing.

"It was an accident, I swear!" he wept. "I couldn't catch it. I tried. I really did! I'm sorry. I'm so sorry!"

"Huh?" Sasha asked, thoroughly confused. At that moment, Mrs. Perkins gathered Jimmy into her arms.

"Oh, honey! Sweetheart, it's not your fault! Not even a little bit. Everyone tried to help Maisy. It just happened too fast."

"But I always help Maisy with dogs," Jimmy dribbled. "Always! I promised her I would always protect her, but I just couldn't this time. It was only a little one, but she gets scared no matter what, and she wanted to see the fireworks so bad, and she took a nap and *everything*. And then that shit dog ruined it all, and now she's maybe gonna die, and she'll never get to see them at all."

Out of breath and words, he turned into Mrs. Perkins, letting her rock him back and forth.

We all felt guilty and responsible. One of us should have somehow been able to stop what happened, right? But no one else bottled those feelings the way Jimmy had. He hadn't wanted to let anyone know it was his fault, not realizing we all felt the same way about ourselves. Usually the awkward one, he had expressed quite eloquently what we had all been feeling, though it had come out with the force of a grenade, and poor Sasha had taken the blast in the face.

"It's not anyone's fault, sweetie. Certainly not yours," Mrs. Perkins choked out, pulling a clean tissue from her pocket and handing it to him. "Sometimes things just happen."

"But it's my job," he protested as he wiped his eyes and nose. "I'm her big brother, and Mom and Dad always tell us we need to watch out for her 'cause she's little."

"And you do," Mrs. Perkins assured him. "But you're not in control of everything around you, hon. We can only do our best."

Natalie, Sasha, and I stood there feeling terrible. We'd been frustrated with our friend for not getting back to normal when we all should have realized what he was thinking. Jimmy took everything to heart, and he watched out for Maisy like no one else. He was a worrier and loved his little sister more than anything in the world. He was her knight in shining armor.

***

We sat in a circle on the Perkinses' living room floor, a box of Kleenex in the middle. Mrs. Perkins had gotten Jimmy settled, and we began to talk about what had happened the night of the accident and what we each thought we could or should have done differently. Turns out, there wasn't much, which helped settle the conscience of everyone present.

As none of us saw Maisy before they'd rushed her to the hospital, it hadn't hit home just how bad things were other than the shock of it all. Of all of us, only Jimmy had seen her since, and he hadn't quite known how to tell us about it. Seeing her so tiny and still in the big ICU bed had scared him half to death, making it seem all the worse that he hadn't been able to save her.

It didn't feel fair to have fun when Maisy couldn't. Still, Mrs. Perkins reckoned that was precisely what we should do.

"You simply need to have an extra bit for Maisy and then tell her about it when she gets better."

It was comforting to sit and talk with my friends about something that scared us all. Nobody cared if we cried, and no one called anyone a sissy. We were more honest with each other than we had ever been before. This was different than whether we cheated at Uno or dished ourselves a bigger portion of a snack. This was important stuff; stuff that mattered; stuff that felt better when someone else knew.

In the end, we decided to get back to doing the things we usually did, keeping an eye out for what we called Maisy Moments. If something happened we thought she would enjoy or find funny, we would write them in a journal to give her when she came home. That way, when we remembered and talked about them later, she could remember them, too, and feel included.

The idea made Jimmy's face light up. He was now on a mission to mend his sister's spirit while her body mended itself. Little did we know, it would heal all of us into the bargain.

Here to Stay

July 8, 1985

M aisy lay in the bed. She'd moved a bit now and then in the week since the accident, but in traction, it wasn't much. The good news was that her vital signs were finally normal, which allowed everyone to breathe a sigh of relief. It was a significant milestone, though she didn't look any different.

Mr. Drummond arrived at the hospital and joined Mrs. Drummond around 6:00 a.m., their measure of excitement matched by an equal measure of terror. What would the path forward look like? How would Maisy feel? Would she be functional? Would she be Maisy? Would she remember anything? The questions swirled dizzyingly around in their heads, exhausting them. But a line of electricity was also buzzing through them that seemed to calm a fraction when they grabbed hold of each other's hand and walked into the ICU.

One of Maisy's doctors met them in the hallway and escorted them to a small room. He began by explaining what the team thought Maisy would be in for now that she'd had several days post-op for observation. It wasn't going to be an easy or entirely predictable road, but he did expect it would be a success. Success, of course, being a relative term.

It would be a long series of small victories, none of which would be too small to celebrate. Maisy was young, a point in her favor. Her vital signs were stable and strong, another tally on her side. But, she'd been very seriously injured and had undergone major invasive surgeries. The long-term effects were as yet unknown.

Possible issues included permanent cognitive, hearing, or visual damage from her head injury, bleeding or clots from the splenectomy—though less common in children—and a lowered immunity to infections since they'd taken the whole spleen. He stressed the importance of keeping her immunizations up to date. Orthopedic issues could arise, of course, but, at this point, he didn't think they would be severe. Both breaks were reasonably straightforward due to Maisy's age and the low speed of the impact.

Maisy would likely be confused, agitated, possibly even aggressive for a little while. Her tiny body was processing and flushing large amounts of medicine. On the bright side, regardless of those things, she would probably be able to move out of ICU soon and likely wouldn't remember her time there at all. Even so, it would be difficult to watch and even harder to know their child was hurting and frustrated. She would be on pain meds, but she wouldn't feel anywhere near a million bucks.

This was the beginning of the long haul.

***

Maisy's eyelids fluttered. It'd been a long morning. They had, of course, felt stirrings as they held her hands over the last several days, and it was always reassuring, but the waiting was excruciating. Just one more flutter, they thought each time. *Come on!* The EEG showed Maisy's brain trying to heal. All signs were positive. But who would they find emerging once she truly came back?

Her lids fluttered again, and her beautiful blue eyes peeked out, not focusing on anyone or anything in particular, but there they were. They closed again, followed by those of Mr. and Mrs. Drummond as tears streamed silently down their faces, and they thanked God for the millionth time that their little girl was still there.

Throughout the day, the doctors evaluated Maisy for neurological issues many times. Each time she woke, she looked around, noticing but not always digesting what she saw. Her fingers squeezed Mrs. Drummond's in answer to questions, newly reassuring each time. The close eye of clinical observations continued.

Her parents kept up a gentle but steady stream of chatter whenever Maisy's eyes were open, and doctors and nurses put her through various observations as she tolerated them. Finger squeezes and blinks had never seemed so important. Despite the recent removal of her breathing tube, she still wasn't able to speak.

Mr. and Mrs. Drummond would sneak out for quick bathroom or food breaks when her eyes would close, one or the other always staying back. It was late in the evening as they sat next to her bed discussing who would stay the night when they heard a rasping sound.

"Mama?"

Mrs. Drummond whirled around to see her baby girl looking at her, knowing her, and calling for her. The inside of Maisy's little throat was raw and irritated. She tried again, but Mrs. Drummond shushed her as she caressed her cheek and wept with joy.

"It's okay, baby. It's okay. Mama's here." The nurse came over and continued with assessments. Maisy recognized her mother and father but remained quite confused and unable to remember other things. She became irritated when she wanted to move and couldn't. But she had survived. She was here. These were the first steps; the rest would come as well.

***

Maisy was moved out of ICU the following day. Her vitals remained stable and strong, and she continued to breathe on her own without issues. She began recognizing more things and communicating more, but "more" was a relative term.

She hadn't spoken since asking for her mother but could sometimes nod or shake her head slightly when asked a question. Barring that, she used her thumb for yes and no. She was confused, not remembering anything at all about what happened or why she was there. It caused her a lot of frustration, which was hard for Mr. and Mrs. Drummond to watch. Sleep was still a big part of her day as her body adjusted and flushed meds. Even the most minor activity tired her quickly. Still, it was a relief to everyone every time she opened her eyes.

PART THREE

Our Time

"Mom, I know Cilla and Nattie started fighting after Jack died, but when was that? Were he and Marlon old?"

"Not really, Will. I mean, they would probably seem old to you and Grace, but to grandma and grandpa, they were actually pretty young. They were both in their sixties."

"That's young?"

"Well, yeah. A lot of their friends were around for a very long time after they passed. Some still are.

"They must be ancient!"

"Hmm ... That depends on your definition, I suppose. But you're only as ancient as you feel, and some of that crew was pretty lively."

***

July 4, 1976

Marlon and Jack sat at the Heilman's Supper Club bar, drinking cranberry juice and seltzer and a Bootleg, respectively.

"Dang sparklers," Marlon wheezed, thumping his chest.

"Damn things always get me, too," said Jack. "You'd think, two old hanger-dogs like us, a little sparkler wouldn't do us any harm."

"Eh, just bothersome, is all." Marlon coughed and cleared his throat.

Outside, Cilla and Nattie sat on the balcony overlooking Boxcar Lake. The foursome had enjoyed the sunset together after a beautiful 4th of July bicentennial celebration followed by dinner. In a rare departure from the norm, Nattie was nursing a frothy Pink Squirrel, a Midwest classic and long-time favorite after-dinner drink of hers, though she didn't imbibe often. Cilla, though still disapproving of overconsumption, laughed any time Nattie ordered one. It contained creme de cacao, creme de noyaux, and vanilla ice cream and looked more like a milkshake than an alcoholic beverage. Like Marlon, Cilla sipped on fizzy cranberry juice while giggling at her friend.

"Oh, who'd have ever thought, huh?" Nattie stretched and smiled; her feet propped on a patio bench.

"What's that?"

"Oh, you know. Two families, in two different parts of the country, brought together by two men meeting in yet another part, during a war, preceded by a depression, who became best friends, started a business together, worked feverishly hard to make it a roaring success, and are now sitting at the bar while their wives rest their feet and sit lakeside, watching the sunset and thanking God that life is good."

Cilla laughed and raised her glass. "I couldn't've said it better myself."

The ladies clinked glasses, savoring the cool drinks and marinating in the sense of security they'd worked so hard for. The kids had all grown and flown. Now was their time. Cilla had long dreamed of this. For all the tumultuous past had thrown her way, now was good. Really good. It had been worth the wait.

***

Back inside, Marlon's wheeze had turned into a persistent cough. He covered his mouth with a cocktail napkin and tried to give one big, resolving bark. When he pulled the thin paper away, gripping his chest where it now hurt, he noticed pink and red droplets that had nothing to do with his cranberry juice. He looked at it a moment and then locked eyes with Jack. It wasn't uncommon for vets to develop lung problems later in life from their time spent in the hangars during the war, but both men knew blood wasn't a good omen.

They stared at each other, willing time to stand still before the next few moments turned the page to a darker chapter. Marlon winced as he grabbed his chest again.

"Get the girls."

Love Lost

S mall cell lung cancer. Well, if it was small, how could it be this bad? Surely, there had been a mistake.

"I'm afraid not. Mr. Prescott, Mrs. Prescott, I'm sure this is a big shock. Unfortunately, this type of cancer is known to develop in smokers and those exposed to high doses of chemical inhalants during the war; guys like hangar mechanics. It's collateral damage no one thought to give any consideration to back then."

"Collateral damage." Marlon thought about the words as his hand clenched and unclenched on the arm of the chair.

"Yes, sir. That's the term used to describe incidental—"

"I KNOW WHAT IT MEANS!" Marlon slammed his fist on the wooden arm.

"Of course, sir."

The doctor gave him a few moments to process and gather his thoughts.

Jesus Christ. He hadn't even gone overseas! Pilot friends had been lost over the Pacific or the Channel. Guys from back in Boston had littered countless battlefields. Others had returned home never to be the same. Every one of them had been in the air or on the ground in Europe or the Pacific theater. Yet, he'd come home without a scratch. His mind was fine, his family whole. Hell, the goddamn war had given him his best friend and the life he loved. And now it was going to take it all away.

"Mr. Prescott, I'd like to schedule some more tests for this afternoon."

"Why? We already know what it is, don't we?"

"Yes, but we need to determine if it has metastasized—spread—and how far, before deciding how to treat it. Unfortunately, with small cell lung cancer, by the time we find it, it has usually spread somewhere else."

"Fine."

Cilla sat next to Marlon, stone-faced and silent, alternating between freezing cold and blazing hot. This was not going to happen again. She was not going to lose someone she loved. Not now. Not Marlon.

"Mr. and Mrs. Prescott, we're going to do everything we can. I want you to know that. You're in good hands here."

"Where do I need to go?"

A nurse came in then and set up a series of appointments for further testing. They had time for lunch beforehand if they wanted to go someplace nearby. Neither was hungry, so they went for a walk instead.

***

The additional tests confirmed the cancer had spread throughout Marlon's body.

"We can begin chemotherapy and radiation immediately to try to slow things down."

"Slow things down," Cilla repeated. "So, stop it from spreading further? From killing him?"

The doctor paused, giving her a long look of regret.

"I'm afraid, at this stage, we can only relieve symptoms and prolong life. We won't be able to stop it."

Marlon sat with his head down, hands hung between his knees.

"How long?"

"A year at the outside. I'm sorry."

Well, This is New

July 1985

S aturday morning, the doorbell rang. I opened the door to find Cilla standing there, hands clasped in front of her. At least, it *looked* like Cilla. But whoever it was, they sure didn't act like her.

"Hello, Annabelle. Is your mother home?"

"Y-yes..." I realized I was staring.

"Could I speak with her, please?"

The Cilla-person grimaced in what appeared to be an attempt at a smile. I backed slowly away from the door toward the kitchen, where Mama sat making out a grocery list.

"Mama? There's someone at the door."

I kept my eye on said person. Mama got up and walked past me, casting a puzzled look my way.

"Oh, good morning, Cilla. How may I help you?"

I knew she was none too keen to do much at all at the moment, after the way Cilla had treated Nattie. But I also knew that she had been a little concerned ever since the last time Captain Nasty had stood in our living room.

"Good morning, Susan. I wonder if you might have time to sit and talk a bit today."

"Uh ... well ... well, yes. Yes, I ... I suppose I do. May I ask what about?" The stranger glanced briefly in my direction and leaned in to whisper.

"I'd rather not say if you don't mind." *If you don't mind?* Mama stared for a moment and caught herself, as I had.

"Oh. Well. Uh, did you have a time in mind?"

"Would three o'clock work? You could come for some cookies and lemonade if you like."

"Oh. Your place, then?"

Mama was utterly gob-smacked, one thing she never was, having seen it all in various classrooms over the years.

"Yes, well, yes. That should be fine. I'll see you at three, then." She nodded and smiled.

"Thank you, Susan." Faux-Cilla turned and walked across the veranda and down the steps.

Mama shut the door. She turned and stared at me, eyes wide.

"Mama, what's the matter with Cilla?"

"Search me."

"Are you really going to go this afternoon?"

"I suppose I'll have to."

Mama seemed only now to realize she had agreed to go to Cilla Prescott's house for cookies and lemonade. The whole thing had a serious *Little Red Riding Hood* vibe to it if you asked me. I was pretty sure a wolf in Cilla's clothing had just visited our house.

"Well, I'd better get going on the groceries if I'm going to go a-visitin' this afternoon!" She winked at me, but I didn't find it funny.

Sitting back down at the kitchen table, Mama stared thoughtfully at the wall, on the other side of which stood Cilla Prescott's house with an unnervingly unusual person inside. Mama shook her head and got to work.

Confession . . . Sort Of

At three o'clock, Mama took a deep breath and headed next door, having absolutely no idea what to expect. She felt understandably anxious. I guess after the whole business with Nattie and her care, I couldn't blame her for being a little apprehensive about getting involved in any more neighborhood debacles. Besides, she'd seriously started to question Cilla's sanity after the visit that morning and couldn't be sure what would greet her at the door. Maybe Cilla wouldn't even remember inviting Mama over.

***

The door opened as she reached for the bell, and there stood Cilla on the other side, looking terrified. She gave Mama a quick, perfunctory smile and ushered her in.

"Thank you for coming, Susan. I wasn't entirely certain you would." Cilla actually sounded timid.

"Neither was I," Mama admitted. "I must say, I was a bit taken aback this morning given our previous encounter. I do apologize for my lapse in manners the other day."

"No, no, not at all. I deserved it."

"What on earth has gotten into you, Cilla!? Oh!" Mama clapped her hand over her mouth. "Excuse me; I'm so sorry! I didn't mean... "

"Yes, you did. It's okay. Shall we sit down?"

Cilla gestured to a side table with cookies and lemonade and directed Mama to one of the armchairs in the living room.

"Please."

Mama sipped as Cilla sat in a matching chair across the little table. Wringing her hands in her lap, she smiled awkwardly. Mama watched wordlessly, waiting.

"I'm afraid I'm a little out of practice at this."

"Take your time."

"You see ... Mm."

Cilla slumped, looking defeated. Regaining her poise, she began again.

"I'm afraid I may have been too harsh."

Mama's eyebrows shot up, and she took another sip, trying to hide her reaction to the understatement of the decade.

"Go on."

Cilla wiped her wet brow and breathed deeply, resuming the wringing of her hands. Her head snapped up.

"How is the little Drummond girl?"

"...What?"

Caught completely off guard, Mama wasn't tracking. What on earth did Maisy have to do with anything? Cilla had been nasty toward a lot of people, but to everyone's knowledge, Maisy was the one person who hadn't been the victim of her wrath. Then again, Fritz certainly could've stood to apologize were he not currently sunning himself on the devil's hot rock down below. Mama glanced around, still not used to the little hell-spawn being gone.

"The Drummond girl. How is she? Will she live?"

"Er ... well ... yes. Yes, they think she will. She has quite a long road ahead but has come through her surgeries well and hasn't had any major setbacks. Cilla, I'm afraid I'm not following you."

"Oh, dear. I am making a mess of this, aren't I?"

"Well, I suppose I could tell if I had the slightest idea what 'this' is," Mama sighed.

"Yes, quite. You see, Susan, I once had a little sister very much like the Drummond girl. Like Maisy. In fact, they are nearly identical in my memory." Again, she stopped to regain her shaky composure.

"I wasn't aware you had any siblings, Cilla."

"Yes, well, I don't. I haven't for quite a long time. Penny, my sister, died in 1919 when I was a girl. The Influenza." She flapped her hand as if to indicate the "how" was of no consequence.

"Oh, I'm so sorry. It must've been terrible for you. Did you have other brothers or sisters, or was it only the two of you?"

"Only the two of us. She was ... She was my best friend."

"Seeing Maisy these past years must have been difficult for you."

"On the contrary! I've enjoyed watching her grow and play. I often wonder if she'll grow up looking as Penny would have."

Mama considered Cilla's frank attitude toward her thoughts on Penny and Maisy. Stepping cautiously, she pressed a bit, unsure where this was going.

"If you'll forgive me asking, how have you been overly harsh with Maisy?"

"Ah, yes. That."

Cilla looked distinctly more uncomfortable, something Mama hadn't thought possible.

"You see, my parents were quite wealthy; old money growing new legs, as it were. My father was a financier in Boston, and my mother was a young socialite visiting her aunt when they met. I'm not sure they were ever really suited for each other, but I got the impression that, at least in the beginning, they made a grand showing.

"Caught up in being children, and protected as we were from outside example, I don't suppose we noticed how abnormally distant they were toward each other at the time. Mother spent hours upon hours with us in Boston Garden and its surroundings. Father would chat with us in the evening before bed, and we would tell him all about our adventures. But then the Influenza came, and he fell ill."

"Oh, dear. Did he pass, as well?"

"No, he recovered."

Mama noted the absence of emotion in this statement; it simply "was."

"For some reason, Mother and I never fell ill, but Penny did. She was fine one day and gone the very next."

"How old were you?"

"Seven. Penny was just five."

"Cilla, I'm terribly sorry. I can't imagine what it must've been like for you. And now, little Maisy being in such a horrific accident must bring back some dreadful memories."

"Yes, well, it got worse."

Cilla sighed. She had never told anyone other than Marlon, Nattie, and Jack about her mother; had never wanted to give her more credence than she had earned. Now that the words were flowing, however, she found a rhythm, and it was all tumbling out.

"My mother took Penny's death terribly hard, as any mother would, I now realize, being one myself. She began drinking heavily and stayed mainly to herself in her room for long periods. I would go days without seeing her.

"When she did come out, she would forget things, looking lost behind her eyes. She would slur her words, even hallucinate. I would hear her and my father arguing downstairs. He became distant, too. Neither one seemed to remember I was still there.

"I began to venture out on my own to escape and became quite self-sufficient if somewhat stunted in social interaction. I even changed my name. 'Priscilla' sounded like a name full of sunshine, and I no longer felt that inside. Anyway, when Mother died, I was fourteen. My father didn't appear to notice me, and I decided that was it. I stole money from his cabinet in the library, set out on my own, and have never looked back."

"*At fourteen?* My goodness! How ever did you survive?"

"Keep in mind, Susan, I'd really been on my own except for tutors and housekeepers since the age of seven. I no longer relied on my father for anything other than food and shelter, and those could be bought. So, I stole away into Boston, created a new me, and went to work in Jamaica Plain, where I eventually met Marlon."

"Goodness. You could write a book."

"Well, I was hardly unique, at least in terms of loss. So many people lost sons or daughters, mothers or fathers back then. Sometimes entire families were wiped out. Anyway, I'm afraid my story wouldn't have a very happy ending."

"Ah." Mama conceded the point, recalling the reason for this most unusual meeting. She was still in shock to be sitting and talking so casually with Cilla as if they chatted on the regular about all of life's problems.

"Mm. You see, my Marlon and Jack, Nattie's husband, were in World War II together. They were stationed in Florida, working as base mechanics. Marlon and the kids and I moved west afterward so he and Jack could start the auto shop. Everett was a friend of Jack's and worked for them, as you know."

"Yes, that I'm aware of."

"Well, Nattie and I became fast friends upon meeting, as did the children, and things took off from there. We had a good life."

Cilla's eyes grew distant. A smile spread slowly across her face, removing years of wear. For a few moments, she said nothing at all. Mama sat silently, enjoying the rare display of happiness and allowing the older woman reprieve from her traumatic and stormy past in the balmy waters of reminiscence.

When Cilla snapped back into the present, the look dissipated, almost as if she'd forgotten and been rudely reminded that she was now alone.

"When my Marlon took sick, we four sold the business to Dicky Hickam and his son, Jamie. Of course, Jack passed not long after Marlon. The doctors said it was likely exposure to all the solvents, paints, coolants, and fuels in the base garages during the war that made them take ill so young."

"But, if you and Nattie were such good friends, what happened? I would've thought you would lean on each other."

Cilla looked at Mama and wrung her hands again.

"You know, Susan, I'm not feeling so well. I'd like to go up and lie down for a while if you don't mind."

"Oh. Certainly. Is there anything I can do to help?"

"No, no. Thank you for coming." Cilla stood and quickly ushered Mama to the door.

"Okay, well, thank you for sharing that with me. I'm sure it wasn't easy."

"Yes, yes. Thank you. Goodbye now."

With that, the door closed, and Mama was left standing on the porch. Whatever had dislodged in Cilla's memories had given her second thoughts about saying any more.

***

Mama walked in our door, unsure what to make of the things she had learned. Indeed, they explained why Cilla had reacted so strongly to word of Maisy's accident. But they hadn't cleared up anything about why she would have been harsh with someone. At least, not that Mama could puzzle together. She suspected she hadn't learned anything at all about the real reason for her visit. Whatever demons Cilla had unearthed, she appeared reluctant to exorcise them.

Fine, I'll Tell You

We hadn't seen hide nor hair of Cilla since her conversation with Mama. She was obviously hurting and processing uncomfortable memories, and Mama thought it best to let her come back again when she was ready. So, when the phone rang on Tuesday, and it was Cilla, she figured it was a big deal.

"Hello, Susan."

"Why, hello, Cilla. How are you feeling?"

"Better, thank you. I'm not sure what came over me the other day."

"Quite alright. I'm glad you're on the mend."

An awkward silence ensued as Mama waited for Cilla to speak again. She didn't.

"Is there something I can help you with, Cilla?"

"Oh! Yes. Uh, you asked a question the other day that I didn't answer."

"I did, yes." Mama knew she could lead Cilla through this and make things easier on her, but she rather thought that if demons were to be exorcised, Cilla best take full charge of it herself.

"Yes, well, er … if you'd like to stop over again, I will try to answer it."

"Certainly. Would you like me to come over now, or would you prefer to put something on the calendar?"

"I think now would be good if you're available."

"As it happens, I am. Why don't you give me a few minutes, and I'll be over."

***

A short while later, Mama and Cilla were once again seated in the armchairs in the living room. Their prior encounter hadn't appeared to calm Cilla's nerves much, and she heaved a sigh and looked Mama in the eyes, pausing as if gathering the spirits around her for strength.

"After Marlon passed and Jack was diagnosed, Nattie began to change. You see, we had always leaned on each other, even in the worst situations. She was never comfortable asking others for help, but our friendship had never been like that. The difference was subtle—I don't know that anyone but a best friend would have noticed—but she would forget little things and get snippy if I pointed them out. I tried to attribute it to the stress of Jack being sick, but it was more than that." At this, Cilla's back stiffened, and her mouth set tighter. Her breathing sped up.

"I'd seen it before in my mother; that lost, distant gaze. Like she couldn't quite figure out where she was or how she'd gotten there. I admit it scared me more than you could ever know.

"The occasional Pink Squirrel had never bothered me, but this was different. Rather than lean on me, her best friend, Nattie began being secretive. Knowing my history with alcohol abuse, she would deny up and down that she'd been at the bottle, but I knew better. We went round and round. The memories it brought back were awful. But she didn't appear to care; she just got nasty with me, and that was it."

"Did you ask her what was going on?"

"Countless times. She just got offended and refused to discuss anything."

"I see. So ... I'm guessing you directed your anger regarding Nattie *and* your mother at Nattie? Does that sound about right?"

"Yes, I'm afraid so. I shouldn't have. I know that now.

"When you told me about the Drummond girl—about Maisy—Penny's death hit me all over again. After all these years, can you imagine? But, this time, it was different. It hit me as a mother and a widow, too, and I began to realize just what my mother and father had been dealing with back then. I started to understand that grief is different for everyone, despite situations that might look the same. Anyway, it made me think perhaps I hadn't understood Nattie's grief as well as I thought I had. I'd just lost my husband, too, but perhaps there were things I hadn't considered for her and had rushed to judgment because of my own scars instead of allowing her to have hers."

Cilla's demeanor continued to morph. From terrified to matter-of-fact, then resigned, angry, and melancholy, she now appeared wholly spent. She and Mama were both crying, a box of tissues between them on the table.

"I've made such a mess of things, Susan. I let my anger with my mother and Nattie spill over to others, as well. And your poor family stuck between us!

"I miss my best friend very much. But I simply cannot tolerate drinking and the memories it brings back. I can't watch another person I love self-destruct. She obviously has no intention of sobering up. Look at her now, nearly burning her house down and pretending her niece is visiting when it's obvious she can no longer take care of herself. It's like watching my mother all over again."

Sitting up straighter and mopping her face, she took a deep breath, determined now.

"I need to make things right, I know, and I'm willing to. But I won't be a party to the booze. I can't. I can make nice, but that's where I draw the line. I was rather hoping you might help."

Mama cleaned up her own eyes and nose and considered the lonely woman across from her. How on earth to tell Cilla she'd been catastrophically wrong on top of everything else she'd been wading through?

"Cilla..." She cleared her throat and studied her hands, thoroughly hating being the bearer of this news and the further devastation it would cause.

"Cilla, you need to know the truth about Nattie."

"Oh? And what truth is that?"

"Nattie is not an alcoholic."

"Hmph! Shows what you know."

"She has dementia. The early stages are what you picked up on and what was causing her to forget things once in a while when Jack was still alive. It frightened her, and she covered by pushing people away rather than asking for help. It's progressed to the point she should no longer live by herself. That's what all the hullabaloo was about after the fire when Parker was here."

Cilla straightened and stared at Mama, still as a statue, as the words sank in. Whatever vigor had remained in her aggrieved, shattered soul drained slowly from her face as her eyelids drooped closed.

"Are you sure?" she whispered. Her body seemed to wait for critical impact or for Mama to change her story.

"I'm afraid so. She's sick, Cilla." Mama put her hand over that of our stricken neighbor. "I'm sorry. I'm so very sorry."

Cilla's shoulders slouched, and she bowed her head, the depth of her mistake and its repercussions slowly sinking in. The shaking started first, followed by silent sobs that wracked her body as she slid from chair to floor.

Regret

Mama knelt next to the broken older woman in front of her, but no words came to mind. What was she supposed to say, after all? Cilla had made a massive, life-altering misjudgment that had cost not only her best friend but the happiness for which she had worked so hard. Not to mention she'd lost the camaraderie of everyone in town, save Mr. Coleman, who was simply too kind to follow suit. She had lived the last several years of her life as an angry, bitter caricature whom people made fun of and avoided at all costs. How did one recover from such a thing?

Lost for words, Mama did as she did for me when I got upset and rubbed Cilla's back. As she lay curled in a ball, Cilla sobbed decades-old tears, still startlingly fresh. Pain from internal wounds still festering with the pus of anger, confusion, and rejection made its way past her vocal cords and out into the world in the incomprehensible language of loss.

She had spent so much of her life persevering, so much energy being strong and capable. So much time had been wasted ignoring the little girl desperate for reassurance, desperate to know that her parents loved her, that their pain wasn't due to her lack. Now, having lanced those wounds with the sharp realization of Nattie's condition and her own terrible misjudgment, she lay prone to sepsis of the soul, which threatened to end her right then and there.

She longed for Penny and the mother who had once been so loving. She ached for the father who had once been there to listen to her share her adventures with him. And she yearned for the best friend whom she had so terribly wronged at a time when she had needed her compassion and unconditional friendship the most.

When Cilla finally began to calm, Mama helped her into the chair again, fetched her a glass of water, and went upstairs. Gathering a pillow, nightgown, toothbrush and paste, and a family picture off the bedside table, she put them into an overnight bag and returned downstairs. Then she walked Cilla out the front door and to our house, where she set her up in the guest room. They would talk about how to move forward later. For now, Cilla needed the oblivion of sleep.

***

Waking late the following day and having slept hard, initially, Cilla didn't feel refreshed. The exhaustion of extreme emotional expenditure had sought reprieve, but her sleep had become fitful toward dawn as she tangled in dreams which both frightened and confused her.

The fog of discomfort carried over into wakefulness. She sat up, taking a moment to determine her whereabouts. Familiar voices drifted outside the room, but she wasn't at home, and they didn't belong to Marlon or the kids. Nattie?

Oh, God. Nattie. The fog lifted, leaving a brutally clear reality in its wake. Her conversation with Susan came rushing back like a knockdown wave, threatening to suck her under again. If only she could sink into a hole in the bed and disappear. Shame and embarrassment burned in her cheeks and insides. How could she ever show her face in public after everything she'd said and done and after having been so horribly mistaken about

Nattie? It was doubtful anyone would have any desire to hear her out, and she certainly didn't want to explain it to anyone again.

Footsteps approached, and she flopped back down on the bed, feigning sleep. The door handle turned. Someone came in, stopping beside the bed. Then, as if trying to torture her, that someone sat down.

"Cilla…"

She tried to breathe heavily as if still asleep.

"Cilla, it's Susan Walker."

Damn.

"You can't avoid the world forever, you know."

Shit. She sighed and opened her eyes.

"Why not?"

"Because you've got work to do. What happened between you and Nattie won't fix itself. I have breakfast or lunch available, whichever you'd prefer, and then you'll need to pull yourself together and get on with it."

"Get on with it."

"Yes. Get on with it. It will only get worse if you don't."

"And, how, exactly, do you propose I do that, sunshine?"

Some of her more usual acidity crept back into Cilla's tone, a habit which would prove difficult to break.

The fact was this was new territory for her … She'd made a good life despite her beginnings and had spent much of it doing exactly that: getting on with it. She had learned to grab situations by the facts at hand and proceed, becoming fiercely independent—entirely on purpose—and shielding her heart from all but a special few. Still, she had never been cold or uncaring, never cruel before she and Nattie had fallen out. She had simply been eminently capable and, while having learned the art of pointed riposte, had never been the perpetrator of first blood.

It wasn't until she had sensed betrayal by her only remaining confidant that she'd lashed out. Bitterness had taken the place of capability and made itself at home over the last several years. Wearing it as a badge laid protectively over the tear in her heart, it incubated the unresolved hurt of the young girl still inside.

Deep down, she'd always known that what happened to her mother wasn't because of her, even though she had still needed to hear it. News of young Maisy's accident had finally made her acknowledge her mother's pain, though forgiveness was still elusive.

In the case of Nattie, however, responsibility was piled high and deep on Cilla's doorstep. She was not the victim here, not the survivor, not this time. In her eagerness to protect her heart from further rupture, she had become the perpetrator, and that was an entirely different labyrinth to navigate. An apology was much more intimidating when she was the one from whom it was expected.

A bit taken aback by Cilla's return to form, Mama replied in kind.

"Well, Cilla, I honestly don't know. You've made a colossal mess of things; I'll grant you that. I certainly understand why you came to the conclusions you did, and I'm terribly sorry about what happened to you as a girl, but I'm afraid how and, indeed, whether you fix this current debacle is entirely up to you."

It was an interesting choice of words. The option of *whether* to fix it hadn't occurred to Cilla. She had simply assumed she must in order to move on. In fact, she needn't apologize at all if she didn't want to. No one other than Susan knew she was aware of Nattie's actual condition.

"I'll leave you to get dressed. Come out when you're ready, and I can fix you something to eat."

Susan left the room, which now felt much too overwhelming in its expectant silence. It was clear that while she had been willing to listen and provide comfort the day before—and Cilla would concede she had been kinder over the last several days than history warranted—she was of no mind to get in the middle of it. Cilla had made this train wreck of a bed and, apparently, she could jolly well lie in it by herself.

***

Gathering up her belongings as quickly as possible, Cilla declined Susan's offer of breakfast or lunch, barely looking at her as she hurried past and out the door.

She thumped down at her own kitchen table and sighed. Her choices hadn't even the slightest glimmer of appeal, save for one, which was to do nothing at all. Simply carry on as she had been, though maybe tone it down a bit.

But Susan knows, which means Ben knows. Does Annabelle? Do all the neighborhood kids and, thus, their parents know by now?

No, Susan was a teacher. She's well aware of how to keep children out of adults' private matters. What about Parker or Piper? What about Everett? Will she tell them she's discussed Nattie's condition with me?

Dear God, this was making her head pound like a piston in a Porsche. But no, Susan didn't want to be involved; of that, Cilla was certain. She wouldn't tell anyone anything they didn't ask directly.

Unfortunately, her choices hadn't managed to pretty themselves up in the last sixty seconds. Doing nothing still appeared to be the most attractive option. After all, while she may well have misjudged the situation, it wasn't as if Nattie herself had been Mother Teresa to the world at large. She'd been just as horrible to people as Cilla. At least Cilla had never fired a starter pistol at anyone.

Restless, she made her way up to the bedroom to put her things away. Passing the dresser, she saw the woman in the mirror and was startled at the figure looking back. Sunken, face drawn, and color pale, save for the dark circles beneath the eyes, the creature was nearly unrecognizable. But the eyes were shockingly familiar. They had stared back decades earlier when the space next to her had been newly and achingly empty.

God, was she really back there, again? Where was the capable woman she had so carefully nurtured all these years? The one who could be thrown into a forge and come out stronger for the firing? The one who so efficiently ran the office of a mechanic's shop, skillfully complimenting stubborn men while managing to get them to pay their bills in full? Where was the Cilla who didn't dither?

She shuffled to the bathroom to find an aspirin for her head, which now felt like a platoon of Sherman tanks was on parade. Deciding a cool shower would likely help as well, she padded back to the dresser and opened the top drawer containing her delicates. Inside, lay Penny's hair ribbon in a small clear container; the one keepsake she had hidden for herself after Penny's death and had allowed herself to bring when fleeing from Back Bay all those years ago.

Memories came flooding back as they always did when she sat with the ribbon. So many good times and not a care in the world until the day when Penny simply wasn't there anymore. Just like that. No chance to say goodbye. She missed her best friend.

She missed her best friend.

The Hill

Pullman Station nestles in a valley between surrounding limestone bluffs that were quarried to make majestic buildings like the library. Streams and small rivers spent millions of years carving out our little corner of the world from the massive deposits. Harriman Hill stands higher than the rest, having been left untouched by the excavators.

One of our favorite experiences, no matter the season, was to hike up "The Hill," as locals call it. It was exhausting and sweaty business and always rewarded with a trip to Bohler's afterward. The best part of the day, however, wasn't the climb or the doughnuts. Instead, it was the park at the top of the bluff. Technically, you can drive up, which we did on occasion, but it made for a more fantastic adventure if we nearly killed ourselves getting there.

You'll find no merry-go-rounds, swings, or slides at the park. It's much better. When you reach the summit, you're rewarded with views of the entire valley and beyond, a breathtaking sight every time you see it, no matter what season or time of day. Miles and miles of undulating bluffs and countryside hide precious gems of nature and civilization tucked between the sleeping limestone giants. It's almost magical knowing that Pullman has its own little place below but that there are others sequestered elsewhere in the nooks and crannies that we can't quite see.

The park was built as a sort of salute to the area back in the early 1900s. Paved paths, benches, and historical plaques discussing the various quarries and the railroad's role in transporting stone were spread throughout to welcome visitors and citizens alike. Lookouts are notched into the protective walls that keep all but the most determined and deliberate from going butt-over-teakettle to the bottom.

The walls can pose a problem for little ones who want to take a gander at the valley. Being the petite little thing that she was, Maisy couldn't see past them. At forty-two inches tall, her view would have been mostly sky if not for the lookouts.

Of course, being fiercely independent, she didn't want help from anyone, though she'd make an exception for Garrett and his shoulders. The city provides step stools for kids to stand on, and Maisy employed these expeditiously. She'd blaze a trail to the nearest lookout, hollering, "I'm going to peek over!" Her little head would pop up into a viewing area notched into the wall and be silhouetted against the view beyond.

It was Maisy, then, who coined the term "peek-overs," and ever since, whenever we wanted to go to Harriman Hill, we'd say, "Let's go to the peek-overs today." None of the rest of us needed stools anymore, but the name stuck.

***

July 16, 1985

As we started to think about how to fill our Maisy Moments journal, "The Hill" bubbled to the top of the list. The tricky part was to do it on a day when somebody's mom could take us and when it wasn't too hot. Rarely given a choice about the heat during a Pullman summer, we at least needed to go before the mercury skyrocketed, and that meant getting up before 7:00 a.m.

Thursday appeared to be the most convenient day, and Mama was available to take us. Since it would be an early call in the morning, we had a sleepover at our house Wednesday night. We got up, packed our backpacks—Mama made us all carry our own stuff, firmly maintaining that she was not a pack mule—and headed out around 7:30. It would be a hot afternoon, but the morning was fresh and clear, and walking the trails in the shade didn't sound too bad.

The thing about "The Hill" was that no matter how many times you climbed it, the views at the top made you forget how steep it was and how long it would take you to get there. Snaking back and forth as you slowly ascended, it was easy to lose track of time. Somehow, it always brainwashed you into thinking it was a marvelous idea, even in the middle of July.

Maybe it's because we didn't always do the climb, and a car ride didn't weigh on our very souls as we went up, or perhaps it was because Maisy made it look so easy. She was small but a powerhouse, leading like a mountain goat and chattering away the whole time. Meanwhile, the rest of us were sucking wind after ten minutes of keeping up with her, having been almost totally silent. Whatever the reason, once again, we'd gotten lulled into doing it.

Mama maintained the caboose position so as not to leave anyone behind. She was in good shape, but I reckon she didn't mind being last, just the same.

Jimmy always took off like a shot, forgetting that he was more a sprinter than a distance man. His enthusiasm was admirable but listening to him whine after he ran out of gas really stunk up the woods. He was always first out of the gate and first to choke.

Sasha, on the other hand, tended to carve his own trail. As such, he meandered and kept a slower, noisier pace, always hollering for us to come see something off the beaten path. Without fail, this resulted in stick-me-tights stuck to our socks, shoelaces—even our hair—and a much higher probability of ticks hitching a ride to the top. Ew.

As for Natalie and me, we were sweepers. We paced ourselves, looking for flowers and other things that we found interesting along the ground. An avid flower-presser, Natalie always brought a book and some paper towels, so she could take half of the nature we encountered home with us.

I was also a collector, but I had chosen less wisely. While Natalie collected things you could weigh in milligrams, I collected rocks. As a result, my backpack was always sagging after only a few minutes, and I usually had to cull the herd a few times as we went up. Natalie had a beautiful display case full of pressed flowers in her room. I had a backyard full of migrant rocks.

As usual, Jimmy took off, hollering back at us about how we were sissies, and he was "King of the Hill." But his voice became distant, and the taunting soon faded. Sasha took off to play Marco Polo by himself among the outcroppings, and Natalie and I were instantly nose-to-the-ground. Mama took out her Pentax camera, stopping now and then to take pictures for her albums and some to accompany our stories in Maisy's book.

As expected, we caught up with Jimmy after about fifteen minutes. Perched on a rock, he was sucking down most of his water. *Idiot.* Everyone knew he'd be asking for theirs before too long. I decided I would be riding the "Nope Train" when he asked for mine; I was already carrying extra weight in my pack and would need all the water I could get by the time we reached the top.

After a rest and another fifteen minutes of strolling more than hiking, Jimmy took off again, a second wind billowing his sails. Naturally, it wasn't long before we found him draped over a boulder as if the world were fading in and out and his ancestors beckoned from the Great Beyond.

Natalie rolled her eyes and sat down to put her flowers between pages. Meanwhile, I dumped my burden out on the ground and began playing favorites. It was peaceful among the quiet of the trees. Too peaceful.

We hadn't heard Sasha crashing around for a while, and no one had been called off the path to go see some weird-looking thing that he considered "gnarly." I caught Mama surreptitiously searching the surrounding woods with her eyes. *Crap.*

Even though the trails were well-traveled, everyone in Pullman Station knew that you had to be careful on "The Hill." It was steep and the unpredictable off-trail footing potentially dangerous.

"Does anyone know where Sasha got to?"

Mama knew how to keep her cool when a headcount turned up one noodler short. We all shook our heads.

"Alright, then it's time to sound off. Jimmy?"

"Hey, dufus! Did you fall down to the bottom?"

"Jimmy…" Mama rolled her eyes and grinned. We listened. Silence.

"Sasha!" I yelled. "Where are you? We want to keep going!" *One-one-thousand, two-one-thousand, three-one-thousand, four-one-thousand, five-one-thousand.*

"Sasha! Come out, you moron. This isn't funny!" She sounded casual, but I could see Natalie's twin tail starting to twitch. Jimmy could see it, too.

"Shit."

"Jimmy!"

"Whoops. Sorry, Ms. Walker."

"*Mrs.* Walker. Okay, how long has it been since you last heard him in the woods?"

We stared blankly at each other.

"I dunno. I was up ahead of you guys. Can I have some of your water, Annabelle?"

"No. And I was looking at rocks, so I'm not exactly sure, either, Mama."

"Natalie?"

Natalie looked pained as she shrugged.

"I don't remember, either, Mrs. Walker. I'm sorry. But I don't think he's messing around."

"Alright. Well, we'll have to spread out and go back the way we came. Form a line, and we'll walk on both sides of the trail and see if we can find him. He probably stopped to look at something interesting."

We did as instructed, Mama and Jimmy on one side, several feet apart when manageable, and Natalie and I likewise on the other side. Every ten yards or so, Mama would stop us, and we would holler and listen. Each time we heard only birds, the knot in my stomach grew a little bigger.

We'd gone about a hundred and twenty yards when we finally heard something different. Faint, but there, nonetheless. We moved around a bit, trying to figure out where it was coming from. As we narrowed in on the voice—yes, definitely a voice—I started to imagine all sorts of things we might find. This could be bad. There'd been a kid in the sixties who tumbled down the bluff and crashed into a tree trunk. He broke his neck and instantly became a quadriplegic. *Please, God, don't let that be Sasha!* I didn't think anybody could handle another tragic accident.

The voice was definitely coming from south of the path. We all moved to that side, and it gradually became apparent that it was, indeed, Sasha.

"Sasha! We're gonna save you, buddy! Where are you?" Jimmy went into full-on G.I. Joe mode. I half expected helicopters to come over the top of the bluff or paratroopers to descend.

We tracked Sasha to an outcropping. Well, to behind one, actually. There, inside a small cave, stood our friend, looking extremely sheepish. His left foot was visibly lower than his right, and he seemed in no hurry to move.

"Dude! Are you okay!?" Jimmy ran up and hugged him. "Are you hurt? Do you need a doctor? Are you dehydrated?"

"He's only been missing for twenty minutes, idiot." Natalie rolled her eyes at me. "And he has water in his backpack."

"Oh. Yeah. So, what's wrong then?"

"I can't get my foot out."

We looked down, and, sure enough, he was stuck. His left foot had gotten wedged in a crack while his right remained on the cave floor.

"Are you hurt?" This, from Mama.

"No, I don't think so. Just stuck."

"Geez!" Jimmy complained. "This place smells like pee. Are there animals living in here or something?"

"Um, I don't think so." Sasha shuffled his right foot and looked at anything but us.

"What are you doing in here, anyway?" Natalie asked.

"Uh ... well ... see, I needed to take a leak, and I was looking at the outcropping, so I stepped back behind it and saw the cave. I figured this would be a good place to do it since no one would see. But then I got stuck."

Jimmy looked down.

"Wait a second. You mean you peed on the floor!? I'm standing in your pee!? Dude!"

"Well, no, not exactly. I did it on the wall so it wouldn't run into my shoe."

"Still! Oh, man, I think I'm gonna barf!"

Jimmy proceeded to gag and choke while the rest of us figured out how to get Sasha loose. Eventually, Mama asked if he could get his foot out of his shoe, which he discovered he could. Then, he simply pulled the shoe out of the hole.

Someone call off the National Guard.

The morning was heating up, and we'd wasted plenty of time finding and freeing Sasha. Rather than continuing up the bluff, we opted to descend back to the car and drive up. Still, it had been fun, and no one had sacrificed any of their water to Jimmy, which was a first.

Heading back down the trail, Mama took the lead, and Natalie and I brought up the rear. We weren't about to let Sasha out of our sight again. The boys chatted while we tried to figure out what to do for the rest of the day. Everybody was glad Sasha hadn't gotten hurt, and it turned out that we got a pretty funny story out of it for Maisy.

"Knob." Jimmy shoved Sasha in the arm, grinning and grateful that his best friend would live to hike another day.

"Shut up, man." Sasha pushed him back with an embarrassed grin of his own, equally happy to be unstuck and back among friends.

***

When we finally got home, we devoured our doughnuts and sat down to write to Maisy. Doing it right away seemed the best way to go about it since it was still fresh in our minds. Everyone would undoubtedly have their favorite details to share, so we decided that each of us would pen a separate letter. And so, Maisy Moments began.

Dear Maisy ...

Sorry, What?

As she lay in her bed, exhausted from the grueling therapy, Maisy's eyelids began to droop. Mrs. Drummond watched as her little girl drifted, thankful she would find respite in sleep.

"Mommy?" Her little voice tip-toed down the sheet.

"Mm-hmm?"

"When is that doggy coming back to see me?" Mrs. Drummond's eyes snapped to her daughter.

"When is that do—What?" *Did Maisy remember the accident?* "What doggy, sweetie?"

"The one who visits me. The one who told me everything was okay."

Mrs. Drummond stared. She had no idea what Maisy was talking about and had certainly never heard her speak calmly about a dog before. Could it be a lingering issue from the trauma, perhaps?

The one who told me everything was okay. Mrs. Drummond wracked her brain, trying to figure it out.

"Maisy, honey, they don't allow doggies in here. Do you mean a stuffed animal someone brought you?"

"No, Mommy! She was real!" Maisy shouted, startling her mother. "She came and saw me when I was scared and couldn't talk. She told me it was okay. She took care of me."

"Alright! Okay, um … Did this doggy have a name?"

"Uh-huh. Her name is Freckle. She's my friend."

What on earth?

Maisy yawned, the drowsiness returning, trying hard to pull her under.

"I'm not sure, honey," Mrs. Drummond stalled. "I'll have to ask around to see where she went."

"Okay."

Thankfully, this appeared to be a satisfactory answer. Maisy yawned again and drifted off to sleep as quickly as she'd flared. Outbursts weren't unusual, but the topic was certainly new.

Mrs. Drummond watched her little girl for a while, trying to make some sense of their conversation. If anything, she figured Maisy would be more terrified of dogs than ever, though the doctors said she likely wouldn't remember the accident at all. She decided to ask her husband and the staff about a stuffed dog since, clearly, no one would bring a real one onto the unit. And even if they did, surely no one would ever be allowed to have it near Maisy.

***

At the very next opportunity, Mrs. Drummond questioned the nurses. None of them had a clue what she was talking about. When the shift changed, she repeated the process with the next group, garnering the same result.

When Mr. Drummond arrived, she filled him in on the conversation, and he was just as baffled as she was. Maisy had never mentioned a dog to him. Certainly not one who was her friend. They resolved to discuss it with the doctor in the morning. Not anything worth a rush, but of concern, nonetheless. Why would she make up something so strange?

Sneaker

Maisy's therapy was exhausting work, and she and Mrs. Drummond were frequent passengers on the Dream Express, but her progress continued. She'd become a bit of a ward mascot, visiting other patients when able and spreading cheer wherever she went. She was bummed when the doctors said she couldn't come home to Pullman yet, but thankfully, we could all visit her now that she was in a regular room on a unit without visitor restrictions.

Mama drove us over twice a week to play a board game with Maisy before her afternoon therapy. It put her in a better mood, which made getting into the hard work of rehabilitation a little easier. Cliff went over with Pansy and Garrett a couple of evenings, and they read to her or colored together until she was ready for sleep.

Of course, Garrett put a bigger smile on her face than anyone else. He drove over by himself one Thursday night. They chatted about all sorts of things: what he'd been up to at the pool, people Maisy had seen during the day, other kids on the ward, things outside her window, what she'd had for lunch, and pretty much anything else that prolonged Garrett's departure. But then it happened.

"Can Freckle come on our camping trip with us?"

I guess that brought Mrs. Drummond's head up in a right hurry. Garrett said her eyes snapped to his, and she nodded. When Maisy got moved to a regular room, Mrs. Drummond had mentioned Freckle to us just in case, but Maisy hadn't said anything to anyone yet. Garrett cottoned on to what Mrs. D. was asking him to do and kept it casual. He selected a burnt sienna crayon from the box while Maisy colored a pine tree with evergreen.

"Who's Freckle?"

"The puppy who visits me."

"Oh. That's nice. What does she look like?" Garrett pretended to concentrate on the log he was coloring in the campsite picture they were working on.

"She's really cute! She's little and has floppy ears and white fur, but she has gray and brown spots on her face and back and tummy."

"Huh. I didn't even know they let dogs in the hospital."

"Freckle sneaks," Maisy whispered. "She comes in and lays down on my bed sometimes when I'm sleeping."

"How long has she been doing that?" he whispered back. "Isn't she worried she'll get caught?"

"Nuh-uh. She's a super sneaker. She's been visiting me since I got here. She told me it would be okay when I was scared and couldn't talk. Promise you won't tell anyone?"

"Oh, I pinkie promise. But she talks?"

"Well, not really. She doesn't have to because our hearts understand each other."

"Oh. Well, that *is* pretty cool."

Maisy combed through the crayons again, and Garrett shot a glance at Mrs. Drummond and shrugged.

"Do you think the tent should be brown or orange?" Maisy asked.

"Umm ... whichever one you'd want ours to be."

"Orange with yellow stars!"

"Sounds good to me!"

"And then, we have to add a doggy house for Freckle."

"Well, yeah, we can't leave an important friend like her without a place to sleep. I'll start on it now. Cool?"

Maisy grinned at Garrett as if he had a big S on his chest and a cape on his back. He always understood.

Mr. Coleman's Salvos

Several days had passed since her meeting with Susan, and Cilla still hadn't decided what to do. Thinking exhausted her. Crying exhausted her. Getting angry exhausted her. It was so much easier just to sleep.

For the umpteenth time, she laid out her options. First, of course, was to do nothing. So far, that wasn't feeling so great. It was one thing to make a mistake, but quite another to continue to hurt someone once you'd realized it.

The most sensible thing would be to bite the bullet and apologize. In her heart, she knew it was the right thing to do, and the possibility of having her friend back in her life in any capacity squeezed her chest tight. But how on earth was she supposed to do that? She couldn't simply go knocking on Nattie's door and expect to be welcomed in. Nattie didn't even want her on her property, not that Cilla could blame her.

Calling or writing were both options, but if she called, Nattie would surely hang up as soon as she found out who was on the other end. She'd attempted a letter several times, but the crumpled paper balls in the wastebasket outnumbered the words she'd been able to get down.

Her final option was to seek out an intermediary. It was clear Susan had enough on her plate to be getting on with, so she was out. That left ... *Shit*. How could she have allowed herself to alienate so many people? How had she managed to let anger and hurt consume her entire life after so many years of putting the past behind her? If she tried to repair things, it might take more effort and energy than she had, leaving her back at square one.

In the end, it was Mr. Coleman who spurred her into action. He stopped by one afternoon on the pretext of delivering bouquets, even though he knew darn well she had plenty of flowers in her own garden. But what he lacked in excuse, he made up for in concern, and it gave Cilla the opening she needed.

Everett had known Cilla longer than anyone else besides Nattie and could be more direct with her than most others without risking life and limb. Granted, he'd technically been an employee during much of their friendship, but it never stopped him from speaking his mind. He leaned against the counter and got right to the point.

"Cilla, I'm worried about you."

"What on earth for, Everett?"

Her eyes didn't move from the flowers as she placed them in a vase. Putting up defenses came all too naturally these days. In truth, she was touched he would have any concern for her at all after her behavior these last several years. But he'd always remained steadfast; whether out of friendship to her or her deceased husband, she wasn't quite sure.

"Well, we aren't getting any younger, are we? Seems to me this business with Nattie ought to wake all of us older folks up a bit. She could've burned her house down earlier this summer. With you two on the outs with everybody and acting like a couple of ninnies, I suppose I'm worried there's no one to look after you once I'm gone, should things go sideways."

Well, he certainly hadn't beaten around any bushes, had he? And he wasn't wrong. Sure, her kids called, and they visited every so often, but in terms of neighbors, it was slim pickings. Yes, Susan checked if she needed anything from the store on the regular, but expecting wellness visits for years to come after all Susan had put up with already seemed like pushing

the envelope a bit too far. Cilla considered this for a moment and then
seized the opportunity before she lost her nerve.

"Everett, your timing is impeccable, as usual."

"It is?"

"Yes. In fact, I've been thinking about just such things of late."

She turned, surprising him by not rebuking his concern. Having decided
to wrap her plea in frankness and bluster in an effort to ward off any
emotion that might dare creep into her voice, she set in.

"You see, it has come to my attention that Nattie and I have had a
rather large misunderstanding, and I've been considering how to rectify
the situation."

Everett, not at all snowed by the blizzard of bravado, dug back in.

"Cilla, you know damn well it was more than a misunderstanding. You
two were far too close for something as simple as that to drive you farther
apart than two butt-ended magnets. Now, it's none of my business what
started it, but I expect plain stubbornness kept it going. You two always
were a couple of old goats about things that got under your skin. Anyway,
I take it you've been informed of Nattie's condition and are looking for a
way to mend some fences without losing too much off your own hide, is
that about right?"

Taken aback by his candor and refusal to entertain any theater regarding
the matter, Cilla dropped all pretense.

"Fine. Please sit. Can I get you something to drink?"

"You can get to the truth if you don't mind."

"Well, good heavens, Everett Coleman! You don't need to be so rude!
If people knew you spoke to me like that, they'd never think you shy and
quiet again."

"Cilla, ain't a person in this town gives two shits if I ruffle your feathers,"
he shot back. "Half of 'em wish they could give you a piece of their own

mind. Now, I'm a very patient man, and I've always given you some extra grace knowin' things weren't easy for you growin' up. But if you think I'm going to sit here and listen to anything other than the God's-honest truth, you got another think comin'!"

Cilla stared at him, stung. He was her only hope. Closing her eyes, she started from the beginning.

The Right Thing

After revealing her hand to Everett, Cilla felt much better about things. He'd known her back when she'd first moved to Pullman and seen how she'd persevered and made a good life for their family. Now that he'd finally heard her backstory after all these years, he was inclined to be gentle with her. Having lost his wife early on, he understood pushing healing aside in favor of simply surviving the next bout of whatever life threw one's way. It felt good to have someone understand her on a very personal level. Her past didn't excuse her behavior, but it at least explained it, which was comforting to have accepted at face value.

Still, Everett didn't coddle her, maintaining a similar position to Susan, though with fewer battle scars to influence his stance. He agreed to help where he could as long as Cilla put in the hard work and was honest with herself and others. She needn't share her story with them, but she did need to express her remorse and set a path forward.

Over the next few days, the two of them spent quite a bit of time discussing how Cilla should proceed. So many years of wrongs needed to be righted, and her head was spinning like a top. She threw ideas onto the table whenever and however she thought of them, and Everett quietly listened as she then talked herself into, and out of, most of them.

They went round and round until Cilla reluctantly agreed that the fire needed to be put out at the source first. Chasing down endless sparks would prove futile.

"It's like the scarlet flesh around an infection," Everett said. "It won't quiet 'til the wound itself is lanced and cleaned."

So, then. She must begin with Nattie.

Everett agreed to call Piper and suggest arranging a meeting in a neutral space for the two women to air their grievances.

"Now, Cilla, if we do this, you have to be prepared to see Nattie in a new light. She isn't the same person as when this all started."

"I understand, Everett. Thank you."

"You're going to have to make emotional allowances for the changes."

"Yes, I realize."

"You sure? It's not a fair fight anymore. You may have to pull punches instead of throwin' 'em, sometimes. Amends and compassion need to be the order—"

"Yes, *I know,* Everett!"

"Well. Alright, then."

***

Forty-eight hours later, Gasoline and Gunpowder met in the living room of one of their oldest friends. Everett set out Nattie's favorite oatmeal raisin cookies and Cilla's favorite lemonade as refreshments; an odd combination, sure, but no less so than the two women awkwardly shuffling about his parlor, avoiding eye contact.

True to his word, he left Cilla in charge of her own destiny as he and Piper stepped into the dining room a few feet away. They would be available if needed, but only just. If things got heated—and it was delicate material sure to provoke strong feelings—they would step in only if it got out of hand. If Cilla thought Nattie might've checked out, so to speak, she was to alert Piper. Other than that, it was sink or swim.

"Now, I want a clean fight..." Everett mumbled, grinning to himself as he stepped into the next room.

***

God, this was uncomfortable. Cilla wrung her hands as she tried to think of how to begin. Nattie wasn't giving her an inch. She could see her friend—could she call her that? —was only here to appease the intermediaries and didn't much care to give Cilla the time of day. And why should she?

"Hello, Nattie," she began, trying to smile. Her tone was hopeful, but her dry mouth made her lips stick to her teeth, and she could feel that it looked strange. Nattie looked at her and cocked her head, raising her eyebrows as if to say, *"Oh, my! Her Highness deigns to speak to little old me!"* Cilla gulped some lemonade and tried again.

"Er, thank you for meeting me. I know I don't deserve it."

A confirming "Hmph!" was the only reply as Nattie turned to stare out the window, cold shoulder evident despite the suffocating heat.

"Nattie, you see, I'm afraid there's been a misunderstanding. I..."

How was she supposed to say this? It'd been so much easier in her head. Of course, Nattie had been much more receptive in her head, too. She tried several more times, explaining where she felt things went wrong and why she had done what she did, but Nattie only continued to stare off. Without so much as a twitch from her, Cilla finally called to the other room.

"Er, Piper? I think maybe she's having an episode."

"I most certainly am not, you ass!" Nattie rounded on her now, her eyes threatening Armageddon. "I'm waiting for an actual apology instead of the horse shit you're doling out! As if your issues are worse than anyone else's! Our entire generation went through that time, remember? And through all the things that followed. But we're still standing here dealing with it. As if your problems somehow make accusing and abandoning your best friend okay!

"But you can't even get an apology right, can you, you old cow? Heaven forbid you seem weak. Heaven forbid someone not be as strong as the mighty *PRIS*cilla Prescott! Well, if you're so damn strong, where were you when I needed you the most? Where were you when I needed your reassurance and trust instead of your judgment? Your compassion instead of your suspicion? Where the hell were you when my world was falling apart?"

"Well, why the hell didn't you tell me what was going on, then!?"

"Because I was scared, you fool!"

Tears streamed down Nattie's face, but they were angry tears, not those of sadness and loss. The fire in her eyes frightened Cilla, not because she feared being struck, but because she had grossly underestimated just how badly she'd hurt her friend. An apology would barely scratch the surface.

Her eyes filled with tears. Her mouth and hands trembled, and her insides became molten, the heat of embarrassment pushing toward the outside.

"Well, so was I," she whispered, her lips finally wet with salty remorse. "I'm so sorry."

Cilla's eyes pleaded with the woman standing across from her, begging forgiveness she now felt even less deserving of. She fell to her knees and sobbed.

"God, Nattie. I'm so sorry."

***

The initial aftermath of the meeting at Everett's was no prettier than the conversation itself. Nattie and Cilla had said and done things over the past several years that were nearly unforgivable. Old habits die hard, and scars ran deep on both sides.

It wasn't easy admitting their faults to themselves, much less each other, and neither was quite ready to do the latter—the temptation to dress elaborate explanations up as acceptable excuses beckoned seductively. And yet, both women knew the difference.

That evening, they sat in their respective homes and reached the same uncomfortable conclusion. The awkward truth slithered in, cold and wretched. The fact was, they weren't only angry at each other; it was disappointment in themselves that stung most of all.

Neither woman had trusted their friendship of more than thirty years or considered the other before themselves. Not even for a moment. Instead, they'd both retreated, frightened, preferring to build impenetrable walls behind which they could marinate in the juices of hate and contempt and self-pity. Marlon and Jack would be mortified. Truth be told, so were Nattie and Cilla.

How, then, to willingly embark on a journey through a minefield of accountability without having it blow up in one's face? It would be painful, agonizing, even. Scabs would be torn off and bleed freely once again. And for what? To be able to say they had made it right? To show others they were, indeed, civil adults worthy of respect and friendship? And how to do so without revealing the truth to the world: that Nattie was sick and would only get worse.

***

For her part, Nattie didn't know if she could forgive Cilla. She had walked out when things got tough. When Nattie was alone and terrified, not knowing what was happening, she had needed her oldest and dearest friend to console her, to add her shoulders to the scaffolding holding up the burden. She had needed Cilla to trust her and believe her, to commit to unconditional friendship despite not yet knowing why. Yes, Nattie should've shared what troubled her, but fear and a lifetime of difficulty asking for help had kept her silent.

Grudgingly, she admitted understanding why Cilla ran. What she endured at the hands of her parents in the aftermath of losing Penny wasn't something Nattie had ever been able to comprehend. Contrary to what she said at Everett's, everybody of their generation hadn't gone through the same. Not really.

Then, of course, there was the most frustrating part of all: she didn't even know if she remembered everything that had happened. How could she remain angry if she wasn't even sure who had done worse? What if the memories she had of everything were no longer accurate? Things had been disappearing for a long time; there was no way for her to know where the gaps lurked.

Since Cilla was willing to bury the hatchet, perhaps she should be, too. If only she'd been honest about what was going on, this could all have been avoided.

***

Cilla paced. Her body simply couldn't be still while her brain wrestled with such a writhing ball of snakes. Nattie was right; their entire generation did deal with many of the things Cilla had. Scores of people in Boston alone lost family members, friends, colleagues. Grief and alcohol had been frequent bedfellows in a post-war boom that many loved ones weren't there to experience. Cilla didn't own the corner on that market. And, so what if Nattie had taken to the bottle? Wouldn't the right thing have been to help her friend rather than write her off and leave her to die? Just look where her quick judgment had gotten them.

Still, Nattie hadn't trusted her enough to tell her the truth. After more than thirty years of sharing their troubles, leaning in and baring their souls during the hardest of trials, she hadn't felt she could be honest in their friendship. That was a slight Cilla didn't know if she could excuse. If she had just put her fears aside for a moment and pushed a little harder, opened her heart a little wider, maybe Nattie would've been able to let her in.

Despite their regrets, forgiveness proved elusive.

Time to Pay the Piper

The time to fulfill their punishments had finally arrived for Jimmy and Sasha. Penance for their Library antics had been put on hold after the accident, but now there was no reason why they couldn't carry out their sentences, beginning with Children's Hour.

The boys selected Wednesdays as their duty day because they didn't want to start or end their week with it and figured they might as well do it on days we'd be there anyway. They wisely chose the afternoon session to take full advantage of the A/C, which Mrs. Chisholm agreed to, though she was fully aware of their reasoning.

We set off, backpacks loaded, and trudged our way over. Mrs. Chisholm had, indeed, decided to make it a learning experience for the boys. Rather than have them check books in and out when the little kids finished with Children's Hour, she had decided that it would be good practice if they did the reading instead of her. They groaned at the news while Natalie and I rubbed our palms in anticipation of watching them squirm.

As it turned out, Mrs. Chisholm knew what she was doing when she set their task. Knowing that neither one of them ever sat still for long, she chose lively and exciting books. The boys rock-paper-scissored for who would read first, and Jimmy's "rock" bashed Sasha's "scissors" to smithereens.

Mrs. Chisholm introduced them as her special guests and let them have the floor. Both were to sit up front no matter which one was reading. The little kids didn't seem to care who read as long as they got their stories. They stared up at Sasha, expectation plastered across their faces.

He began quietly and quickly, without much inflection. The performance wasn't well-received.

"That's not how you read it! You hafta make the noises," said a little boy in the front row. Sasha glanced at Mrs. Chisholm, who smiled her best "go ahead" smile from her chair in the back. Thinking fast, he put Jimmy on sound duty before starting again.

"I can't see the pictures! You hafta do it like this." A little girl promptly got up and showed Sasha how to correctly hold the book, showing it back and forth in front of the group so everyone could see.

"Um, okay. Thanks."

"I hafta go potty."

Poor Sasha looked helpless. He glanced over at Mrs. Chisholm, who again nodded approval.

"Um, yeah, go ahead."

He began again, this time accompanied by Jimmy's noises. The kids started to giggle, which seemed to boost Sasha's confidence, and he read a bit louder.

Between the two of them, Sasha and Jimmy soon had every kid eating out of their hands and begging for another story. Before they knew it, they'd swapped positions three times. In front of them sat eleven grinning faces, looking up with enthusiastic approval. The boys reflected them back.

When they'd finished reading, the children cheered and asked for more. Mrs. Chisholm stood and told them it was time to pick out books. Their moans of disappointment were quickly replaced by several kids grabbing either Jimmy's or Sasha's hand and asking if they would help. Some even asked Natalie or me. Since they were kind of used to us all being one unit,

I guess they assumed we were special guests, too. Mrs. Chisholm walked back to her desk, trying to hide the grin on her face.

Children's Hour was a smashing success, and Natalie and I had enjoyed the antics, too. We'd seen our friends do a lot of silly things over the years, but that was the first time we'd seen them do anything goofy because it made them proud. Really proud.

Mrs. Chisholm thanked the boys for their hard work and said she'd see them again the following Wednesday for an encore. They talked non-stop the whole way home, high-fiving each other over their favorite noises and planning for the next time. They even started a list of books to read if Mrs. Chisholm let them. But what they really wanted to do was read for Maisy. It appeared Mrs. Chisholm had created a monster.

Dear Maisy ...

Up a Creek

H aving derailed on our trip up Harriman Hill, another hike was in order. This time, though, we made a Saturday of it and picked a different location.

We had long ago taken to asking Mr. Coleman for stories about the adventures his kids had at Hillman Park so many years earlier, and we weren't above carrying on the tradition ourselves. With parents in tow, save for Mr. Drummond, who insisted Mrs. Drummond come and take a little break while he stayed at the hospital with Maisy, we headed out.

The park was still lovely, though the toilet situation hadn't improved much from the looks of things. However, in addition to enjoying the usual activities, we'd taken to exploring where Hillman Creek came from. As such, we had created our own tradition of following it back into the hills.

We had memorized the route long ago, but storms and flooding often changed things slightly from year to year or even month to month. Once we got back to the gigantic trestle bridge along the tracks outside the park, we'd climb up and follow them back until we reached the stone pavilion.

The sun beat down that morning, and the thought of hiking in the shade of the woods was quite appealing. The creek twisted and turned through the trees, requiring us to cross it at least twice on our journey. Having gouged its path as it trickled along and swelled to the point of flooding several times a summer, the terrain might be anything from dry and rocky to wet and boggy. One thing was for sure, though: if you were the last one across, and anyone before you had fallen in, you were going to be walking in their soggy footprints, and that dramatically increased your chances of soaking up a bit of the creek yourself.

In many places, tree canopies overhung the water. This served us well in two ways. First, the dense growth often required that we hang on to branches as we rounded boulders, stumps, or anything else in our way, lest we fall off the bank and into the water. Second, it usually meant a downed limb or two from a strong summer storm would be available as a makeshift bridge for crossing. Without those, it was strictly rock-jumping and another shot at going *sploosh*. Maisy had joined us for the first time last year but had spent quite a bit of time on Mr. Drummond's shoulders. It had made for an interesting hike for him!

Mrs. Perkins was the resident champ at getting unintentionally soaked, while Jimmy simply expected to after all these years. He knew it would happen again at some point and didn't bother being all that careful anymore. Being the sprinter he was, he ran ahead to check things out, frequently returning with an enthusiastic update on treacherous terrain or sitting down to rest until we caught up.

Sasha, always the explorer, constantly tramped off into the woods, sure he'd found a stellar path. Not always right, but never in doubt, he had a reputation for getting stuck in a snarl of brambles and also held the record as our number one burning nettle victim. We figured, one of these years, he would realize staying with the creek would always be his best bet and would always lead us back to the trestle bridge without fail.

Natalie and I always saw lots of things we wanted to collect, but we knew it was a bad idea. I didn't want to get bogged down with extra weight on slippery terrain, and Natalie didn't want to get her pressing books wet if she fell in, so it was eyes only for the two of us.

***

Our troupe crossed to the back end of the long park—minus Mama and Mrs. Drummond, who stayed back to watch camp—and headed in. We knew the entry point like the backs of our hands by now, but new brambles and snags always caught us unawares. We'd changed into jeans since poison ivy and burning nettle liked to hide in these parts, not to mention thirsty ticks. As soon as we entered the trees, the mosquitoes sent out an APB and hunted us mercilessly. Thankfully, we all remembered to put on heavy-duty bug spray.

It would be hard to end up well and truly lost with the bluff always to our right. In fact, "lost" took on a completely different meaning in there. It wasn't unheard of for Jimmy to lose a shoe in the muck and have to go digging for it or for someone to lose their balance and tip into the creek. Nor was it hard to lose our sense of time as we traipsed through weeds, rocks, and water. But we always had a relatively good idea of where we were.

We laughed ourselves silly at near misses, unintentional butt-slides down muddy embankments, and parents who couldn't quite scamper up things like us kids. It was the great field-leveler, as everyone had different advantages and weaknesses.

Parents, Cliff and Pansy all had longer legs and were more likely to make a broad step from log to embankment successfully, while Jimmy, Sasha, Natalie, and I all scampered up the hillside more easily. While the grown-ups were tall enough not to get thoroughly soaked if they stepped in the water by accident, the rest of us might get waist-deep in certain parts, depending on rain.

We hiked along the creek bank, feeling the cool of the water radiating toward us in the thick fug of humidity and mosquitoes. As we approached our first trek over the water, Sasha and Jimmy took off to find a suitable crossing point. Cliff and Pansy, wise to the follies of the other two, began a careful and slow search of the bank to find boulders or rocks that would work. Not being very deep there, finding a downed tree didn't matter all that much. However, if we went much farther upstream, we'd come to a turn that resulted in a much deeper pond. We could hear Sasha and Jimmy giggling near it as they searched.

"Hey, guys!" Sasha's voice echoed along the valley wall. "We found a log! It doesn't cross the whole way, but I think—*aargh*!"

A huge splash and riotous laughter from Jimmy, who was congratulating himself, followed.

"It wasn't me! It wasn't me this year! It wasn't me! You guys—*argh!!*" Another splash, courtesy of Jimmy, followed by giggles from both boys.

"Never mind!"

Down on our end, we shook our heads and decided to try our luck with the boulders Pansy and Cliff found. After picking our way across, we caught up with the sodden idiots on the other side.

The boys got relegated to the back of the line until they stopped dripping. No one else wanted to put their footing in jeopardy because of those two monkeys. Our shoes got lapped at while we crossed on the rocks, but no one else was making audible squishing sounds with every step.

Daddy and Mr. Perkins took the lead. Adequately sure-footed and cautious into the bargain, they always made sure everybody got across the water okay and held branches out of our way on the trail before they followed along again. In the event we got to a deeper, rushing part of the creek, they walked in before us and let us hang onto their arms and hands to cross without being knocked over. Extremely wet years could be a bit dicey.

The boys always had to stop to take a leak in the woods somewhere, apparently fulfilling some sort of ancient male ritual. I always thought it would be funny if they did it amongst the burning nettle, though. It would serve them right. Alas, it was way easier for them to pee in public than for us girls—one of the great inequities of life.

Walking beside the creek was relaxing. We stopped to examine interesting rocks and play along the edge when we needed a break. Bugs skittered across the surface of the water, and tiny flowers popped out here and there as we crashed through the underbrush.

The day was a wonderful reprieve from the trials awaiting us back home in the coming week. We just missed Maisy.

***

The hike passed pretty uneventfully for a decent stretch. The creek wasn't high, though we could see it had been earlier in the summer. Swarms of mosquitoes buzzed in for a quick investigation and then moved off when we got closer to the water. If we hit an open area, the breeze off the water cooled us for a few moments.

Just before our halfway point, we discovered that the rains in May had carved out a massive chunk of the bank as it turned left toward the park. It had swelled and rushed and resulted in quite a drop-off to the current water level. As such, there was only one way to cross: jump down, wade across, and climb back up.

Mr. Perkins and Daddy jumped in and assisted as we picked our way across the shallowest part. Everybody's shoes got soaked, but that wasn't so bad. That's what creek walkers were for anyway, and it cooled us off after hiking in jeans.

Before crossing, it didn't occur to us that we would have to climb back up the other side—dripping wet. The flooding had carved out a steep embankment roughly six feet high, so we needed to be creative about how we went back up. Looking around, I found a branch hanging down that could be used as a sort of "helper's arm" as we pulled ourselves up, but that only worked for the first two of us.

I managed to pull myself to dry, solid ground, as did Mrs. Perkins. After that, the grass was so wet from our shoes no one else could get a foothold. Finding another spot where everyone else could climb and land on open space proved a challenge.

Pansy finally crawled up the embankment in a narrow place free of trees. Jimmy followed her and managed to soak the entire area. He made it up, but that left Sasha, Natalie, Cliff, Mr. Perkins, and Daddy still down on the creek bed. Things were about to get interesting.

Cliff tried to get a foothold and climb up, so he could help from the top, but nothing doing; it was a mess.

"Why doesn't Natalie give it a try since she's the smallest and driest of us," Cliff said to Daddy and Mr. Perkins. "Then Sasha can give it a go, and you guys and I will bring up the rear."

Daddy and Mr. Perkins created a basket step for Natalie and hoisted her up the embankment. Sasha tried the same method, but he was too wet to boost without slipping.

"Okay, we're going to kind of swing you and toss you up, alright? You sort of jump and grab hold and then pull yourself up," said Mr. Perkins.

"I dunno, Dad. I'm not sure that'll work."

"Just give it a whirl. You can do it."

They gave the heave-ho, but Sasha's foot slipped at the last second. He met the muddy embankment with his chest and stomach, practically knocking the wind out of him. Pansy and I ended up each grabbing a hand and dragging him over the edge, but it worked. Six down, three to go.

Cliff decided a running leap might be worth a try seeing as how Sasha was now head-to-toe mud and grinning like an idiot as he waited to see who got it next. Cliff backed up a few steps and braced for a run. After his first step, he began choking and coughing and sputtering, doubling over and trying to catch his breath. He hocked a loogie into the creek and peeked up sheepishly.

"Sorry. Inhaled a mosquito." Everybody laughed; a common hazard to avoid out here.

On his second try, he did fine until stepping in the mud at the bottom of the wall. His intended launch ended as more of a flop, and he scrabbled his way up, grabbing grass and dirt and our hands when he could. He looked like a taller version of Sasha.

With only the dads left, and neither relishing a sludge bath, they discussed the situation further. Daddy glanced down the creek.

"Hey, Alex, why don't we go grab those boulders and bring them over here to use as a sort of step?"

Mr. Perkins leaned to look past Daddy. Down the creek bed lay several decent-sized boulders. They walked over and began testing to see what they could carry. Between the two of them, they managed to roll a boulder over to the base of the embankment and then lodge some smaller rocks under the back side so it would stay put. Then they took turns stepping on it and jumping up to the edge where they could hoist themselves over. It worked perfectly. Neither one got terribly dirty save for their hands and a bit on their pants.

As they turned to the trail, they noticed Sasha and Cliff staring at them.

"What?"

"Really?" Cliff and Sasha shook their heads.

Daddy and Mr. Perkins laughed like hyenas. "Sorry, boys. Sometimes it takes a few guinea pigs to find genius!" Daddy cackled.

At that, Sasha and Cliff stepped forward and gave them tight, muddy squeezes, covering them in yuck from chaps to nave. Turnabout was fair play, after all.

***

The trestle bridge marks the start of the journey back. It was the only way to go unless we retraced our steps. Having left a slippery mess in our wake, no one wanted to run that gauntlet again.

The most straightforward way up lay just this side of the bridge. It was steep and required secure footing if we could find it. By the time we got to the top, everyone stood bent over, sucking wind.

We caught our breath and looked over at our task. Maybe fifty yards across, but with an intense and dizzying drop, it was a challenge even if heights didn't bother you. Problem was, they *did* bother Mr. Perkins.

He did the hike with us every year, saying it was productive to face our fears. And every year, he regarded the bridge like he was about to lose his lunch. Maisy had shown him up last time by prancing across as if she was skipping down the sidewalk. He needed to redeem himself, and we couldn't wait to tell her if he turned chicken again.

It was a two-track line without much grace on either side. Not horrible if you stayed in the middle, but none of us would have advised looking down while walking, regardless. Most of us made it across without issue, but Mr. Perkins always had to psych himself up for the journey across the open-slatted ties. Everybody else waited patiently and pretended not to hear him as he muttered, "Oh-shit-oh-shit-oh-shit…" and minced his way across.

The walk back along the track was much quicker and entirely flat until we climbed back down the final hill behind the pavilion. It was a pleasant wind-down from all the exercise of the trek out. We arrived wet, filthy, exhausted, and grinning from ear to ear.

Mama and Mrs. Drummond feigned horror at our condition, especially that of the four mud runners, but then shook their heads and laughed. They had cleaned up most of the pavilion while we were gone, and everybody just needed a snack and something to drink before we packed up for home, another Hillman Park adventure in the books.

We'd managed several good stories for Maisy. The best part was that we'd get to do it again next year with her along.

Dear Maisy …

Onward

True to his word, Everett left Cilla and Nattie to their own devices to work things out. He stayed close and provided an ear when needed, but the work was theirs alone to be getting on with.

Cilla, tired of struggling with how to proceed, decided the best way to determine their path was simply to ask. Now that she had a chance to change things, ugly as that chance was, she wasn't about to pass it up. Courage in hand and stomach in her throat, she marched over to Nattie's, remembering to switch to a more gentle approach only as the door opened. It was going to take some practice.

It was Piper who answered.

"Hello, Cilla. How are you? Please, come in."

"Thank you. I'm well," she lied, stepping into the tiny foyer.

In fact, she felt like she might throw up. Alternating hot and cold, with her vision going fuzzy around the edges and sounds becoming muffled, she plunked down on the small pouf next to the shoe tree.

"Cilla! My goodness, are you alright?" Piper pushed her head down and told her to stay put while she fetched a glass of water. Upon her return, she graciously pretended not to realize it was nerves causing the trouble.

"I tell you, this heat is just beastly. It's a wonder we don't all shrivel up from dehydration. You must remember to drink enough water, Cilla."

It was a lovely gesture, and the water did help. Two big gulps, and it was gone.

"There. You'll be right as rain in a minute or two. Now, what can I do for you?"

Cilla sat straighter and took a deep breath, gathering what gumption she could muster.

"Well, I ... I thought maybe ... you see..."

Damn it! Why did her composure keep high-tailing it at the most inconvenient times? This babbling-like-an-idiot business was for the birds and made her feel like a fool—not that she needed any help in that department.

"Oh, hell! I need to ask Nattie if she wants to try to fix things or not. There. That's it. That's what I want to know. Just tell me straight so I can get on with it or not."

A ghost of a smile flashed across Piper's face. Poor Cilla looked like a child waiting on the punishment stool, bracing for consequences.

"Well, I'm sure Nattie would have a word with you either way, but today might not be the best time to ask."

"What? Why not?"

"She's having ... a bit of trouble this morning."

"Oh."

"You can still come in and visit if you'd like. I imagine she'd welcome the company."

"Even from me?" Cilla eyed Piper suspiciously, doubting her presence would make Nattie's bad day better.

"Maybe *especially* from you."

"How do you mean?"

Piper considered her for a moment.

"Come with me." She turned, calling, "Nattie, I'm going to step out for a second. I'll be right outside."

***

Piper put a hand on Cilla's arm, leading her out to sit on the front steps.

"Cilla, when patients like Nattie have an episode, depending on where they are in their illness, a few different things can happen. They often sense something is off but can't put their finger on what. Perhaps they're aware that they know a visitor but can't quite recall how or remember a name.

"On a good day, Nattie is very aware of what has passed between the two of you in recent years, as you saw at Mr. Coleman's house. And keep in mind, she did agree to meet you on that occasion, so she's not entirely opposed to reconciliation.

"However, on a tougher day like today, recalling that information may be quite difficult. Memories become jumbled and tangled. More recent ones tend to be the first to go, while older ones are more concrete. As the disease progresses, patients favor spending more and more time in the past. When they're experiencing that, reminiscing with someone they've known a long time can be calming and reassuring for them.

"Now, on a good day, Nattie may seem completely normal, and you might think she should be able to discuss things as she would have before she got sick. But even when she's capable of doing that, any upheaval of emotions could trigger anger or aggression, like at Mr. Coleman's.

"I know he spoke to you about the altered playing field here, but you need to understand it isn't black and white. It's not 'good day equals normal; bad day equals Froot Loops.' It's more fluid than that and can fluctuate at any time. It requires a good amount of grace, as well as letting a lot of things pass without mention."

"Like what?"

"Well, say Nattie tells you that Parker was here in April. We all know he visited near the end of June after her incident. But correcting her or reminding her of what happened would cause undue frustration and embarrassment. The error is of no consequence, so it's best just to let it go.

"Another example in your case would be arguing about something as you two work to repair things. You might really want to be right, but belaboring a point would be counterproductive. Nattie may or may not remember details on any given day, so you have to tread lightly, even when you think she's tracking just fine."

Cilla sat quietly, taking in all this new information. Piper watched for a moment before laying her hand on Cilla's knee.

"Listen, Cilla, I know what you're seeking here, and I truly hope you can find the kind of healing you need between the two of you. But you must be prepared to accept that Nattie might not be capable of giving you what you need the way you need it anymore."

"I don't know what to do."

"Why don't you come in for a little while and just chat. Keep things lighthearted and follow Nattie's lead. I'll be there to help, but you can get an idea of what an episode looks like and how she functions within them."

The women stepped back inside and joined Nattie in the living room. She was watching a gardening program about tropical plants native to Central America.

"Nattie, you have a visitor. Cilla is here to see you."

"Oh!" she said, looking up. "How nice."

Her speech was a little slower than usual. Not quite simple, yet with an air of apprehension about it; nearly childlike in that she seemed to give each word ever-so-slightly more thought than usual. It reminded Cilla of the hippies they used to see in the city, zenned out on who-knows-what.

The happy welcome felt both disconcerting and oddly comforting. They hadn't spoken to each other like that in years.

Piper nodded, encouraging her to sit. This living room had been witness to thousands of their chats. Still, Cilla was caught wrong-footed by the attitude that things were the same now.

"Hello, Nattie."

"Have you seen this program? I think I might give some of these a go in the garden next year."

Nothing in the show would stand a chance of overwintering in the harsh upper-Midwest winter. Emotions warred within Cilla's heart. On the one hand, such casual, friendly conversation is what she longed for. On the other, it was jarring and heartbreaking to watch Nattie's gears strip. She glanced at Piper, who nodded, indicating she should play along.

"Er, no, I haven't. I'd be glad to help you put them in next year, though." Again, she looked to Piper, seeking approval, which was granted in the form of raised eyebrows and pantomimed clapping.

"Orchids will look so lovely in the back, and I think passionflower will be just gorgeous on the trellis. I don't know why I haven't thought to do it before."

"Yes, it will look beautiful."

They chatted for another twenty minutes or so while the program played out—nothing heavy or of any importance. Once finished, Cilla politely excused herself, thanking both Nattie and Piper for a lovely chat. It was all she could do to not run to the door. By the time she reached home, her cheeks were wet with tears.

***

The shock of seeing her best friend in such a state made Cilla's head buzz with confusion. Nattie's eyes had revealed a childlike uncertainty that even Piper's frank warnings had left her grossly unprepared for. Accustomed as she was to Nattie's supreme capability during all their years as business partners, the incongruity with the person she had just witnessed seemed almost comical, save for its tragic magnitude.

Nattie suddenly appeared old, something that had never occurred to Cilla before. They were nearly the same age, after all, and she certainly felt like she had several good years left in her. But it was another implication staring her in the face that troubled her more: how on earth did one go about receiving forgiveness from someone unable to grant it?

If She Can Do It . . .

F ew things in life had gut-punched Cilla like the devastating realization of her error. Having now seen Nattie during an episode, it
was clear why she had been unwilling to share what had undoubtedly
been a terrifying shift when things had begun to go fuzzy.

Guilt heaved and threatened to flatten Cilla with the ferocity of a
prizefighter out for blood. The fact that her actions had been informed
by terrible, deep-seated personal trauma did nothing to assuage it. No
amount of creatively worded excuses or prettied-up caveats would buy
back the time they had lost. Nor would it replenish Nattie's capabilities
for the time they might have left.

Cilla's own experiences and coping mechanisms during her mother's
battles had been those of a desperate child. Engulfed in her own juve-
nile struggle with grief, and without assistance from her parents, she
hadn't had the skill set to process what anyone else was going through.
That the pain of abandonment should come rushing back nearly sixty
years hence and cause the end of her most treasured friendship seven
years ago was galling.

News of Maisy's accident had instantly refreshed her grief over Penny's
death; the two girls were inexplicably linked in her mind. This time, her
parental understanding of loss compounded things. It had taken nearly
a lifetime, but Cilla was finally beginning to understand the true ramifi-
cations of the childhood she had struggled to leave behind. She, too, was

swept off her feet in reaction to the idea that a small child might be so callously expunged from this earth.

But Maisy, it appeared, had other ideas and would not be so easily courted by death. She was a fighter. Though her injuries were severe, her spirit was not among them, and she continued to sass back at life's great challenges. Cilla was reminded of her own determination as a young girl of fourteen, carrying on in desperate challenge of fate, in part because Penny would never have the chance.

Through the processing of Maisy's accident, Cilla began to understand her own mother's grief. The realization that Sarah had been unwillingly crippled released the grip around Cilla's own throat, allowing her to breathe in new compassion toward her mother and the engulfing loss she had suffered. She, too, had been without support. They all had.

Suddenly, Cilla wanted nothing more than to forgive Sarah, to hug her and hold her. To let her cry the tears of anger and sadness and emptiness that no one had been willing to hear all those years ago. But time had passed, and so had Sarah. Still, there was work to be done. It occurred to Cilla that the one thing she could still do for her mother was to let the demons die.

It was ultimately Maisy, then, who unwittingly convinced Cilla that she, too, must fight. Fight for release, for freedom from the hurt and loneliness that had haunted her these last eight years. Fight for her friendship of more than thirty. She would look the demons in the eye and say, "No more." Her weapon of choice would not be harsh words this time but her heart. Not anger, but compassion. She would not bow to defeat but rise with hope and seek what she could salvage from the wreckage of pain. If a little girl of nearly six could do it, then, by God, so would she.

Heal Thyself

Over the course of many more visits, Cilla and Nattie found themselves walking when the days finally cooled off, talking, exploring, crying, nurturing, and healing. Piper was never far but allowed them the courtesy of space in which to find a rhythm again. As hard as Cilla had anticipated it being, the two women fell into familiar grooves quite quickly. While they had never agreed on everything—and still didn't—both craved the quenching cool of camaraderie over the heat and scorch of animosity. For Nattie, finally sharing her fears felt like settling into a squishy chair or warm bath after a long day. Her muscles and attitude relaxed. Her guard slowly came down.

When able, she would talk about the early days of her dementia. Describing the fear even helped her cope a bit, though it didn't change or ease what was coming.

"When Jack was dying, everything flipped upside-down," she said one day as they walked. "I'd watched you during Marlon's illness, and it petrified me. I didn't know how I'd live without my Jack.

"At first, when things started to disappear, I thought I was just tired and stressed. But the things that went missing weren't just 'where I'd set my coffee mug.' It was things I'd done hundreds, even thousands of times before that I should have known without even having to think about them. When other people began to notice, I knew it was more than stress. Whatever it was, I would have to deal with it without Jack."

"I can't imagine what that must have been like. But why didn't you tell me what was happening? I would have helped; you know that. We would have faced it together."

"I should have, I know." Nattie paused, looking embarrassed, and sighed.

"From the first time we spoke, even while uprooting your life to move to Pullman Station, you were confident, solid. Nothing ever made you flinch. You could stand up to people and just carry on when life threw things at you. It's something I've always admired and envied. I've never been good at asking for help, and I didn't want anyone to see how weak I felt, especially you. You'd dealt with Marlon's passing with such grace, and there I was, coming apart at the seams."

"Oh, Nattie!" Cilla grabbed her friend's hand and squeezed. "I've never had a choice. Life never asked how I felt about what happened when I was a girl. If I hadn't developed a thick skin, I imagine I would have just dissolved into nothingness. Fighting for myself was the only way I could survive. And I couldn't have made the move to Pullman without your help. As for Marlon, I suppose I just pushed it down. I'd gotten pretty good at that. But I'm just as scared as anybody on the inside."

Nattie smiled and leaned her head against Cilla's shoulder. Maybe they weren't so different after all.

***

Patience came more quickly than Cilla had expected. When Nattie was having a hard time, she found herself willing to support rather than judge, letting it be about Nattie instead of herself. They would reminisce and find comfortable pockets of events long past for Nattie to rest in. As is the case in most friendships, they exchanged occasional sharp words, yet the balm of healing was too soothing for anger to get a grip.

It was confusing, then, that Cilla still felt so much guilt. Much progress had been made in a very short time. Still, something was missing. She began keeping two diaries, one for herself and one chronicling their daily activities together to help Nattie keep track.

She looked forward to their time, but an apprehension began to creep in that she couldn't put her finger on. The more she ignored it, the worse it got, beginning to fester and ooze when she was alone in the quiet.

She often roamed the house, avoiding the heat outside, feeling an uneasiness under her skin. Sitting down at the kitchen table, she would deliberately try to find anger at her mother or overwhelm regarding Penny, anything familiar that would explain her restlessness.

But she had forgiven Sarah, truly, freely, and completely. The scars were there but had loosened and no longer restricted her movement. (As for her father, she had long since made peace with her choices there.) Likewise, she had forgiven Nattie. Slings and arrows from the recent past had lost their sting. Perhaps Maisy twanged her heartstrings, then, except her prognosis was good, and her doctors expected a complete recovery.

***

When the heat of the day had withdrawn enough to be tolerable, Cilla went for a walk. Knocking around inside the house left her vulnerable to fears that threatened to trap her in a moment of stillness, suffocating her with a thick, viscous atmosphere. Walking provided a steady rhythm she could get lost in as her thoughts tumbled like rocks in a polisher. They would still be rocks when she returned home, of course, but with luck, the edges wouldn't be as sharp.

The perfume of oriental lilies mixing with the tang of hot asphalt beginning to cool created an oddly reassuring bouquet on the warm breeze. Solid, practical, yet promising beauty even amongst the harsh, unforgiving surfaces of life. Two scents as polar as her emotions battling within. The sidewalk's concrete ensured a grounding for her soles as the heady wafts of lily acted like a salve on her battered heart.

The heat instructed a more leisurely pace, lest she fall victim to heatstroke. It felt good to move and have her heart beat harder for a reason other than panic, her blood at least stirring up the stagnant sludge weighing her down.

As always, the familiar waves of guilt washed over her as she replayed the last several years in her mind. She had said and done some horrible things, made all the worse because of Nattie's actual condition. Stuck as Cilla had been in the whirlpool of refreshed trauma, she'd instinctively flailed against it. Paddling like hell and becoming hysterical, she'd exhausted and angered herself in the struggle. Had she forced herself to calm, plunge into the truth below, and survive in the less turbulent, rescuing currents there, she would have been carried to safety, clear of mind, and able to provide aid to her best friend. Instinct had not worked in her favor.

The more she thought, the faster she walked, and she eventually found herself quite a ways from home. Still, she was far from done thinking, so the distance didn't bother her.

The remainder of her journey, however, would need to progress differently. Going 'round and 'round in eddies of guilt wasn't doing her any good, and it certainly wasn't solving any problems.

Practicality had always been her way of life. Never spend more than necessary. Never over-promise to get someone's business. Never buy a pair of shoes simply because they're pretty. Never waste time dwelling on what should have been. She had spent far too much time being practical in order to survive. So, why was she so damned emotional now? She needed to return to that cool-headedness so she could finally move forward completely.

Subconsciously, she was laying out the issues to Everett in her head. It was dark by the time she arrived home, but his light was on. She threw caution to the wind, headed to his house, and knocked on his door. Let people talk; it'd give them something to do as they lay awake in the heat, anyway.

The front door was wide open, the glass on the storm door raised to allow cooler night air to move throughout the house. Everett arrived at the threshold barefoot, in thin pajama pants and a tank-top undershirt. Seeing Cilla, concern immediately clouded his face.

"Cilla! It's late. What's happened? Is everything alright?"

"No. No, it's not, and I could use some wisdom from an old friend, Everett. My apologies for the hour. I've been out walking."

"*Now?* In the dark!?"

"Well, it wasn't dark the entire time. I began some time ago and am only finishing up now. I couldn't sit in my house any longer."

"Well, first things first, then—let's get you some water."

"Yes. Thank you. I hadn't intended to go quite so far."

Everett led her to the kitchen and filled a glass with ice and water. Turning, he handed it to Cilla and motioned to the table.

"So, what's on your mind, then?"

She drank, then sat quietly, tracing the beads of condensation as they ran down the outside of the glass.

"I don't know what to do."

"About...?"

"Nattie, of course."

"I thought you were already doing it."

"Well, yes, but this is different. I can't put my finger on it."

"Is she getting worse? Piper hasn't mentioned anything."

"No, no. Just ... something is missing. I don't know."

"Cilla, she isn't going to get better. It won't be like old times. You do know that."

"I know, I do, it's just ... I thought it would feel different."

"Different how, exactly?"

"I don't know ... freer, maybe. I realize she can't absolve me of things she may not remember, but I feel like it's not good enough, even though we've reconciled. I still feel terribly guilty."

Everett considered her, thinking.

"Cilla, you've been visiting Nattie a lot, right?"

"Yes."

"And you two have had words, as well as reminisced? Laughed and cried?"

"Yes."

"And Nattie has been welcoming when not agitated, correct? She doesn't bring up the things that happened?"

"*Yes*. Everett, please get to the point."

"My point is, Nattie's behaving in ways that indicate she's forgiven you and that she enjoys having you back in her life."

"Yes, I know. That's what's so frustrating." Cilla heaved a sigh. "I guess I just wish she could remember everything, and then I'd know that she truly wants to forgive me for *all* of it."

"Maybe it's not her you need to hear that from."

Cilla's eyes flashed to her old friend across the table.

"What do you mean?"

"Well, seems to me, Nattie's forgiven you entirely. But it appears you have yet to forgive yourself."

***

Everett's wisdom kept Cilla awake for a long time that night. It had never occurred to her that forgiveness could be—or needed to be—granted to oneself. She had worn it as a shield, a weapon protecting her heart. The world had hurt her so profoundly. She had viewed forgiveness as a thing to be clutched tightly, greedily withheld from others until such time when they had finally suffered enough, lest she give the impression that their crimes were of no importance. If she gave it away, she would be vulnerable, unprotected, weak.

She had always held herself to a higher standard, promised herself she would never hurt anyone the way she had been hurt. And yet, look what she had done. Not intentionally, of course, but it had happened anyway. Perhaps it was inevitable. After all, her mother hadn't intended to persecute her. Instead, she had been a victim of her circumstance. Nattie was the same. Fear had kept her from divulging that which was debilitating. Scorn had never been her intent.

Forgiving them both had lifted Cilla's soul in ways she had never imagined possible. Lowering her shield had lessened the pressure on her chest, and she could breathe again. Perhaps it was time to set it down entirely.

The Milk Pail

The following morning, Cilla and Nattie packed a picnic and headed to Boxcar Lake as they had done many times early in their friendship. Piper joined them, though Nattie didn't require her services just then.

Nattie was having a good day. Words and conversation came easily, and they relaxed in the cool shade of the big willows near the water. Red-winged blackbirds called from the reeds, their trills dancing over air currents bringing an earthy and pungent, yet not unpleasant, smell of decay and renewal from the shore.

The two older women sat in silence on a bench, watching the water and savoring what would too soon become the chill of autumn carrying woodsmoke on its wings. Piper lay nearby reading.

"Did I ever tell you about the time Russell and Carver dumped the milk pail?" Nattie asked.

"No, I don't think you did." Cilla turned, smirking and curious. She had met Nattie's siblings over the years, but all were quite a bit older. Russell and Carver were twins closest in age to her, though it was a wonder Nattie even came to be after they arrived. Once those two boys walked the earth, their parents having relations again seemed like a reckless tempting of fate.

"It's only that sitting under this tree reminds me of that day. I haven't thought of it in ages."

"How old were they?"

Nattie snorted. "Old enough to know better. I don't think I'd ever seen Pa that angry. Scared me half to death."

She stared off, giggling.

"Well, go on then!" Cilla prodded. "Don't dangle that dastardly duo's antics in front of me all day."

"Oh! Yes, well…"

Nattie settled herself and leaned back, closing her eyes.

"Now, let's see. I must've been about six years old, so that would've put the boys around eleven or twelve, I suppose."

Cilla watched her best friend bask in the freedom of lucidity. It was bittersweet. These moments would become fewer and farther between until they disappeared altogether, along with the woman Cilla knew almost better than herself. There was no telling how much time was left; it could be months, it could be years. Pray, God, it was the latter.

"I had my chores, of course, but the boys always thought Pa favored me. They'd get prickly and start teasing whenever they saw me sitting under the big willow while they worked. 'Poor baby Natasha can't do anything herself,' they'd say. Probably why I've always found asking for help so difficult. But I loved it under that tree. Pa hung a rope with a piece of wood for a seat, and I would spend hours sitting or swinging, thinking up all sorts of stories about the creatures around me.

"Mother had me in the kitchen with her and Elenore whenever it was time to make butter or jam but, other than that, I always finished my chores early. I made my bed, swept the front porch, and changed out flowers on the table every day. Mother always wanted her flowers. She said a happy kitchen made for a productive one.

"Mother didn't want me underfoot, though, and as soon as I finished my work, she'd shoo me outdoors with Jip, our old hound. He had a special spot in the dirt by the willow to keep me company."

Nattie stared off again, a wistful smile spread across her face.

"Why, it's been forever and a day since I've thought of old Jip."

"He sounds like a boon companion."

"He was that. I reckon he knew every secret in my heart." Nattie sighed.

"Pa was a blacksmith, you know, and shared the old homestead with his younger brother, Brian, who ran the dairy farm. Pa and Allen, my oldest brother—you'll remember him—"

"Fondly."

"—they worked in the shop, and Owen—he was after Elenore, of course—and the twins helped Uncle Brian with the milking when they weren't attending school. Brian never married and didn't have sons of his own, and it was more economical for him to utilize the boys in the summer.

"Anyway, Mr. Finch came by with the creamery truck every morning and evening. Uncle Brian was quite particular about keeping track of volume and prices. His ledger was neat as a pin, and you could ask him any day, and he'd know exactly how much each milking had produced and what milk was fetching.

"Course, the Great War had a significant impact on milk prices, and Pa was severe in his lectures that not a drop go to waste. 'Liquid gold,' he called it. The smell of a dairy farm was always the smell of money to him, though his own passions lay in metalwork.

"I don't know what all got into Russell and Carver that day. They'd recite Pa's lectures word for word on the way out to the barn, shaking their fingers at each other and trying to make their voices deep. But, Lord help 'em, when the devil got hold of one, the other was always in the soup with him, sure as water's wet.

"See, when Jip would hear Mr. Finch's truck coming along the road by the back pasture, he'd get to bellering something awful. The boys couldn't hear the truck in the barn, but they could sure hear him, and they knew they had just about two minutes to get the milk cans out to the yard.

"Owen said Russell and Carver were goofing instead of milking that day, and he'd had to get on 'em a fistful of times. There were still pails to dump when Jip started in, and the cans weren't ready. While Russell and Carver got to dumping, Owen got to hauling cans. He told Pa later that he could hear them laughing all the way out in the yard while they scrambled.

"Mr. Finch gave the horn a squeeze to announce himself. Must've been a habit as it was clear everybody at the farm knew when he was coming down the road. Anyway, I watched him pull in and then turned to watch Owen head back for the last of the cans. That's when Russell and Carver shot out the barn and into the field like their trousers were on fire. A few seconds later, Owen shot back out, too, only he was making more noise than Jip.

"The last big pail of milk had spilled all over the floor, and poor Owen was left the task of telling Uncle Brian, Pa, and Mr. Finch. He was in a heap of trouble, being in charge of the twins while they milked. Pa came charging out of his workshop to see what had happened. My land, Owen turned about eight shades of puce before getting the news out.

"As you well know, my Pa was a good man."

"Kind to a fault and gentle as can be," Cilla informed Piper, who was now sitting on the blanket, listening.

"Still, there wasn't anything worse than knowing you'd disappointed him. Not because he'd get violent, of course. Though, Lord knows it might've knocked some sense into those two idiots. It was the silence. Sitting in the quiet with the disappointment nearly killed a body, and Pa knew it. He expected us all to do our best, and wasting milk was far from it.

"We didn't see the twins again until they tried to sneak back into the house for bed. They missed evening milking, which caused a load more trouble and double duty for everyone else, not to mention holding up Mr. Finch's route.

"Well, I think Pa was too angry to deal with them that night, so Mother told them to wash and get to bed. Elenore told me later that Owen and Allen nearly turned themselves inside-out, holding their tongues against complaining there was no punishment. Didn't matter, though, because the next morning, the hammer came down.

"When the boys showed up for breakfast, both Pa and Uncle Brian were still at the table. They'd shooed Allen, Elenore, and Owen out. I expect those three would've given their eye teeth to stick around. I was listening through the pantry door, and Mother was at the sink pretending to wash dishes.

"The twins looked scared stiff and shuffled to the table with their heads down. They didn't dare look at an adult, poor fools. It was so quiet you could've heard a pin drop, and Pa just let 'em hang for a spell. When he finally spoke, I had to press my face right up to the crack to hear him.

"'Well?' he asked. 'What have you got to say for yourselves?' The boys mumbled something or other, and Pa got quiet again. 'You're to be Brian's sons for the next week,' he finally said. 'You'll do anything and everything he asks without complaint to make up for the lost milk. After that, you'll be Allen and Owen's for a week. That's on top of the milking, mind. You created a lot of work for all of us last night.'

"Land sakes! Their eyes got big as saucers, but they didn't say a word other than 'Yes, sir.' Uncle Brian got up, and they followed him out, and that was that.

"I tell you, I never saw two boys work so hard as they were made to for the next couple of weeks. Uncle Brian was hard on them, but Allen and

Owen nearly killed 'em. They were even too tired to pester me, but they never spilled the milk again."

"Did they ever say what happened?" Cilla asked.

"Not a word. Owen said he knew, but I doubt it. He just wanted to sound important to Pa. Russell and Carver were like an old Ironclad when it came to presenting a united front. Wasn't a person alive could ever land a punch hard enough to make either one rat the other out."

The three women sat smiling and thinking.

"Nattie," Cilla said after a while, "what would you think about us writing that story down?"

"What for?"

"Well, lots of reasons, I suppose. It might be good to have on hand when you're having a hard day. To be honest, I've been keeping a diary of sorts recently about our time together. I got the idea from the journal the kids are making for Maisy. I've been having a think, and, well, it might be nice for Parker and his family to have some stories from your life written down before you can't recall them anymore."

Nattie looked down at her hands, picking at her cuticles. Her lips moved in and out as if she wanted to speak, but nothing came out. Cilla was immediately contrite.

"I'm so sorry, Nattie. If I've overstepped, please forgive me."

Nattie looked up then, eyes moist, and put a hand on Cilla's.

"I think that would be just fine," she whispered, nodding and squeezing her old friend's fingers hard. "Thank you."

***

It became routine, then, for Nattie and Cilla to visit the willows at Boxcar Lake. On days when Nattie was doing well, she would share stories from years gone by, and on days when she was lost within, Cilla would often pull out a story to soothe her and give her familiar ground in which to sink her feet. Unbeknownst to both, it was the beginning of a legacy that would reach far beyond the two of them.

Voodoo Dolls

August 1985

Maisy was to be discharged on a Tuesday. Mr. and Mrs. Drummond were looking forward to having their whole family under one roof again. Even Cliff would be home, having enrolled in engineering classes at the community college in the city.

The City Council had long been planning to hold a *Welcome Home* event for Maisy, complete with fireworks to replace those she had missed on the night of her accident. Once her discharge date was set, the council scheduled a party for two weekends later and got to work. Dicky Hickam, Treasurer, and Margaret Chisholm, Secretary, headed up the effort.

Pullman Station being such a small town, many people wanted to help in some way. Volunteers from St. Mary's and First Congregational quickly put together a silent auction to be held the night of the party. All proceeds would go to the family to help cover medical costs. Businesses donated generously to the items up for grabs.

Restaurants in town organized all the food, and Marta Heughan, a piano teacher who lived down our block, and her husband, Rusty, rounded up a couple of bands to play.

The local Clown Club volunteered their face painting and balloon animal services, as well. Everyone was glad that what began as every parent's worst nightmare had reversed course and was now going to have a happy outcome.

***

When Maisy learned she would be headed home in a few weeks, she became quiet and withdrawn, actually causing concern. She eventually confided to Garrett that Freckle had never been to her house and didn't know where she lived. It was still strange for us to hear that Maisy loved a dog, real or otherwise.

While not active in Cilla's personal reparations, Mama was keeping her abreast of Maisy's recovery. During one of their conversations, Mama mentioned that Maisy would be home in a few weeks. While relieved by the news, Maisy's concerns over Freckle troubled Cilla. The next evening, she made the trip 'round to the other side of the block for the first time in years.

***

The Drummonds' front door held a large brass knocker, which Cilla employed. Unsure whether her idea would be met with enthusiasm or scorn, she fidgeted. Thankfully, Mr. Drummond opened the door, and she didn't have to explain herself to one of the children.

"Well, hello!" he said, momentarily caught off guard.

"Hello, Max. I apologize for not calling first. I wonder if you might have a moment. There is something I'd like to run past you for approval."

Thirty minutes later, Cilla left the Drummonds' with a spring in her step. She'd been right to take a chance, and for the first time in what felt like forever, she knew exactly what to do. She marched home, grinning the whole way.

***

Cilla visiting the Drummond house was immediate news, of course. The following morning, Jimmy and the twins came hurtling over the fence, tripping up to our back door to spill the beans. The fact that they didn't know why she had visited made the story that much juicier, and we spent our day coming up with all sorts of wild theories.

It wasn't until a couple of days later, however, that things got a bit out of hand. The scene played out very much like earlier in the week, except in slow motion. All three of my fellow conspiracy theorists cleared the back fence, looking horrified. Clearly, there was more news.

This time, Jimmy held a bag out in front of himself, and the three of them were eying it like it contained Medusa's head. I met them at the door but didn't allow them inside. No way something nasty was coming into my house.

I stepped out, now staring at the bag as hard as my friends.

"What is it?" I asked, keeping my distance. I couldn't smell anything unusual but didn't want to get close enough for a good sniff, either.

"Part of Maisy's blankey." Natalie squinched up her face as if it hurt to say the words.

"Maisy's blankey?"

"Yep." Jimmy stared at me, the bag still held out in front of him.

"What's it in there for? Why isn't it with Maisy?"

Horrible thoughts raced to my mind. I'd given voice to a question for which I wasn't sure I wanted an answer. Sasha spoke with the seriousness of an FBI agent, drilling his eyes into me, waiting for a reaction.

"Mr. Drummond's making Jimmy give it to Cilla."

"What!? Why?"

"Dunno."

I had to hand it to them. If they were pulling my leg, they were playing it flawlessly. I didn't think they'd joke about Maisy, though, especially Jimmy; she was off-limits.

I struck out for the fence, gesturing for my friends to follow. Once over it, we all crouched on Mr. Coleman's side, staring at the bag sitting in the grass in front of us.

"What do you think?" Natalie asked me.

"I dunno." I looked at Jimmy. "What did your dad say?"

"Just to give it to Cilla."

"And you're sure that's what's in there?"

"Cross my heart and hope to die."

"It's creepy, isn't it?" Even Sasha, who loved a good horror flick, was feeling the crawlies.

"Yeah. Are you gonna do it?" I eyeballed Jimmy doubtfully. Chances were pretty good that he'd pass out way before he got to Cilla's front walk, and there was no way he'd ring the doorbell.

"Hafta. Dad already said."

"Can you leave it on her porch?"

"Nuh-uh. Gotta ring the doorbell and hand it to her. No ditching allowed." Poor Jimmy stared at the bag as if it were going to explode.

"We'll go with you."

"What!? OW!" Sasha rubbed his arm where Natalie had backhanded him.

"Of course we will." I glared at Sasha, silently daring him to chicken out.

"Why can't you do it for him, Annabelle? You go over there all the time."

"Because Maisy's not my sister and, no, I don't. Mama does."

"I think I'm gonna throw up," Jimmy said to no one in particular.

"No, you're not," I continued. "You're going to stand up, and we're going to get this over with. Then we can all go to the pool and forget about it."

"But what if she's making a voodoo doll or something?"

"Jimmy. Would your dad give Maisy's blankey to Cilla Prescott if he thought she was going to make a voodoo doll out of it? Cilla's been weird lately. Maybe she's trying to do something nice for a change. Yeah, it's creepy, but I think we've gotta trust your dad on this one."

"Fine. But I want it on the record that I did not agree with this."

"Done. Now, let's go."

***

We marched over to Cilla's and stopped on her front porch. Well, Natalie, Jimmy, and I did. Sasha stopped at the bottom of the first step. Jimmy, sweating buckets, stared bug-eyed at the door. Eventually, I reached over and rang the bell. A small squeak escaped Jimmy's throat, and Natalie rolled her eyes. Cilla opened the door and smiled.

"Well, hello, children! This must be what Mr. Drummond and I discussed."

Jimmy didn't move. Or speak. Or look at Cilla. Her smile faded a bit as she stepped out and took the bag from him. He squeaked again.

"Well, yes, thank you!" She smiled once more and scanned all four of us in turn. Sasha smeared a toothless grin across his face, gave her a chin-up nod, and waved from his position in the next county. Natalie smiled shyly.

"You're welcome, Mrs. Prescott." I began moving away, then stepped back toward the door and nudged Jimmy. He turned tail and ran down the steps, back over to my house.

"Tell Mr. Drummond I said thank you, won't you?"

"Sure thing!" Sasha hollered and then burned rubber to join Jimmy.

Idiots.

Discharged

On Sunday afternoon, Natalie, Sasha, and I headed over to the Drummond house to help prep for Maisy's return. They decided to move her bedroom down to the den, so she didn't have to do a lot of stairs every day. She was getting stronger, but the last thing they needed was for her to take a tumble.

We spent the afternoon moving furniture, cleaning, making everything cozy, and ensuring her favorite things sat within reach in her new space. Then we made adjustments to the living room so she could do her schoolwork on the couch and lay down comfortably if she got sleepy and needed to rest.

It was exciting to get everything ready, and the atmosphere buzzed. None of us could believe she was finally coming home. Summer was over. It had been so long since she'd tagged along, our cadence had changed. It would be nice to get back into the old rhythm, though it would be slower than before.

While we helped at the Drummonds', Mama, Mrs. Perkins, Mrs. Chisholm, and Mrs. Hickam spent the afternoon in the kitchen of St. Mary's church basement making more freezer meals to replenish the stock at the Drummond house. Maisy would still require therapy and need extra help for a while, so they made full dinners and wrapped a lot of single-portions. The kids would be able to grab them as necessary to take the pressure off Mrs. Drummond. They also made several casseroles to toss in the oven for a no-mess dinner that would yield leftovers for lunches the next day. By the time they finished, the freezer was full again.

***

September 10, 1985

Maisy came home on Tuesday, as planned. A long day filled with paperwork and instructions, the transition exhausted her. By the time we got home from school, she had passed out in the living room.

It felt great to have her home again. Granted, she looked a little different than before, a bit skinnier, and her hair was a little patchy in places where they had drilled or shaved. Still, if you tried hard, you could almost pretend she hadn't ever left.

Of course, it wasn't lost on any of us that seeing her there was a blessing, and tears threatened, but none of us cared about showing our emotions anymore. She had been lucky, still a strange thing to think considering all she'd been through. Lucky was for four-leaf clovers and catching a fly ball at a baseball game. Not for horrible accidents and terrible injuries. But she might not have been there at all if things had gone differently, so lucky it was.

***

Over the next week and a half, Maisy got stronger and more comfortable in her surroundings. With ongoing therapy, her walking continued to even out, and she could be on her feet longer. She started to get downright cranky, which the doctors saw as a good sign. She wanted to run with us big kids and missed Freckle terribly. There wasn't much we could do about either of those things.

No one understood how the whole Freckle thing worked. She obviously wasn't real but had been an enormous comfort to Maisy, nonetheless. Maisy certainly considered her to be the real thing. The doctors figured her brain had created Freckle as a way of helping her cope with trauma too difficult to process. It sort of erased the things she wouldn't be able to deal with and replaced them with something palatable. They predicted she would eventually move on once she got used to her surroundings at home again.

The doctors were *wrong*; I'll tell you that for free! No amount of distraction or consoling diverted Maisy's attention away from that dog. Mr. and Mrs. Drummond didn't seem to think too much of it, but it started to drive the rest of us nuts. For Pete's sake, she'd been terrified of dogs before! Now, she wanted nothing more in the world than to go back to the hospital to see Freckle.

Mr. and Mrs. Drummond finally relented, promising her they would go back and visit the Sunday after her Welcome Home party. None of us could figure out how that would make things any better.

Fireworks

Maisy's Welcome Home party began at 6:00 p.m. Saturday, with a picnic-style barbecue and silent auction. After dinner, everyone roamed around, visiting the various booths, bidding on items, listening to the live music, getting their faces painted and balloon animals made, and setting up their spots for the fireworks.

At 9:00 p.m., the sky would light up in celebration. The City Council reserved a special spot on the fishing pier for the Drummonds to ensure a clear view and a different feel for Maisy from the last time.

At about 6:15, the Drummond family arrived by firetruck with Mac and Jeannie, the paramedic team who'd taken care of Maisy. After depositing her at the head table and getting her settled, the paramedics returned to the truck. Kids got to walk through and see the inside. No lights or sirens, but they all loved it anyway.

It was a pleasant mid-September evening to stroll the lakeshore. The bugs weren't as bad as in June—gosh, months ago! —and the breeze was still warm enough for us to be in shirtsleeves. Thankfully, no one brought any dogs this time, by specific decree of the planning committee.

At 7:30, the Drummond family gathered at the fishing pier, and Dicky Hickam came over the public address system asking for people to gather around.

"Now, everyone here tonight feels just terrible about what happened earlier this summer during Pullman Days. Everybody's been prayin' six ways from Tuesday for a healthy recovery for young Maisy, here. We on the City Council wanted to do something to help make things easier for the family.

"As many of you know, we've been doing a little collection over the last couple of months, taking donations at businesses downtown and in the churches. And so, I'd like to present Mr. and Mrs. Drummond with a check in the amount of eleven thousand, fifty-three dollars, and seventy-one cents."

The crowd cheered as Mr. and Mrs. Drummond stepped forward, disbelief evident on their faces.

"What on earth?" Mrs. Drummond started, her hand going to her mouth as Mr. Drummond accepted the check. Mr. Drummond looked out at everyone and tried to speak but stopped. He stared at the paper in his hands and back at the crowd, only able to nod in gratitude. Mrs. Drummond said thank you to Dicky and nearly suffocated him with a hug.

"And now," said Dicky, "there's a young man here who would like a word."

Garrett stepped to the microphone and cleared his throat.

"Hi, Garrett!" Maisy shouted. A chuckle spread through the crowd.

"Hiya, squirt," Garrett began. "All the folks at the Pullman pool felt bad that you couldn't be there this summer, and we wanted to do something for you. So, we started a penny collection at the concession stand.

"You guys probably noticed that kids have been bringing their pennies all summer," he said to Jimmy and Pansy. "We ended up with enough to buy a family pass for you next year along with a bunch of vouchers for snacks. It's not much, but it's from everybody that used the pool this year." He reached down and gave the envelope to Maisy, then gave her a squeeze.

"I love you, Garrett!" she said, beaming at him.

"I love you, too, squirt!"

Finally, Mrs. Chisholm stepped up. This time, Natalie, Sasha, Jimmy, and I all grinned. We knew about this one.

"This summer, I had the pleasure of working with the City Council on a wonderful new philanthropic effort. The Pullman Station Public Library is pleased to present the very first Maisy's Courage Award to Ms. Maisy Drummond for displaying heroic courage in the face of adversity.

"This award, to be presented annually, provides the recipient with seventy-five dollars worth of new books for themselves and seventy-five for their classroom, as well as an additional two hundred and fifty dollars for their class to choose books to be given to the children's wards at Pullman Memorial Hospital and St. Michael's Hospital in the city.

"Maisy, we are so proud of you for your courage and the joy you spread everywhere you go. We missed your smiling face at Children's Hour this summer and can't wait to have you back again."

Mrs. Chisholm presented Maisy with the newly minted award. We all knew which books she would be ordering for herself. She grinned up at Mrs. Chisholm, thrilled by the prospect of so many new stories and being able to deliver books to the kids in the hospitals. Everyone else delighted in her enthusiasm and the fact that she had no idea how genuinely courageous she had been.

As the brief ceremony drew to a close and people settled in to wait for dusk to pass, a murmur rolled through the crowd. Heads began to turn, and a few people gasped. Coming out of the pavilion toward the lake was Cilla Prescott. On her right arm was Nattie Dennings, being gently led to a blanket and chair. Behind them, Piper followed at a distance.

It had been years since anyone had seen these two women together at an event without sparks shooting from their eyes and a good distance between them. Cilla glanced up and saw everyone staring. She quickly waved her hand in a shooing motion.

"Oh, pooh! Haven't you all ever seen two old ladies before?" She tried to hide how pleased she was and failed miserably. People began to smile and remark to each other, and eventually, a round of applause broke out. Cilla ducked her head bashfully and waved them off again.

"Now, go on and settle yourselves. We've got fireworks to watch and a little girl to celebrate."

"Used to be you two were the fireworks!" someone hollered, and everyone fluttered with laughter.

"Well, not anymore!" Cilla beamed and helped Nattie into her chair. Then she pulled out some oatmeal cookies and a thermos of lemonade, and they settled in for the show.

An Unexpected Gift

Sunday morning, Maisy woke bright and early, ready to see Freckle. She didn't want to go to church first, but her parents insisted. There was a lot to be thankful for, and the time had come to get back to attending services.

The Drummonds had invited the neighbors over for a quick informal lunch afterward as a small thank you for everything we had done for them during Maisy's time in the hospital. Maisy fidgeted with impatience at being detained from her date, but she did need to eat.

***

Mama, Daddy, and I arrived as the Perkinses walked over, and everyone gathered in the backyard, bypassing the house interior. The picnic table was set with a cheery tablecloth, buns, pickles, olives, chips, and a meat and cheese tray from the Piggly Wiggly. A large plastic jug of lemonade sat at the end of the table, along with plates, silverware, napkins, and cups.

"Hi guys," said Mr. Drummond. "I believe we're waiting on a few more guests before we can bless this mess and eat."

Just then, Cilla walked around the back of the house with Nattie and Piper in tow. Mr. Coleman brought up the rear. In his hands, he held a large, beautifully wrapped box with a bow on top.

"Well, hello! We're so glad you could make it!" Mrs. Drummond said. "Maisy, can you say hello to Mrs. Prescott and Mr. Coleman, and Mrs. Dennings and Piper?"

Maisy waved shyly, tucked in close to her mother's hip. Cilla took the box from Mr. Coleman, walked over, and set it on a chair in front of her.

Jimmy started forward, instantly defensive of his sister, even if he was headed toward Cilla Prescott. Mr. Drummond held out his arm to stop him.

"Hello, Maisy." Cilla smiled a smile that appeared genuine.

My eyes met Natalie's.

"I think I found something of yours at my house," Cilla continued. "I'd like to return it to you if that's alright."

Maisy peered up at her mother, who nodded. Maisy, likewise, nodded shyly to Cilla.

"Go ahead; open it," Mr. Coleman grinned mischievously.

Maisy looked at him and stepped forward carefully, putting her hands on the box. She looked up at Cilla again, just to make sure.

"You can pull the top right off if you'd like."

Maisy glanced at her mother and then at the box again. Gently grasping the sides, she lifted the lid. Her eyes got huge, and her face broke out in a brilliant grin.

"Freckle!"

Inside the box sat a tiny puppy, white with tan and gray spots and shaking to beat the band. Completely out of character, Maisy reached for the creature, and Mrs. Drummond helped her pick it up. The little pup sniffed her, licked her chin, and snuggled in, immediately soothed.

"She remembers me, Mama!" Maisy grinned from ear to ear while the rest of us tried to understand what we were seeing. Cilla retrieved Maisy's partial blankey from inside the box and laid it on the puppy. Everything finally made sense.

"Some voodoo doll, huh?" I nudged Natalie, and we giggled.

Maisy sat in a chair with Freckle, and we all gathered around, reaching out to pet the adorable fluffball. She was a Miniature Schnauzer, sweet as can be and more precious than anything we had ever seen.

Mama walked over to Cilla and smiled, putting her hand on the older woman's back.

"Well done, Cilla. How ever did you keep that a secret?"

"Well, Dicky Hickam helped. We have a mutual acquaintance from several years back who is a breeder. I made a few calls, and it fell into place. The pup has been staying at Dicky's house since Everett and I picked her up a couple of weeks ago. She's had Maisy's blanket to sleep with and imprint on, so she would recognize her right away."

"You clever old girl, you," Mama grinned. "I think that might be the sweetest thing I've ever seen anybody do for another person." Cilla flushed, the compliment a balm for her soul.

"Thank you, Susan. I may be a bit out of practice, but I hope to keep remembering how it's done. I owe that little girl more than you know."

Hello, Again

June 2005

The air was changing as we left the interstate and headed into Pullman Station. We passed Dicky Hickam's, now a hardware store and service shop run by Jamie and his son, Mason. Many of the houses, which now have new owners, had been painted or sided in different colors over the years. The evening scents of earth cooling, recently cut grass, and imminent dew settling in the valley tell me I'm home.

Turning onto Maple Street, I noticed Mama and Daddy's yard contributed to the cut-grass bouquet. It's neat and tidy, and the house looked the same as it always has. Nattie's house is still to the left, though it's been years since she passed, and the new owners have made it their own. Cilla's house still sits on the right and, from the outside, there is no difference from our last visit.

Daddy was chatting with Noah Prescott and Parker Dennings in the yard, and Teeny's husband, Marshall, made his way across the lawn to join them. There is much to do, but no one seems rushed this summer evening. After all, it's not as if tomorrow hasn't been expected and planned for some time now. Nearly everything is prepped.

Parker pointed to the car as we pulled in the drive, and Daddy turned to look, a big smile lighting his face. Grace and William spilled out and ran to him, grateful for "Papa" hugs and a good leg stretch. Mark and I followed, equally as happy to see everyone. We joined the little group, instantly enveloped in kinship.

The kids and I went off in search of Mama inside Cilla's house. We found her in the kitchen with Teeny, along with Noah's wife, Gretchen, and Parker's wife, Sam. Again, hugs were shared, though with slightly longer holds and a few extra squeezes for Teeny. Losing one's mother is something every woman dreads, no matter her age.

After snuggles, Mama handed Grace and William each a canning jar, telling them she'd be out shortly. They ran out the back door, eager to catch lightning bugs before bedtime. We watched them go, Teeny and I each remembering our own times in these yards.

"So," I squeezed Teeny's arm. "How are things?"

"Oh, you know how it is," Teeny waved. "Not unexpected, but not much fun, either. Still, it was time."

"Ninety-three. Who would have ever thought!?" Gretchen asked.

"Not us, back when Marlon and Jack passed, and then Nattie got sick," said Mama. "There was a time I wasn't sure her heart could take any more."

"She's certainly been through more than anyone else I've ever known." This from Sam. "To think of all that sadness, all that loss. By herself, no less. And then to pick herself up for the umpteenth time, at her age, and start again ... *again*."

"When Nattie passed so soon after they'd patched things up, I wasn't sure what would happen." Mama turned to me. "They had, what? Two years? Two-and-a-half?"

"About that," I said. "Thank God for Mr. Coleman."

"That man is a saint here on earth," said Teeny. "It's a wonder he never remarried. Though I'll tell you, I suspect he had a lady friend he visited in the city for quite a few years."

"Not that we would ever have known!" laughed Mama. "He's like Fort Knox to this very day. But I do hope he's had someone to share things with."

Mama looked out back. "Okay, I'm going to go play with the kids for a few minutes. Annabelle, we'll meet you at home."

"Thanks, Mama."

***

I chatted with Teeny, Gretchen, and Sam a bit longer and then moseyed home, snagging Mark on the way. Morning would come soon enough and, with it, goodbyes, hellos, and a reunion many years in the making.

Goodbye, Old Friend

C illa and Nattie had, indeed, had about two-and-a-half years together after their reconciliation. Cilla once again became Nattie's constant companion, helping, doing, steadying, and comforting in her times of need. It seemed to bring a new youth to Cilla herself.

As for the rest of Pullman Station's citizenry, it took some time, but many people were willing to give both women another chance, especially after they learned the reason for Nattie's behavior and how Cilla was taking care of her. It would prove only the beginning of a new and embracing relationship between the former Town Nasties and the community itself.

***

A few months after Maisy came home, Cilla reached out to Mrs. Chisholm to help increase funding for the Maisy's Courage Award. It had touched her deeply, and she felt it was a way she could honor both Maisy and Penny. It wasn't the only program on her mind, however.

The seeds of a new venture had been germinating ever since she had first seen Nattie during what she finally understood to be an episode. The new program was entitled the *Friends of Individuals and Elderly Living with Dementia Project*—the *FIELD Project* for short. It was run through the adult library and began as a small group of older folks willing to spend time with their less-abled peers, listening to their stories and writing them down to preserve for generations to come as well as creating soft places for the memory-holders to land when things got difficult.

The work gave Cilla a new purpose and vigor. She felt useful, needed, and productive. For the first time in her life, she wasn't worried about what the future held. Her biggest concerns were making sure her friend enjoyed what time remained and providing a way for the stories of the Greatest Generation—her generation—to be preserved and studied. The first stories completed for the *FIELD Project* were hers and Nattie's.

The program eventually spread to include several nursing homes in the city, as well as other care programs. It was frequently employed as a tool to soothe those whose more recent memories had become fuzzy or incomplete as dementia slowly worked its way backward in time and eroded their past.

Many story sets had been made into books that were now available to the public via the adult library, while others were added to compilations containing stories from several people. The schools in Pullman Station and the city used many of them in history classes as first-hand accounts of the early part of the twentieth century.

It wasn't quick work writing down a lifetime of memories, but it was beautiful work. Nattie remembered things from her childhood that Cilla had never witnessed, and Cilla was able to help her with anecdotes from her middle years and more recently. Those were the ones most likely to have fuzzy or missing pieces. Of course, some days were a wealth of information, while others were nothing but white space.

It was a collaboration then and a labor of love. Many townsfolk awaited their stories eagerly, wanting to know the scuttlebutt. Still, curiosity quickly turned to compassion as they discovered what the two women had lived through in their younger years, particularly Cilla.

Over time, Cilla's nagging feeling of something missing dissolved. Perhaps it was giving back that proved a balm to her soul, or maybe it was taking stock of exactly what she'd been through and allowing herself some grace. Either way, she enjoyed being back on solid ground.

***

One especially cold February evening in 1988, Nattie and Cilla sat watching *Wheel of Fortune* after dinner, as had become their practice. Piper listened from the kitchen as she cleared up. Nattie was no longer able to play with any skill or attention, but she liked the familiarity of the routine and watching the wheel and Vanna's dresses spin around.

The puzzle that evening was a Before & After, Cilla's favorite kind. The letters E, A, and C had been called, and she solved it without a doubt.

_ E A C _ C _ _ _ _ E _ ' _ _ E _ C _

"Well, now, there's an oldie but goody, wouldn't you say? I wonder how many peach cobblers I've made over the years; most of Teeny's birthday cakes for a start. She never liked cake. Still doesn't, in fact. Must have gotten that from Marlon's side."

Nattie stayed quiet, as had become customary as more and more of her mind went missing.

"I'd like to buy an 'O', please," called the contestant on the TV.

"Call a 'B,' you boob! It's PEACH COBBLER'S BENCH. Stop wasting good money! What a twit, don't you agree, Nattie?"

Still, Nattie remained silent.

"Can I get you a blanket, honey? You look cold sitting there, and that wind outside is ferocious."

But a blanket would no longer help Nattie. Where she was, it was warm and sunny, and she embraced Jack and her mother and father and Jip, whom she had missed for so very long.

Realizing this, Cilla sat looking at her friend. A tiny sob escaped her lips.

"Oh, Nattie," she whispered. "How I will miss you, dear friend, how I will miss you. Say hello to my sweet Marlon for me."

Last Man Standing

June 2005

Today's the day. Cilla left instructions that she was to be cremated, and not a lot of fuss made, but that isn't about to keep people away.

Daddy, Mark, and Parker have been moving picnic tables into the backyards. Mr. Coleman had the red board fence removed after Maisy came home from the hospital all those years ago, lest she climb it and risk further injury. The chain link between Mama and Daddy's house and Cilla's came down just a few years ago to make it easier for Daddy to cut Cilla's lawn while he was cutting his own. As such, the three yards make for a lovely park-like area with lots of room for a party.

Mr. and Mrs. Perkins are heading up the catering and potluck efforts with Mr. and Mrs. Drummond. All four have been running back and forth all morning, doing a final checklist of who has what in which refrigerator, accepting drop-off items, and getting the sloppy joe meat and pulled pork started in several crockpots.

Mama's in charge of buns, drinks, cups, cutlery, paper plates, and napkins, while the kids and I have been tasked with making sure there is plenty for little ones to do later while adults chat. We set up bubbles, chalk, and hula hoops under Mama's clothesline earlier, watching as everyone buzzed around us.

Teeny and Noah and their families are meeting with the funeral director for the graveside service. It will be a short and straightforward do, with only family present, as Cilla wanted. Then, it will be a matter of honoring a rare woman who few knew as well as they thought, but who taught us all more than we realized about ourselves.

***

As I was heading back to Mr. Coleman's yard, Natalie and her family arrived. We've all kept in touch over the years, though we spread out after graduation like feed thrown for chickens. Our children found each other immediately, and the two of us happily embraced. Being back in these yards with her brought a flood of emotion to my heart. So much time had passed, and yet, none at all. *What a day this will be!*

Just behind Natalie was Jimmy and Sasha and their families, and we exchanged a mess of hugs and grins.

"Is it really going to be all of us today?" asked Jimmy.

"I think it is if you can believe that," I answered. "Gosh, what's it been since everyone was home at the same time?"

"Thirteen years?" Sasha calculated.

"Longer than that if you include us." We turned to see Cliff and his wife walk up, followed by Pansy and Garrett and their kids.

"And us!" said Garrett, looking around. "Geez, either we got bigger, or everything else got smaller."

"Isn't that the truth!" This from Jimmy.

We stood looking around and taking in our old scene. Some things have changed, but the bones are still there. Nattie no longer lives next door to Mama and Daddy, and Mr. Coleman's gardens aren't what they used to be, but in our momentarily quiet circle, we could almost hear Jimmy calling a game as he chugged toward first base.

***

People began to arrive in earnest. Kids were chasing each other with bubble wands as Mama, Mrs. Drummond, and Mrs. Perkins carried food from the houses. Casseroles, Jello salads, glorified rice, seven-layer salad, Cilla's peach cobbler, and plates of oatmeal raisin and chocolate chip cookies adorned the buffet tables set up against Mr. Coleman's garage. Mr. Drummond and Mr. Perkins followed with crockpots. No one was going to go hungry today.

"I hope Maisy didn't have flight issues this morning," said Pansy.

"Nah, the elite just like to make an entrance," replied Jimmy, snickering. Garrett punched him in the arm.

"You leave my Maisy alone, now. She'll be along. In fact, speak of the devil."

All heads turned, and we watched across the yard as Mr. Drummond opened his arms wide for his youngest child. She'd been away at medical school, and trips home were few and far between. She gestured wildly about what must have been a close call at the airport while Mrs. Drummond squeezed her tight. Then, seeing us, she squealed and ran over, hugging everyone in turn.

"Nice of you to make it, Dr. Drummond," Cliff teased as he set her down.

"Oh, stop, you! Besides, I'm not a doctor yet," she grinned. "Gosh, am I the last one? I almost couldn't get away, and I'd have felt horrible missing it. Are we really all here?"

"Every last one," I said. "We're finally back together."

"The only thing I need now is to hear Mr. Coleman laugh," said Sasha. "Has anyone seen him yet?"

"Daddy was going to go get him from Pullman Manor a little while ago. He moved over there last month," I answered. "They should be back any minute."

***

Teeny and Noah and their families arrived back from the cemetery shortly after noon.

"Good thing. I'm starving!" said Jimmy, ducking his wife's smack upside the head. "What?"

Everyone gathered around the buffet table, and Noah stepped forward to say a few words.

"Thank you for coming today. It means an awful lot to our family.

"As most of you know, our mother lived a rather interesting life. If you've read her book at the library or worked with her on the *FIELD Project*, you know she dealt with a lot from very early on and experienced quite a bit of loss over the years. She was a survivor, though, constantly popping back up like a Weeble, wobbling, but never falling down.

"She was tough as nails, our mom. And a strict disciplinarian, to boot, making sure we knew how to live right and keep our heads above water. It was hard to put one over on her. Believe me, Parker, Marty, Jamie, and I tried many, many times. Still, she always had a warm hug at the ready any time Teeny and I, or any of our friends, needed one.

"Mom wasn't always an easy person to be around. Some of you remember the rough years after Dad and Jack passed. I'm looking at you, Walker family. I've filed the paperwork for your eventual sainthoods with St. Peter." At this, he winked at Mama, and a low rumble of chuckles rolled through the crowd as Daddy held his glass aloft in acknowledgment.

"Mr. Coleman, I'm holding off on yours as I suspect you may be immortal." The rumble exploded as people laughed and nodded their agreement. Mr. Coleman grinned, raising his hand in a dismissive wave.

"Most of this town turned their back on Mom after she and Nattie fell out," he continued, "and no wonder why. Those years were the darkest of her life, aside from those just after Penny died."

Noah looked around, taking in all of the friends gathered. The majority were generations behind Cilla but had rallied around her as she began her work with the library. Many had fond memories of her telling stories or simply sitting with them as they listened to a relative of their own.

Noah bowed his head and cleared his throat, taking a moment before speaking again.

"Looking out—a-hem. Looking out at all of you today, it's clear to me how wonderful the people of Pullman Station are. You gave Mom another chance when she needed it desperately, and you'll never know how much that meant to her.

"She loved this town; loved everything about it. When she learned of Nattie's illness and worked so hard to make things right, you embraced her, encouraged her, forgave her, and, ultimately, helped her heal. When she passed, it was with a joyful heart. I can think of no greater gift than that of grace given from one to another. And so, from Teeny and me, and Mom, thank you."

"Here! Here!" Parker called. "To Cilla!"

At that, everyone raised their glasses of lemonade and made a beeline for the buffet.

***

Sitting at our picnic tables, we reminisced about those crazy years with Nattie and Cilla. What a ride it was!

Daddy was pushing Mr. Coleman around in his wheelchair to chat with various friends, and they finally made their way to our table.

"Hi, Mr. Coleman!" we cheered. A grin spread across his wrinkled old face, and he let out a "Hooo!" nearly bursting every one of our hearts.

"Would you just look at all of you!" he croaked.

"Us!? What about you?" Natalie cried. "My goodness, you look wonderful!"

"How old are you now, Everett?" Daddy asked.

"I'm 95, and the tank's still full."

"Geez! You're gonna outlive us," Sasha joked.

"It's the ladies that keep me young, son. Got me a girl, ya know."

"Is that right? When you gettin' married?"

"Oh, we figure we'll give it a few years. Make sure it'll last," he winked. "No point in rushing things."

"Well, if she won't marry you, I will," said Maisy.

"Likewise, little lady. But you better polish up those wheelchair skills, 'cuz I'll be chasin' you. I might need me a doctor someday."

"I can't think of a better man to catch me."

Daddy and Mr. Coleman moved on, and we continued to chat at our table.

"Oh—I almost forgot!" Maisy reached down into her bag and pulled out her Maisy Moments book.

"You're kidding—you still have it?" asked Natalie.

"Of course I still have it. I love this thing!"

Maisy passed it around, and several of us read stories aloud and laughed as we rehashed our adventures from the summer that changed us all so profoundly. Funny how the same story can be told from four very different perspectives.

As I handed the book to Cliff, two pieces of paper fell out of the back pocket.

"What's this?" I asked.

"Oh, that's from Cilla," Maisy answered. "She sent it to me a few years ago."

"Really?"

"Yep. You can read it, though, now that she's passed. Leave it to Cilla to surprise us 'til the end. It's incredible the things we never realize about others; fascinating what heals the heart."

EPILOGUE

*A*ugust 28, 2000

Dear Maisy,

I so enjoyed seeing you last month while you were home for a visit. You've grown into a beautiful young woman with so much ambition, and I know your parents are very proud.

When you were little, I imagine you thought me downright scary. I let anger and sorrow be my compass, something I regretted terribly once I finally found peace. But I didn't start out angry. In fact, I began as a little girl just like you, and I had a younger sister named Penny, as you may know, whom I adored with all my heart.

Penny had been gone a very long time when you were born, but you always reminded me of her. I watched you grow and felt her with me. Your curls, your energy, even your mannerisms brought back so many beautiful memories. Of course, you weren't aware of that, and I hope you never saw me watching and got scared, as frightening you was the last thing I intended.

I'm writing today to say thank you. It's funny how life nudges us with little reminders and moments of gratitude. As I've worked on the FIELD Project over these last many years, it's become evident to me that we must take time to say what we feel when we feel it, rather than waiting to find the courage, which may happen too late or not at all.

I've made many mistakes in my life and haven't always been good at admitting them. I've hurt people I love. Things that happened after I lost Penny terrified me, and I let my fear get the better of me even as an adult all those years later.

When you had your accident, you must have been scared, too. But you didn't give up or let your fear guide you. You fought back and worked hard, and just look at you now! You showed me what strength and courage looked like and how to fight back against fear, and you were barely six years old!

Many, many people who care so much for you loved you through that trial. Your friends and neighbors never stopped cherishing, encouraging, and cheering you. It reminded me how much we need other people, that pushing away isn't the answer. We must come together and help each other when things are hard. It's not our challenges that limit us, but how we choose to meet them; not our missteps that define our character, but how we decide to amend them.

That summer changed my life. When I heard you were worried that Freckle might not know where to go, I knew I could help ease your anxiety just a little. It wasn't much, but it was something I could do, and it felt so good to do something nice again for a change. You helped me repair a treasured friendship and heal before it was too late. I owed you more than I could ever repay.

I hope you are old enough now to understand and that you will accept the thanks of an old and grateful woman. You are remarkable, Maisy Drummond, and you will make a fantastic doctor. From one fighter to another, thank you.

Sincerely,

Mrs. Priscilla Prescott

Sticks and Stones

The Pullman Station Series Book Two

Jen Telger

Zinger

Pullman Station, Minnesota

April 1986

Two things went through my mind.

One: getting punched in the face isn't nearly as cool as it looks on TV.

Two: a punch sounds way different from inside a head than from outside.

A third thing landed about the same time I did: asphalt is no softer than concrete.

I lay on the ground, hand over my eye, as Cameron Schulz and his buddies laughed, and everyone waited to see what I would do.

"You're such a dweeb, Perkins! Real tough guy, spazzing on the blacktop, aren't you? If I were you, I'd be more careful about who I hang out with."

The little crew cackled and sauntered away as best as twelve-year-olds could.

Truth be told, I wanted nothing more than to drill Cameron and his cronies into the pavement and show them what was what, but it would only make things worse. We weren't on school grounds, but Mr. Anderson would certainly hear about it.

Jimmy Drummond, my best friend in the world, reached over and held out a hand.

"I *hate* him! You alright?"

"Yeah. I just wanna go home."

"Why didn't you hit him back, man? You know you could take him, easy."

"I just wanna go home, okay?"

"Yeah, alright. Still..."

My other best friend, Micah Howard, was supposed to meet us at my house a few minutes later. I looked over and saw him behind the tree in Mr. Palinski's front yard across the street. He must have seen the whole thing. Our eyes met, and I gave a chin-up nod. He knew why Cameron came at me all the time. Even though it hurt like hell, I'd gladly take the punch for him anytime. He was my friend, and that's what friends do. He looked at me and turned away.

Jimmy and I started off toward my house, expecting Micah to dovetail with us, but he started walking back the other way instead. I would've chased after him to catch up, except it would have embarrassed him. It had taken me a long time, but I finally understood why.

June 2005

Pullman Station is a sleepy town—it always has been. From the outside, you'd think nothing much happens here. We don't make the national news. Our sports teams don't make big headlines, though we'll occasionally have a runner or gymnast make the state trip. We don't have a booming industry or hot political candidates. Besides the best pool in the tri-state and a library with legendary glass floors, there's not much flash-bang to our little stop in the road. But like any place where people gather, there are differences: prejudices, blind spots, and sharp edges that keep things interesting and people talking.

We've gathered to bid a fond farewell to Mrs. Priscilla Prescott, a woman who taught us all more than we imagined her capable of. A woman who suffered enormous loss and hurt in her life and who had succumbed to the seductive bitterness of anger and animosity and destroyed a nearly lifelong friendship. Yet, somehow, she clawed her way back above it all to repent and comfort a friend who didn't have much time left, changing the trajectory of her own life and of those around her.

Most of the elderly who were around when we were young have passed. Cilla was the second-to-last of the legends to leave us, but there is one man who fascinates us to this day. Mr. Everett Coleman is ninety-five and, to hear him tell it, "the tank's still full." Even has himself a girlfriend. In fact, it's his yard we're currently sitting in as we reminisce about our years together; it being the highway of our youth, perfectly positioned between our houses and saving us from perilous treks around to the other side of the block.

Mr. Coleman looks good for ninety-five; attitude must really be everything. He only recently moved to Pullman Manor near downtown and is being pushed in a wheelchair by Ben Walker, Annabelle's dad, since his own kids can't make the memorial. He can still get around alright, but the yard is uneven and could prove treacherous, even to someone we're fairly sure is immortal.

A quiet man who doesn't judge and never gossips, Mr. Coleman provided many words of wisdom to each of us during our time here as kids. By the time we came along, his own children had grown and flown, and he loved having us around to keep things lively. Kind and generous, he'd always laugh and let out his characteristic "Hoo!" as we ran through. In fact, it's just that sound that melted our hearts only moments ago as he visited our table.

"Back in a bit, guys," I say, standing up. "Looks like he's gotten to all the tables now, so I'm gonna go have a chat."

Of our crew, I was the closest to Mr. Coleman. We spent a lot of time together during my first year of middle school and beyond. I can't wait to talk to him alone.

The summer of '85 is not one we'll ever forget. It shaped who we became and how we lived and taught us to think about what really mattered to us. Sitting in these yards, surrounded by these people, resurrecting feelings we felt not only as individuals, but as a group of kids becoming familiar with the ways of the world, isn't something I ever imagined we would reproduce. Yet, here we are. Older. Wiser. Stronger. Wearier. And still as cohesive as those seasons twenty years ago.

Some people think you can't go home again. They've had the rose-colored lenses of their childhood removed and think it's impossible to revisit the days of yesteryear with the same fondness. Infinitesimal smudges have appeared as life experience dusts for prints in places once thought pristine. But this crew, my best friends from Pullman Station, had the prints exposed long before most. We're not fooled by the notion that our childhood was without trial. In fact, it's those very trials we treasure that bind us for life. We know things about each other that others never will. We all walk with them in our hearts, each of us pieces of a patchwork. Coming together again simply combines us into a quilt. Some of us are the batting that keeps us warm; others, the bright and varied top fabric that makes us smile; still others, the strong stitching that holds us firm. As a group, we're comforted and warmed by an almost magical past as unique as the prints on our fingers. Back then, we learned who we were, and that we had a choice about who we became.

Ch-Ch-Ch-Changes

During the summer of 1985, right before middle school, Jimmy's little sister, Maisy, was in a terrible accident. She got hit by a car at the annual Pullman Days fireworks at Boxcar Lake after a dog chased her, and she ran out into the road. At first, we weren't even sure she'd survive. Hit by a heavy 1970s beast mobile, she'd taken the brunt of it in the midsection and suffered a ruptured spleen, broken pelvis and leg, and a fractured skull and spent the rest of the summer in the hospital. That accident set off a series of events no one could have predicted and is actually the reason we're all sitting here mourning Cilla Prescott instead of her dying alone and lonely with no one to notice. Life's kind of funny that way.

While Maisy's accident and its aftermath changed us all in ways we never imagined possible, it also impacted our entry into middle school, which we started that fall. None of us had had much time to worry about it as we spent the summer adventuring and filling our *Maisy Moments* book, chronicling our adventures so she could remember them with us later on. She was younger than us by several years but still part of our crew, like a little sister to all of us, and we hadn't wanted her to feel left out. Middle school hadn't seemed as important as making sure we got her back.

Her homecoming happened on our first day of sixth grade. While our minds should have been on all the new things we were experiencing, like changing classes and being the underdogs again, we were most concerned with what we would find when we got home.

***

Micah's family had moved to Pullman in August 1985, and upon starting school, he quickly joined Jimmy and me as one of our best friends. Of middle height, a thinnish stature, and wearing glasses, he was super smart, funny, and loved video games. He fit right in. We'd all fallen in love with Pac-Man on the rare occasions when we got to go to the Ground Round in the city and play in their arcade. Plenty of allowance quarters disappeared as we played, trying to best Inky, Blinky, Pinky, and Clyde, or when wielding a cord-tethered Duck Hunt rifle. Jimmy had a Nintendo, and we all played whenever we could. Micah held the best Pac-Man score of anyone we knew. He said he was going to ask for the new Super Mario Bros. game for Christmas, too.

Sixth grade brought a lot of firsts with it, and Micah happened to be one of them. He was the first Black kid we'd ever had in our school, though his parents were white and he'd been adopted as a baby. Our little town was a melting pot of Polish, German, Norwegian, and all of that, but the most diverse we got in terms of color was if one of the high-schoolers dyed their hair purple or someone's family went to the Bahamas over Spring Break and came home with a tan. Sure, we had skinny and stocky, blond and brunette, short and tall, but other than that, Pullman Station was as white as the food served after a Lutheran funeral.

Micah added a unique element to what we saw every day, but it wasn't long before we didn't see it at all. I doubt it would have mattered much, regardless, as Jimmy and I pulled him into our fold immediately.

Sixth grade brought another change to our class, as well. That was the grade when the district consolidated surrounding areas into Pullman Station for middle and high school. It meant our class grew to several times its original size, and there were a bunch of new kids we'd never met in addition to Micah. The good news was that most of them were really nice, and our social circle expanded quite a bit. Jimmy and I had been best friends since we were little, as had my twin sister, Natalie, and her best friend, Annabelle Walker, who lived on the other side of our block. We'd known other kids for years, but living so close gave us a ready-made team, available and accessible at a moment's notice. We trusted each other with everything. Branching out would have felt weird if we hadn't bonded so quickly with the others. Being a bit wiser than our years for what we'd gone through the summer before, not much of the new stuff bothered our crew the way it would have a year prior. We welcomed the new kids and opportunities to participate in extracurriculars and even got to visit the surrounding area once in a while as a result.

Of course, the consolidation also meant the kids who had been the smartest in class before now had competition, and it gave the bullies fresh meat to pound on. Cameron Schulz was our biggest class bully. He didn't like anybody, save for a select few he could control and who would laugh at everything he said or did. To be fair, he came by it honestly. He'd hit every I-don't-like-you-because branch on the way out of his family tree and likely couldn't have avoided it save to be dropped off by a stork. Still, it hadn't much mattered to us *how* he came to be such a jerk. We just tried to stay out of his way.

In addition to Micah, Jimmy and I quickly joined forces with Anthony Petrowski and Clay Hostettler. Anthony and Clay were from the contradictory little town of Hill Valley down the road. By the end of September, all three boys were regulars with our gang. Micah hot-footed it over to my house with his latest games on Saturday mornings, and we would go over to Jimmy's for tournaments on the Nintendo or the computer. Clay and Anthony joined us if someone could bring them into town.

It wasn't until a few weeks in that some things began to rankle. For me, changing classes, having new teachers, and new subjects weren't really things that bugged me. I always got along with everyone I met and pretty much rolled with the punches, but I took issue when we arrived as the fresh meat of the school, and I stuck out in gym class as being long and lanky. Other boys had grown muscles over the summer or somehow no longer looked like little kids. Not yours truly.

Jimmy had taken me down with a head to the torso a couple of months earlier when he was still trying to figure out how to deal with Maisy's accident, but it had still only been Jimmy. Maybe him crying and snotting all over the place had made him look less foreboding, and we simply hadn't noticed, but even he had started to thin out and become more defined. Our classmates had begun to change, and I hadn't. It pestered my self-confidence like a mosquito in a dark room. I never knew when it would sneak up on me, but it was always lurking.

Of course, the seventh- and eighth-grade boys had a year or two on us. Some even had the beginnings of facial hair, which freaked Natalie and Annabelle out. They thought it was disgusting and that the guys looked greasy, but Jimmy and I and most of the sixth-grade boys worshiped them. In our minds, anybody that had to shave before school was either top of the cool kids' food chain, or had flunked a few grades, and we figured we could tell the difference.

By the end of September, I was feeling like the winner of a county-wide wimp contest. I was strong, but not developed, and I spent a significant amount of time in the bathroom posing in front of the mirror, trying to find nonexistent muscles, which drove Natalie crazy. It didn't matter that everyone liked me. I just wanted to *look* like everybody else.

Dad and I began going out for a boys' afternoon once a month, and Mom did the same with Natalie. Nothing fancy, just time to hang out and do guy stuff. Sometimes we went bowling, hiking, or into the city to the batting cages. Once in a while, we'd catch a movie and go out for ice cream. It was nice to have that time together.

Looking back, I suppose it was about becoming a man and all that. Still, I appreciated having him to talk to when things got weird, and they got weird in a big hurry. In fact, our very first guys' day at the end of September was the catalyst for why I'm sitting with Mr. Coleman today.

Mr. Coleman

June 2005

I see the man I admire so much tucking into sloppy Joe and potato salad. As I said, he looks great for ninety-five, but for the first time in my life, he seems old. Not "sad" old—he's sitting at a picnic table smiling to himself. I'm fairly sure he's going to skid into heaven someday with a grin on his face followed by a "Hoo...!" But he's hunched more than I remember, and the wheelchair off to the side bears silent witness to his increasing need for caution. Dad and Mr. Walker are heading back toward the table with their plates and stop short when they see me making a beeline for the chair next to Mr. Coleman. They give me a nod, indicating they'll find another seat, and I appreciate the consideration.

My hero looks up.

"Well, Mr. Perkins! How're you doin', son?" He slowly unfolds and reaches out a hand, legs less certain than in years prior.

We shake, my heart easing a bit at the firm grip under the tissue-paper skin. Clearly, he's as good as ever on the inside.

"I'm doing well, sir. Still getting back up every time."

"Of course you are! I never had any doubt about you."

"Well, that makes one of us!"

WHAT HEALS THE HEART

"Nah ... integrity! You've always had it, son, even back in your scrawny days. Your whole crew is the type of good eggs hard to come by. But you, you have a special heart, Sasha."

"Thank you, sir."

"Aw, you can do away with that 'sir' business now. We're both adults and equals."

"I'm not sure it'll ever feel that way. You'll always be the Yoda to my Luke."

Mr. Coleman lets out a guffaw, and the "Hoo..." that follows nearly brings me to tears. This man carved a big part of who I am.

"How's Mr. Howard doing these days?" he asks, referring to Micah as he sits back down.

"He's well, sir, and sends his hello. Moved the family to Massachusetts recently for a job promotion at a large IT firm. Computers, you know."

"Well, that's just fine. Never doubted that young man for a second, either."

"You championed us both."

"And was very happy to do so. I enjoyed watching you both grow."

"Thank you. I'm sure you have no idea how much you influenced our lives, but we're eternally grateful for your guidance and wisdom. I can't tell you how often you sit on my shoulder as I mull over how to handle something."

Mr. Coleman's eyes are the rheumy red of old age, but I sense more moisture than usual. He's a sensitive soul, though quiet, and many people aren't aware of just how deep his rivers run.

"Sit down, sit down. Tell me all about what's been going on with you," he says. It's an invitation that fills me with warmth and comfort, and I am mindful that its days are numbered.

***

Continue the adventure! Order

Sticks and Stones: Book Two in the Pullman Station Series

today!

***

Read on to find out where to leave a review for What Heals the Heart, how to join my mailing list, and learn fun facts about several special locations and characters in this book in the Author's Notes.

Please Consider Leaving a Review

If you enjoyed *What Heals the Heart*, please consider leaving an honest review on Amazon, Goodreads, or wherever you prefer to read and write reviews and tell the world what you think of Cilla, Nattie, and the Maple Street gang. Reviews do not need to be complicated – a simple, "I (fill in the blank) this book!" does wonders. Reviews are what help an author continue to provide you with stories you love.

Thanks so much!

–Jen Telger

Want the inside scoop on Pullman Station? I enjoy your questions and keeping you all informed about what is happening in the neighborhood. You can join my mailing list here: https://www.subscribepage.com/pullmangazettefor the latest news, giveaways, and upcoming events.

Feedback is food for a writer's whirring mind, and I love and appreciate hearing what you have to say. Drop me a comment on social media, or visit my website and let me know your thoughts. I'd love to hear what your book club thinks about the club questions, what you're doing in your town to remember the history of the great people who came before you or anything else you'd like to share about this experience.

You can contact me in any of the following ways:

Email: jentelgerbooks@jentelger.com

Website: https://jentelger.com/

Facebook: Jen Telger Books

Instagram: @JenTelger_Writer

Author's Notes

Though this story is fictional, some people, places, and things are based on real people, places, and events.

The Thomas G. Plant Shoe Factory in Jamaica Plain, Massachusetts, was a real place located at the corner of Bickford and Centre Streets and functioned as explained in the pages here. Mr. Plant was quite progressive for his time. After acquiring the business, the United Shoe Company followed his philosophy and policies and continued operations out of the building until the 1950s. Arsonists destroyed the Plant Factory building in 1976. Twenty-three Metropolitan Boston communities responded to fight the blaze. Visit the Jamaica Plain Historical Society at for more information.

The Continental Dye House on Brookside Avenue really did turn the brook various colors as a result of the dyeing process, creating a rather unique feature of Jamaica Plain.

Most other landmarks, hotels, and businesses—including Back Bay, Boston Garden, Filene's Basement, Loews, Franklin Park, Michel Kazan Beauty Salon, the Beauty Balcony, Fairmont Copley, Lenox, Omni Parker House, Massachusetts Transit Authority, and Franklin Park Zoo—are real places, some of which still exist today. Creative license has been taken with some characteristics, services, and activities conducted in these places.

The Pullman Station Public Library, Pullman Pool, Harriman Hill, Hillman Park, Windham Park, and Bohler's Bakery are all based on real places in and around Winona, MN. And, yes, the glass floors of the library are real, as are many of the other features described herein, and can be seen to this day. It was and is a magical place for this little girl to visit.

Cilla and Nattie are loosely based on the two women who lived on either side of my house growing up. While they did not like each other, and things did get colorful on occasion, the relationship between Cilla and Nattie here is a complete fabrication. That said, my mother really did run into "Nattie's" house when smoke came billowing out due to a bone that had burned dry on the stove. The real-life Nattie responded much like her fictional counterpart.

Book Club Questions

1. Do you think Cilla would have believed Nattie if she'd disclosed what was happening after Jack died? Why or why not?

2. Do you think Cilla's actions toward Nattie and her diagnosis would have been different if Maisy hadn't gotten hurt that summer? If so, how?

3. Do you think Ben Walker (Daddy) handled his discussion with Annabelle appropriately regarding why Maisy got hurt? Why or why not?

4. Do you think Cilla needed to forgive her mother in order to move forward with Nattie? Why or why not?

5. Do you think Mr. Coleman was right not to intervene in the rift between Nattie and Cilla for all those years? If not, what should he have done?

6. How do you think Maisy's accident changed Jimmy?

7. What do you think was the most important lesson Annabelle and her friends learned that summer?

8. What do you think was the most important lesson Cilla learned that summer?

9. What do you think would have happened to Cilla if Maisy had died?

10. How do you think the Maisy Moments journal helped the older kids deal with their grief?

11. Do you think Cilla would have started the FIELD Project if the kids hadn't kept a journal for Maisy? Why or why not?

12. Why do you think Cilla wrote to Maisy all those years later? Would it have been the same if she had written sooner?

Book Club Activity

While the *FIELD Project* in this story is entirely fictional, why not start one in your town? Libraries, churches, high schools, and community groups are great candidates for connecting the elderly in the community with a world that needs to hear their stories. Those with dementia can benefit from having their stories written down as a place to rest in when days get tough. There is no teacher more valuable than one who has lived a life full of lessons, both big and small. Nor is there a greater love than the validation of one human being by another.

Acknowledgements

So many people have helped to make this book possible, and I am grateful for every one of them. Little did I know as a young girl that Hazel and Stella would become Nattie and Cilla some forty-odd years later! Or that a quiet painter named Everett, whose yard abutted ours at the red board fence, would become a fictional confidante and savior to a neighborhood full of kids looking to bypass the hazards lurking on alternate routes. My adult heart is eternally grateful to all three of these people for the inspiration they have provided the little girl in my mind. My apologies for any liberties taken a touch too far (to my knowledge, no one ever flung poo)!

To my parents, who raised us to value all people, regardless of their differences or challenges, and who taught us the value of older generations and the meaning of love, thank you. You created a wonderful childhood for us and have instilled the importance of acknowledging our mistakes and working to make things right. I love you more than you can ever know.

To my husband and children, who have frequently giggled about my childhood experiences living between "Gasoline and Gunpowder" and who put up with my late-night writing and frequent disappearances during this project, I love you times infinity, plus one.

To my brothers, who helped wear first base into the pampas grass, and with whom I enjoyed many backyard moments, I love you dorks.

Dan Davis, my very first WHTH beta reader and eternal cheerleader, thank you for being my sounding board and encouraging me as I traveled this path. Your unfailing confidence in my abilities and this story have been a tremendous boon when I wasn't so sure. To the rest of my beta reader crew, thank you for your time, honest input, and thoughts along the way.

Dr. Macaran Baird, thank you for taking time out of your busy life to provide insight and advice on all things medical. I couldn't have done it without you! Jeannie Culbertson, I appreciate your guidance more than I can express. Thank you for helping the little town of Pullman Station and its residents shine! Dominic Holland, thank you for creating a venue in which I have connected with fantastic new writer friends around the world and for allowing me to be a part of your MIE process via Patreon. It has taught me much about myself and my own writing process into the bargain.

To the city of Winona, MN, and the surrounding area, thank you for all of the beautiful places for a kid to make memories.

And, finally, to the Self-Publishing School family, who have placed the bar so incredibly high when it comes to helping authors find their voice and send it out to the world on their own terms, thank you for your guidance, expertise, excitement, encouragement, and camaraderie during this journey.

About the Author

Jen Telger is a writer and avid people-watcher who loves to figure out what makes people tick. She believes the beauty of writing lies in her stories expanding exponentially as readers make them their own, finding solace, inspiration, familiarity, and new adventures in which to play.

Having grown up in the small Midwestern town of Winona, MN, she has a keen eye for quirky characters, what makes a town a community, and the you-won't-believe-this quality of stories that happen when residents upset the local apple cart.

In her Best Seller and #1 New Release debut novel, *What Heals the Heart*, readers are treated to the down-home realism of small-town life that Telger experienced growing up in the mid-80s. The nostalgic free-range days of yesteryear that just can't be found anymore come alive on her pages.

In *Sticks and Stones*, Book Two of the Pullman Station Series, she invites you to discover just what it is that makes these people who they are.

Telger currently resides outside of Madison, WI, with her hubby, two children, and two miniature Schnauzers. When she's not working on the next installment of life in Pullman Station, she can be found puttering in her gardens, playing with her cameras, designing homes, browsing bookstores, creating fantastic worlds in Minecraft, and drinking way too much chocolate milk (a.k.a. Elixir of Life). She is available for Book Clubs, podcasts, interviews, and event talks. You can find Telger on Facebook at Jen Telger Books, Instagram @JenTelger_Writer, email at Jentelgerbooks @jentelger.com, and you can explore her website at www.jentelger.com.

Made in United States
Troutdale, OR
04/13/2025

30557459R00194